A PROPER CUPPA *Tea*

KG MacGregor

BELLA BOOKS

2018

Bella Books, Inc.
P.O. Box 10543
Tallahassee, FL 32302

Printed in the United States of America on acid-free paper.

First Bella Books Edition 2018

Editor: Katherine V. Forrest
Cover Designer: Judith Fellows

ISBN: 978-1-59493-607-4

Other Bella Books by KG MacGregor

Anyone But You
Etched in Shadows
The House on Sandstone
Just This Once
Life After Love
Malicious Pursuit
Moment of Weakness
Mulligan
Out of Love
Photographs of Claudia
Playing with Fuego
Rhapsody
Sea Legs
Secrets So Deep
Sumter Point
T-Minus Two
The Touch of a Woman
Trial by Fury
Undercover Tales
West of Nowhere
Worth Every Step

Shaken Series

Without Warning
Aftershock
Small Packages
Mother Load

Acknowledgments

Fifteen years ago, I wrote a novella called *Shaken* and posted it online for the Xena fan fiction community. Within days, my inbox exploded with hundreds of notes from readers all over the world sharing their thoughts on the characters and the story. Most of it was flattering; all of it was engaging. Seeking to repeat that head-swelling experience, I wrote another...and another...and more. Operant conditioning, that's called.

And now *A Proper Cuppa Tea* is my 25th book! It was so much fun to write, especially the research trip last spring to Cambridge to study the setting. I love my job!

This may sound trite, but it's certainly true that I wouldn't be writing today if not for the ongoing encouragement I get from readers, whether through notes, reviews, social media or book events. Not only does it create a marvelous sense of community with other authors and fans of lesbian fiction, it's an ever present reminder of the names and faces on the other end of my books. I write with confidence knowing you're there.

Thanks as always to my editor, Katherine V. Forrest, whose encouraging voice has spurred me through the last fifteen books. Not only did she sharpen my prose on this one, she drew a big red circle around a plot hole in my first draft. You'd be cursing me over that. You can rest easy knowing Katherine approaches every editing job as your advocate.

I'm not usually one for beta readers, but some books need a special eye so they won't land sideways on a discerning reader who knows way more about the subject matter than I do. My biggest concern with this book was British-isms. Longtime reader Jac Hills, resident of Devon UK, was kind enough to check all my "bloody's" and "blimey's," and to steer me clear of clichés.

My partner Jenny gets a mountain of appreciation just for putting up with me while I write. She also put the finishing touches on this manuscript in her hunt for dropped words, extra words, basically anything she could find to question. She loves her job too.

Finally, a big thanks to the professionals at Bella Books for pulling this all together in such a great package, and for all you do to help books and readers find each other. Let's go do some more of these.

About the Author

KG MacGregor is the author of twenty-five books, including the romance saga, *The Shaken Series.* Her works feature strong, career-minded lesbians, and blend romance with intrigue, adventure and dramatic events. She has been honored with eight Golden Crown Awards, a prestigious Lambda Literary Award, and the Alice B. Medal for career achievement. She served as president of the board of trustees for Lambda Literary, the world's premier organization for LGBT literature. A native of the Blue Ridge Mountains, she now makes her home in Nashville, TN. Visit her on the web at www.kgmacgregor.com

CHAPTER ONE

"Hundred bucks says her tits aren't real."

From a quiet corner of the British Airways lounge, Lark Latimer glared in the direction of the paunchy, middle-aged businessman who'd uttered his sexist slur loud enough for several others to overhear. It was a singular brand of catcall, the sort hurled by a loser who knew when a woman was out of his league.

She too had noticed the woman in black. Her breasts appeared perfectly natural, raised to form a gentle cleavage by what probably was an ordinary push-up bra. What stood out to Lark was the way she walked in murderous three-inch stilettos. The rhythmic tap of her steel-tipped heels on the marble floor was like a techno-soundtrack to her sensual glide. *Hip...shoulder...hip...shoulder.* Chest high, chin out. And an unflappable steely gaze.

The brash man's two companions added wolf whistles and a shouted invitation to join them, their flattery dripping with contempt. To call it adolescent was an insult to teenagers.

"G and T, please. Sapphire if you have it," the woman said to the bartender, her melodic British accent adding charm to an already alluring persona. She took her drink to a bar table by the window, beyond which a Boeing 747 loomed like a beluga whale.

Unfortunately, Lark noted, the woman's snub of the businessmen did nothing to dampen their lewd behavior. A pack of dickheads performing for one another. The loud one squeezed his crotch and grumbled to his companions, "Think she'd like to use my stir-stick?"

"You're sick, Fred."

And repulsive too, Lark thought. She'd scrupulously watched the three over the past hour as they grew louder and more vulgar with each trip to the self-service beer cooler. Making matters worse was the near certainty that Fred and his pals, like the forty-odd others scattered in various alcoves and work carrels throughout the lounge, were on Lark's late-night flight to London.

Fred continued to sneer, as if personally wounded by the woman's indifference. "Go over there, Jimbo. Check out them tits."

The younger man he prodded had baby-smooth cheeks already splotchy from alcohol. Jimbo, as he was called, hardly seemed the sort to approach a strange woman, let alone inquire as to the authenticity of her breasts. He kicked at the third man. "You do it, Vic. You're better at this than I am."

With a sleazy chuckle, Vic replied, "Just tell her you're TSA and you need to check her for liquids."

Lark cleared her throat and gave them a scolding look. Deplorable, all three of them.

Fred shot her a contemptuous glance as he drew a crisp Ben Franklin from his wallet and crumpled it to make sure it wasn't stuck to another. "Go on, Jimbo. A hundred bucks just for asking her. That'll get you a blowjob in Soho."

Sitting with her back to the room, the elegant woman nursed her cocktail and scrolled through her phone, oblivious to their loathsome scheme. It occurred to Lark to hurry over and strike up a conversation—safety in numbers—but before she could collect her belongings, Jimbo rose to make his move. The two who stayed behind chortled, gleefully anticipating her impending humiliation. Jimbo perched on the adjacent stool at her table, red-faced and grinning, furtively glancing back to his buddies as he plied her with fatuous chitchat. His words were inaudible from across the room, but there was no mistaking the moment he let fly his ill-advised inquiry—it was answered by the sudden dousing of his lap with her cocktail. The stain spread quickly on his tan slacks, even down his leg. To the casual observer, he'd pissed himself.

"London passenger Latimer, please see the agent."

Lark had been waiting for word on an upgrade to business class but she hesitated now to leave the lounge in case Jimbo lost his temper. Her dilemma was solved when the woman picked up her shoulder bag and relocated to another section without fanfare, leaving the men to guffaw at their buddy's sullied state.

"I'm Dr. Latimer," she said at the desk.

"I'm so sorry. I was unable to accommodate your upgrade request. But I snagged you a seat in the first row of World Traveler, and I'll bump you up to the second boarding group as a courtesy."

World Traveler was British Airways-speak for economy class. Tiny seats that reclined an inch or two at best. At least in the first row she wouldn't have to deal with someone leaning back into her lap. "I don't suppose there's anything open in first class?"

This was Penny from Plymouth UK, according to her name tag. She clacked away on her keyboard. "I could issue a new ticket for an additional…thirty-eight hundred. That's US dollars."

Ouch! "That's what I get for missing my flight. Lesson learned. Thanks for the bulkhead."

"We always do our best to accommodate Silver Executive customers. We just received word from the crew. They'll begin boarding at any moment."

Jimbo waddled by toward the restroom holding his wet pants out from his crotch.

"Penny, I hate to make trouble but I probably should give you a heads-up about a certain situation. Three men in the back room by the bar—I assume they're on this flight too—they've been drinking for a couple of hours at least. They've gotten out of hand, harassing a woman because she wouldn't talk to them." She jerked her thumb toward the men's room. "That guy who just walked by said something nasty to her and she dumped her drink on him."

"Oh, dear. I know exactly the men you're talking about. They're regulars on this route." Penny crinkled her nose and lowered her voice to a whisper. "Our beverage manager says they drink all the Harvey's Ale. Did you happen to notice who the woman was?"

"Really pretty. Kind of tall, reddish-brown hair down to here." She drew an imaginary line at her shoulder to indicate the length. "She got up and moved away from them. I think she's sitting just around the corner now. Black jumpsuit…spiked heels."

"Oh right…Miss Hughes. I checked her in."

Miss Hughes. Lark jotted that down in her mental black book. "Just to be on the safe side, you might want to have a look at the seating chart and make sure she's not sitting next to one of those sleazebags on the plane. That could be trouble."

Penny waved her off. "She's in our first-class cabin. Once aboard, they won't even see her again until they get to London."

Of course, first class. That should have been obvious. There was little about Miss Hughes that said business traveler. "That's good. Let's hope she taught them a lesson."

"I'll inform our club manager and get word to Jeremy on board to cut them off. Thank you for letting us know."

A nice feature of the British Airways lounge at Boston's Logan Airport was its priority boarding and departure gate with a private Jetway, saving club members the trouble of returning to the concourse to line up with the mob. An agent had already propped open the door in preparation for the call to first class.

Boarding pass in hand, Lark located the object of her concern and took a seat a few feet away in the opposite row.

From this new vantage point, she had an unfettered view. Miss Hughes was about her age—late twenties, early thirties—with blue-green eyes so bright they popped against her smooth peach complexion. Her sculpted nails were painted light coral, the same shade as her lipstick, and a dazzling sapphire ring decorated her left hand. The epitome of *chic*.

More remarkable than her features was her expression. Where Lark had expected to see aloofness or irritation after being so brazenly harassed, there was surprising vulnerability. Her vacant gaze and furrowed brow suggested faraway, sorrowful thoughts. That she might be anguished made Lark even more furious at the men who'd so boorishly pestered her.

The announcement for first class passengers to board created a stir throughout the lounge as travelers gathered their luggage and moved closer to the gate in anticipation. Moments after Miss Hughes proceeded down the jet bridge, angry voices erupted around the corner in the reception area. One of those voices was unmistakably Fred's, the Dickhead in Chief who'd bribed Jimbo to act on his insult. "Christ Almighty! You can't even tell a woman she's pretty without her yelling sexual assault."

Penny's manager had wasted no time in confronting the men over her complaint. Lark anxiously heeded the call for Group Two, hoping to be well gone before they realized she was the one who'd reported them.

A flight attendant greeted her as she stepped aboard. "Welcome to British Airways. I'm Jeremy." After checking her boarding pass, he leaned in and added, "Penny says I'm to look after you, luv. You'll let me know if there's anything you need?"

"Of course, thank you." Walking past, she craned her neck for one last peek at Miss Hughes, but a gauzy blue curtain had been drawn to obscure the view of the forward cabin. For an obscene number of frequent flyer miles, Lark could have wrangled first class. She was too stingy for her own good.

After trudging longingly through business class, she located her seat on the aisle in the center section, quite a good location if one had to fly in coach. The biggest downside was the view forward, where she'd have to watch with envy as business

travelers dined on a gourmet meal before folding their seats flat
to sleep. If only she'd made her earlier flight...

She lifted her small wheeled suitcase to the overhead bin and
stooped over to see if there was room for her backpack beneath
the seat. A pair of feet came to a stop only inches from her head.

"It was you."

"I beg your pardon?" She rose to find Vic looming over her,
his beer breath fouling the air. Apparently his seat was in the
back row of business class, barely three feet in front of hers.

"You had to go and tattle like some femi-nazi social warrior
bitch. I hope you're satisfied—you got Fred and Jimbo kicked
off the plane."

"Hunh...how about that? I *am* satisfied. Thanks for letting
me know."

"You cow...I bet you're a lousy fuck."

"Not what your wife says," she replied, preening with a
brush of her nails against her lapel. His befuddled expression
was priceless.

Jeremy appeared suddenly and wedged all hundred-thirty
pounds of himself in front of Vic. "Is there a problem here?
Because I can sort it with one call to security."

Vic's eyes smoldered with drunken fury but he smartly bit
his tongue.

"That's what I thought." Over his shoulder, he said to Lark,
"Where's your bag, luv? I have another seat for you."

* * *

Channing waved off the flight attendant's offer of champagne,
a fine Grand Siècle. Bubbly was for celebrating, and she was
having none of that today. "Gin and tonic, please." She'd try not
to dump this one in some wanker's lap.

Most of her first-class companions were tucked into private
compartments along the window. Her suite was paired with
another in the center row, these designed for couples traveling
together. As if she needed another vicious reminder of her
wretched life. Seated alone in the open space, she felt exposed.

How bloody fitting that she'd completely forgotten to cancel Payton's reservation. Now she could stare at the empty seat for the next seven hours. One last twist of the knife. Asserting matter over mind, she forced her shoulders to relax against the cushy leather. Her suite was replete with a workstation she didn't need, a state-of-the-art entertainment system she didn't want, and a set of plush knit pajamas with the ostentatious *First* stitched onto the chest. Payton Crane would have appreciated such pampering.

"To expedite the boarding process, please step into your row to allow others to proceed."

Squeezing her eyes tightly shut, she stifled a groan. A hundred years of commercial aviation and people still didn't know how to board an aeroplane. How hard could it be to find a seat and sit your arse in it?

The interminable delay to takeoff compounded her misery. Getting out of Boston was the necessary first step to putting her life back together. How many women through the ages had thought *their* affair with the married boss would be the one in a million to end happily?

"This is you, darling—five-F." A male flight attendant abruptly appeared in the opposite aisle, gesturing toward what would have been Payton's seat.

The young woman who followed him stopped short, her eyes wide with surprise. "Are you serious?"

"Didn't I promise to take care of you, luv?"

In the muted cabin light, Channing first thought her a teenager. The most obvious clues were the backpack on her shoulder and short honey-colored hair that looked, to put it bluntly, unattended. A pretentious coed setting off on a gap-year tour through Europe's youth hostels on Mummy and Daddy's dime.

Except instead of shredded denim, she wore neat ankle trousers with a cropped jacket, and gray textured flats. Office casual. Once she sat beneath the reading light, the faint lines of her smile were more apparent, putting her closer to Channing's age.

So not a coed.

"Jeremy, this is incredible. Thank you." She went to work right away manipulating her footrest and entertainment screen. "I was planning to sleep all the way to London but now I'll have to stay awake so I can appreciate the perks."

"Enjoy it, darling. I'll speak with Muriel so she knows to treat you like a princess."

Absolutely not. Channing couldn't abide a chirpy seatmate fidgeting all night with her seat controls. She waved her fingers to catch the flight attendant's eye. "I beg your pardon…Jeremy, is it? I do believe there's been a slight mistake. I don't mean to be inhospitable but I actually purchased both of these seats, you see. I assumed that meant I'd have the space to myself." Her voice withered slightly under the woman's incredulous glare.

"Oh dear, my paperwork shows it as open, Miss…" He ran his finger down a folded list. "There you are, Miss Hughes. Did you inform the ticketing agent of your intention to purchase a two-seat ticket for single travel?"

"I'm not familiar with the particulars. All I know is—"

"See, I show that five-F was originally ticketed to a Passenger Crane. Your intended companion perhaps? Except Mr. Crane failed to check in so his seat was returned to inventory. Those are the particulars I have."

"*Those are the particulars I have,*" she snipped, mocking him under her breath. Then with gritted teeth, she added, "I don't suppose you have another suite available…perhaps one by the window with a bit more privacy."

"I'm so very sorry. It's a full flight. But Miss Latimer's previous seat is available in our economy section if you're interested. Just hit that little button and Muriel will be happy to assist you with the move."

As he disappeared behind them, Channing noted with displeasure that her face was warm, thus probably red. Humiliation always announced itself. Not only had she been condescendingly upbraided for what she considered a perfectly reasonable request, she now was left sitting in the company of someone who likely thought her a misanthrope. Not that she wasn't.

"Well…*that* was awkward," Miss Latimer said passively, her lips tightening in a barely discernible smile. She ran her hands along the armrests and wiggled her outstretched toes, the playful rejoinder of a bratty child who'd just tattled on her sister. Channing was in no mood for such impishness…though she'd probably not get away with chucking another drink. "My apologies. I've had quite the miserable day and had deemed myself not fit for human company. I assure you it was nothing personal."

"No offense taken." Checking herself in a compact mirror, the woman tamed her disheveled hair with her fingertips, sweeping the curls into an orderly bob. Like any good haircut, it had the instant effect of raising her refinement level a notch. "If it makes you feel better, I've been on kind of a lousy streak too."

"Please, I wouldn't want to be the sort of person who'd feel better because someone else was miserable as well."

"Like I said, no worries. Considering I've stacked a seven-hour flight on top of a fourteen-hour workday, I'm pretty sure I'll be lights out right after dinner."

Lovely. So on top of feeling like utter shite for what she'd already faced today, she could add embarrassing herself with a temper tantrum.

Muriel returned with her cocktail. Annoyingly pert in her trademark ascot and garrison cap, she squatted beside Channing to speak softly, "Did you happen to notice who's on our flight? It's Terrence Goff."

Recognizing the name, Channing followed her eyes several rows ahead where the chiseled television star, a rugged Hollywood hero-type whom the gossip rags linked to starlets half his age, was hanging his blazer in a small closet next to his seat. Payton's secretary gushed like a schoolgirl over his popular series, a firehouse drama filmed on location in Boston. Channing was utterly unimpressed.

"I only point him out because he asked if you were someone special."

Oh, for the love of — "What did you tell him?"

"That all of our first class passengers are special, of course." From Muriel's coy smile, she relished her role as potential matchmaker. "I'd be quite pleased to make an introduction if you like."

"I would *not* like, actually." She'd rather be doused in petrol and set ablaze. She twirled the stone of her sapphire ring downward so it looked like a wedding band and positioned her hand so it was prominently displayed. "If he should ask again, would you please just inform him that I'm no one he should know?"

No sooner had Muriel walked away than Goff caught her eye and flashed a blinding smile. To her horror, he strutted the few steps toward her seat, teeming with self-assuredness.

"Oh, bloody hell," she muttered, swiveling abruptly toward the seatmate she'd just abused in hopes of dissuading him with the appearance of being engaged in conversation. A pointless exercise, she realized, as his spicy cologne announced his arrival.

The woman, Miss Latimer, reached casually across the dividing console and took her hand. "Sweetheart, did you remember to stop the newspaper?"

"I..." Seconds ticked by before she grasped that she'd been thrown a lifeline. "Yes...yes, I called them this morning."

As the actor's footsteps made a hasty retreat, Latimer held her gaze. And her hand as well. By her devilish smirk, she was exceedingly pleased with herself. "That should keep him out of your hair."

Stunned to silence, Channing drew her hand back ever so slowly, as though she'd been petting a dog she was worried might bite. Or maybe she was the dog, too fearful to trust a simple gesture of kindness.

CHAPTER TWO

There was always that one arsehole. In this case it was Terrence Goff, who'd raised his window shade to enjoy the Arctic sunrise. Never mind that it was still the middle of the night in Boston and everyone else aboard the flight was trying to sleep.

Not everyone, Channing conceded. Her seatmate had kept her promise to go to sleep immediately after dining but now was up and about, presumably in the loo preparing herself for arrival. On her seat was an unzipped overnight bag, its luggage tag identifying her as Lark E. Latimer, MD. Perhaps on her way to an international medical conference.

Her snap judgement of Latimer as a privileged slacker obviously had been well off the mark. To say nothing of the fact that her own impending inheritance of millions hardly left her in a position to scoff at someone else's entitlement.

Muriel materialized at her shoulder with a breakfast menu. "Tea or coffee?"

"Tea, please." Of the things she missed most about England, a proper cuppa tea was high on the list.

Latimer returned, a fresher version of the woman who'd plopped into the seat last night on the verge of exhaustion. She'd changed into a shirtwaist dress, its hem well above her knee. A touch of makeup smoothed her complexion and highlighted her unusual eye color, an amber tint that almost perfectly matched her hair. Quite attractive, Channing decided. A pleasant personality would easily carry her across the line.

"Here you are," Muriel said, depositing a tea tray. "And for you?"

"I'll have tea also," Latimer replied.

Rested and in a more charitable mood than the night before, Channing felt compelled to prove she could be personable. "I'd have pegged you for coffee."

"A few years ago, you'd have been right. I switched to tea when my work started taking me abroad. Turns out there's a lot of really bad instant coffee out there."

"And a lot of bad tea as well."

"I suppose, but my tea palate isn't refined enough to know bad tea from good." She put away her toiletry bag and swapped her flats for woven leather pumps with sturdy heels. Other than the daring hem, it was an understated business look that didn't boast of power. If she was headed to a conference, she clearly hoped to blend into the background. Except eyes as remarkable as hers wouldn't allow her to go unnoticed.

"Then I take it you've not yet come to blows over when to add the milk," Channing said.

"How about I take my cues from you, assuming you're the expert?" She proffered a friendly smile and held out her hand for a shake. "I'm Lark Latimer, by the way."

Channing took her hand, remembering its spirited warmth from when she'd briefly held it the night before. By her mental calculation they were almost two hours from landing. A bit long for mindless prattle, but it was too late to retreat from a conversation she'd initiated. "Channing Hughes."

"You're heading home?"

Escaping Boston was more like it. "It would seem so, yes. Not exactly the prodigal return I'd planned." Her dream for this particular trip had been two years in the making, a chance at last to show Payton some of the people and places that meant so much to her. That fantasy was now a steaming pile of—

"That's the movie for you. It never quite measures up to the book," Lark said.

"You have no idea." Deflecting the subject, she nodded toward the small suitcase. "Looks to be a quick trip for you. Conference?"

"Oh, this is just the stuff I needed for the plane. I checked a monster suitcase. No telling where it is now though. I was supposed to be on the earlier flight but I got hung up in security. Logan drives me crazy sometimes."

"Logan's a walk in the park compared to Heathrow. Glad I'm not connecting."

"Ditto." Lark stowed her suitcase just in time for Muriel to deliver her tea. "All right, I'm ready for my tea lesson. How much milk and when?"

"First, you must allow the tea to steep for four and a half minutes. No more, no less." She seized Lark's forearm as she grasped the tag that hung from her ceramic teapot. "Leave it be. It's not swill."

"Sorry, my bad."

"While you wait, you might start with a few drops of milk—a tablespoon should do nicely." She meticulously prepared her own cup in demonstration and took a sip. "There, perfect. Sugar if you must, though a more sophisticated palate might prefer a biscuit on the side."

"Really, what kind of savage would add sugar?"

"Certainly not a proper tea snob." Channing mentally conceded that Lark's appreciation of her sardonic humor redeemed her overall as an otherwise unwelcome seatmate. "Yours should be ready soon."

"I have twenty-eight more seconds…twenty-two…sixteen."

"Oh, go on. Don't be such a literalist."

Lark poured haltingly as the jet skipped over a couple of bumps. "I don't suppose anyone has ever pointed out that you're kind of intimidating?"

"Yes, that… I truly am sorry for trying to have you evicted from first class. You struck me as a tad over-stimulated. I thought perhaps you should be somewhere more restrained. For your own safety, of course."

"That's really quite touching, such concern for someone you'd never even met," she replied drolly, proving she too could play the sardonic game. "Seriously though, I get why you might have been annoyed. You weren't expecting company and then I came and crashed your space."

"Crashed my pity party is more like it."

"Any chance it gets better now that you're heading back home?"

"Hard to say, actually. Home isn't what it used to be." With her beloved Poppa now gone, she was the last leaf on the Hughes tree. "My grandfather's not here anymore. He died in early March."

"I'm so sorry."

"Very kind of you to say." Though Poppa's death had little to do with her current mood. "Barely two days after I returned from his funeral, my relationship ended—not my idea—so there's another loss to process. A rather disastrous office affair… as if there's any other kind. It makes for a wretched working environment once it's over. So wretched that yesterday morning I cleaned out my desk and resigned."

"Wow. And you're already sitting on a plane to London."

"Oh, I was going anyway to settle the estate, but I'd hoped Payton was coming too, which is why I'd purchased two tickets." Such blathering was so very American. Yanks vented their emotions at the slightest provocation, whereas the British were more stoic. Channing was neither and both, having lived half of her life in each place. "And I have literally no idea what I'm going to do next."

"Look at it this way—you get to start over. The world is your oyster."

"I suppose if one fancies mollusks… I know, I know. Crack one open and perhaps there's a pearl inside."

"Exactly. And there's only a moderate risk of contracting hepatitis." A deadpan delivery, very British. "So an office romance, huh? We have a gross saying for that…something about not making a mess where you eat."

"That would have been helpful advice if I'd thought to heed it. Especially since it was my boss," she whispered. "My married boss."

Lark wrinkled her nose ever so slightly.

"Oh, I saw that—bit of a sneer."

"I didn't sneer."

"You most certainly did. But I won't hold it against you. Everyone judges. It's precisely why we keep such affairs secret, even after they've run their course. There's no such thing as a sympathetic home wrecker."

"I'm sure it's never as simple as people make it out to be."

"Simply ruinous if we're being honest." The worst of it was the complete surrender of her self-respect. "It never had a chance really. There was always Payton's loving family, Payton's important job. An imbecile could have predicted it would end horribly. I blame myself for allowing her to string me along for two bloody years. All the while she got to have her cake and eat it too."

"It's not like any of us have control over who we—" Lark's jaw went suddenly slack, as if frozen before a glib thought could escape her lips. "Her?"

Channing couldn't help her wry smile. Payton had been right about that—no one would ever suspect an office affair between women, especially if one was married to a man. That presumption had provided them the necessary cover to carry on under everyone's noses.

Amused by Lark's flummoxed expression, she stood and stretched. "Now if you'll excuse me, I should freshen up before all these men realize they smell dreadful and need a shave."

* * *

In a million years, Lark would never have guessed a woman like Channing Hughes batted for her team. Funny how first impressions took root. The context in which she'd first seen her—with the "three little pigs" harassing her in the lounge— seated her firmly in Lark's mind as a woman whose style and seductive sway invited the appreciation of men.

"My bad," she mumbled, chiding herself. "My *so* bad."

Channing had gone curiously quiet following her startling admission, busying herself with a magazine after returning from the lavatory. Completely stupefied by the arousing mental image of Channing with another woman, Lark had blown her chance for an appropriate reply. Anything she said now would sound contrived or gratuitous.

As the jet touched down on the runway, she reviewed her landing card and made sure the rest of her documents were easy to access. The worst part of the journey was still to come. First was getting her extended work permit through passport control. Then she had to clear customs with her gigantic suitcase and somehow get all of her luggage from Heathrow to King's Cross and onto a train. Stairs and ramps and doors and tickets.

Pointing toward the burgundy passport that marked Channing as a citizen of the UK, she casually offered, "Lucky you. You'll be home having lunch before I'm even out of the airport."

"Likely not, but I suppose *that* process is rather a series of hoops, is it not?" Channing nodded to Lark's lap, where the papers related to her work visa protruded from her US passport. "Looks as if you're planning to stay a while."

"Three or four weeks at least, maybe longer. One of the projects I've been overseeing went sideways and I need to figure out whether it's just a run-of-the-mill fiasco or a colossal…"

"Clusterfuck?"

"Good word. Perfect word, in fact."

"Yes, the etymologists really outdid themselves on that one. I noticed your luggage tag. You're a medical doctor?"

"I am…sort of. No, I am." It was nuts that she couldn't seem to answer such a straightforward question. "I went to medical school but decided not to do a residency. Practically speaking, that means I have four years of medical training that I'm not allowed to use on anyone. So don't go choking on a grape. I'd have to watch you die."

"That would be bloody awkward."

Lark laughed, relieved by Channing's smile and willingness to chat again.

Muriel announced a welcome to London, where the local time was nine thirty-five a.m. It would take several minutes to taxi to their gate. Meanwhile, chimes erupted all over the first class cabin as phones connected to wireless networks, including Lark's. She quickly texted confirmation of her arrival to Wendi Doolan, the woman who was to meet her at the train station.

"Oh look, it's a notification from British Airways that my baggage is now available at Carousel Five—three hours ago. It must have made the flight I missed."

Absorbed in her own messages, Channing showed no sign of having heard her remark. "I see… Let the games begin." She jabbed at her phone to delete the offending note.

"Problem?"

"Not for me. Someone has her knickers in a twist because I resigned without explanation. Far more sensible than the actual truth, don't you agree?"

"I don't know how you stayed there at all, even just for a couple of months. Working with an ex…" She cringed at the idea of having to face Bess every day at the office, even though their breakup had been mostly civilized.

"It wasn't pleasant but at least I was professional about it, which is more than I can say for her. We used to travel a lot together—client meetings and the like. Made quite a good team, actually. All of a sudden she can't do that anymore, because evidently we can't be alone together, not even in the bloody copy room. So she hired an absolute pillock to our team—Boyd Womack—who must be someone's nephew. There's no other explanation for how he made it through the door."

Lark didn't dare say it, but she could see why Payton wouldn't want to travel alone with someone as tempting as Channing. Perhaps she was worried about her resolve.

"But now apparently even that's too much." She stowed her phone and began collecting the personal items she'd brought aboard in a Louis Vuitton shoulder bag. "I'd been looking forward to this trip home for months, a break from all the melodrama. Then Payton sends me a bloody email from her office ten feet away to say she'll not be traveling anymore, that when I return, I'm to take over client meetings and Boyd will accompany me. Her top analyst reduced to being a bloody nanny. So I dumped all of my office knickknacks into a rubbish bin and left my resignation on the desk."

"Gutsy." Her top analyst. Funny how only hours ago Lark had assumed she couldn't possibly be a businesswoman. "I don't blame you a bit. I'd have done the same thing."

"But now Payton is having to field queries about my sudden departure. She's rather desperate to have me confirm with Human Resources her version of events—that I became homesick for England, what with my grief over Poppa's unexpected death. Mustn't have anyone think it had anything to do with sexual harassment, no matter that she deliberately drove me to quit."

"You don't have to play her game." Which sounded ridiculous coming from Lark. Women like Channing already knew that.

"I don't intend to. I have my own game this time."

"Does it involve dumping a drink in her lap?"

"You saw that?"

"It was epic."

"It was, wasn't it?" Channing pursed her lips in a half smile, but it didn't last. She was clearly still annoyed by Payton's message.

Upon arrival at the gate, Muriel directed those in the first class cabin toward the exit. Jeremy, who was holding back business and coach passengers to let them pass, gave her a small wave.

"Thanks again," Lark told him. "You're the best."

In the unending corridors of Heathrow, Lark once again found herself mesmerized by Channing's sensual gait, now synchronized with the thump of Lark's rolling suitcase along the seams of the tile floor. It was devastatingly sexy, especially now that Lark knew she was gay.

Furthermore, she'd accidentally confirmed that her lovely breasts were quite real. In the night, she'd lingered on a fleshy mound through the gap in Channing's jumpsuit while she was dozing upright in her seat. No unnatural curves, no sculpted spacing. Gravity in action.

Channing, the enigma—at times almost friendly, then instantly irascible and aloof. The top analyst who dressed like a model for *Elle*. Who'd had an adulterous affair with her lady boss. And who now waffled between cynicism and spite, with an occasional hint of hopefulness.

Lark was taken aback by her emotional investment. It was irrational to feel such empathy for someone who'd admittedly earned her misery through her own questionable choices. Yet from the moment Channing had walked through the British Airways lounge, Lark had been captivated. Then Fate had dropped her in the adjacent seat. Now she wanted to trade phone numbers and meet up in the city for—

"God, this walk takes forever," Channing suddenly groused, her first words since leaving the plane. "Terminal Five might as well be in bloody Wales."

"And here I was thinking how nice it was they gave us all this time to stretch our legs."

"Are you always so cheery in the morning? I should think that would be bothersome for the cohabitant."

The word surprised her, leading her back through their conversations of the last seven hours. Though she'd taken Channing's hand to dissuade the attentions of Terrence Goff, she hadn't explicitly revealed herself as gay. Not even when Channing said she was. As squandered opportunities went, that one was mammoth. "My ex-girlfriend found it annoying too."

Channing cast a sidelong look as they neared a sign directing European Union citizens one way and everyone else the other. "So you're gay as well?"

"I am."

"Hmm...odd that I missed that. Though I suppose I should have known when you clutched my hand so aggressively and called me sweetheart."

"My secret signal. It's a little too subtle for some people."

Channing ignored her remark as she came to an abrupt stop. "Looks like my queue is this way, Dr. Lark Latimer. I wish you a pleasant stay in jolly old England, though I can't promise my fellow countrymen will return your morning cheerfulness. Most are like me, I'm afraid, a bit on the stiff side."

"Don't be so hard on yourself. You weren't a *total* bitch. There was that one moment when you were asleep..."

Channing rolled her eyes and actually laughed. "Very well, I deserved that."

"Seriously, I have a feeling this will turn out to be a good move for you. Payton's loss is some lucky lady's gain."

"Thank you." She walked backward a few steps, giving Lark one last chance to appreciate her gracefulness. "Don't forget— the milk always comes first."

"Got it." Gripped with disappointment at goodbye, Lark blurted, "I don't suppose there's any chance you'd like to..."

Too late. Channing had turned away.

A familiar hollowness enveloped her as she continued alone down the hallway. Some days her life felt like a string of random scenes that never added up to a book. Thwarted plans, fleeting relationships.

Her mood lifted as she turned the corner and instantly noted her favorite perk of flying first class—she was at the front of the line for passport control. The agent scrupulously processed her work permit, but she still made it through in record time and picked up her lonely bag from the deserted Carousel 5. With nothing to declare to customs, she turned in her card and breezed through the arrivals area looking for signage to the Piccadilly Line.

A small crowd waited to greet arriving passengers, a scene she rarely noticed except for today. An elderly gentleman, smartly dressed in a three-piece suit and driving cap, held a hand-printed sign: *Lady Channing Hughes.*

Lady Channing Hughes.

CHAPTER THREE

It was ten a.m. on the nose when Channing exited customs and spotted Cecil's warm smile. The placard in his hand triggered a rush of poignant tears, which she blinked back so as not to embarrass herself. This first trip home since the funeral three months ago marked her grudging acceptance that nothing would ever be the same.

She took a moment to bask in familial bonds, shrugging off a nagging sense of humiliation at returning to England alone—again. This was not the homecoming she'd daringly planned with Payton last February over room service at the Park Hyatt in New York. Payton had promised that day to set her divorce in motion soon, before Channing's thirtieth birthday on the first of May. By summer they could vacation together without the elaborate charade.

Though Channing had tried that night to ignore her doubts, her gut had warned her not to get her hopes up. A month later their relationship was in tatters.

"How are you, dear one?" Cecil asked, enveloping her in a fatherly embrace.

"Much better now, Cecil. I've been so homesick for Horningsea."

It surely must have looked strange to those who saw her step into the arms of an elderly gent who so obviously was her limo driver. Cecil Browning was much more than that. He and his wife Maisie had run the Hughes household at Penderworth Manor since before she was born. It was Maisie who'd found her beloved Poppa in his study after he'd died, an open book of Keats poetry against his chest.

Cecil looked about as if expecting to spot her companion, since at the funeral Channing had floated the possibility she might bring someone home.

"It's only me." She'd always been deliberately vague where Payton was concerned, never quite knowing how to describe their relationship. It strained credulity to think they didn't know she was gay. A thirty-year-old woman who'd never had an actual boyfriend? Of all the women she'd dated, only Payton had been worth the anguish of possibly coming out to Poppa. What sense did it make to tell the Brownings now?

He eyed her single suitcase and shoulder bag. "This can't be all your luggage, Miss Channing. You haven't changed your mind about an extended holiday? Lord Alanford seems to think it could take a month or more to settle the estate. I'm sure there is much to talk about…many plans to make."

"Not to worry. I plan to stay a few weeks at least. I shipped my summer clothes a couple of days ago. They should arrive soon."

Sadly, her plans probably included a decision on whether the time had come for Cecil and Maisie to claim their pension. She couldn't bear to think about replacing them, but both were in their late sixties. The day-to-day work of maintaining a manor house was taxing.

A curly-haired woman with a backpack scurried past, reminding Channing briefly of Lark. She couldn't believe she'd been so oblivious. How on earth had she not known the doctor was gay? Even more idiotic was the realization, as she'd waited for her bag, that Lark had been chatting her up on their walk from the plane. And she hadn't responded at all.

She could have had an actual date with someone who fancied her. Lark's flattery felt so much better than Payton's dispassion of the last few months. Why hadn't she fallen for someone like Lark Latimer in the first place? Someone pretty, witty, and smart. Someone closer to her age. Someone single, for bloody's sake.

"What about your work?" Cecil asked, breaking her train of thought. "Can you continue from Penderworth?"

"I've taken an indefinite leave of absence." She'd have to venture back to Boston eventually to pack up the rest of her belongings and sell her car. Her apartment lease was good through November.

And there still was the matter of what she'd do next. Her expertise in corporate valuations was of little use in the tiny village of Horningsea, though it was but a stone's throw from the bustling university town of Cambridge. It remained to be seen if Albright Trust would enforce its noncompete agreement, which tied her hands from going back into a similar line of work. She needn't let that concern her—inheriting the Hughes family fortune ought to give her several options.

With her arm looped in Cecil's they crossed the skybridge to the parking garage, where her grandfather's ancient but functional black Mercedes sedan was parked mere steps from the ramp. She could almost see him inside, peering down his nose through his bifocals to read *The Telegraph*, London's conservative daily.

Cecil guided her toward the backseat.

"You don't have to chauffeur me, you know. I'm more than happy to ride in the front seat beside you." She didn't stand on ceremony like Poppa, but oh, how she'd looked forward to impressing Payton with her own private limo.

"Another time, perhaps. Maisie gave me strict instructions for today." He gestured inside to a small basket. "She's packed a little something for you. And I've a pillow and blanket in the boot should you wish to nap on the way home. Let me get them for you."

One sniff and she knew what the basket contained—fluffy homemade scones. There'd be jam too, and no doubt a thermos of hot water for tea. "I don't know what I'd do without you and Maisie. Now that Poppa's gone, you're practically all the family I've got."

As they pulled onto the M25, Cecil inquired, "Is there news from your mum?"

Her Mum...to use the term loosely. Elizabeth Trilby Hughes. Guillory. Blumenfeld. Liz to everyone who knew her.

"She's still annoyed that I didn't fly down to Florida and collect her for the funeral. She won't fly alone, but she refused to ask Irwin to come with her. Apparently it was awkward to have him see where she lived with her first husband." Irwin Blumenfeld was husband number three, a retired bankruptcy attorney. They lived at a marina in West Palm Beach aboard a 36-foot cabin cruiser Liz generously referred to as a yacht. "I don't expect to see her anytime soon, if you want to know the truth."

She closed her eyes to savor the taste of Maisie's black currant jam.

Cecil caught her eye in the rearview mirror. "What's happened to Calvin and the twins? Are they still in Boston?"

With her mouth full, she replied, "I've honestly no idea what's become of the Guillorys. Ever since the divorce, I've been forbidden to mention Calvin by name. Not that I ever would. I loathe the man."

They shared a chuckle over their mutual distaste for her stepfamily. It was practically a scandal that Liz had married Calvin Guillory so soon after Channing's father died, but then he'd made matters worse by uprooting the family from England to his hometown of Boston. Her half-brothers had come along when she was four. Annoying to no end, the pair of them. With endless squabbles in the household, Calvin thought it best that Channing return to England to live with her father's family. Eight years old and miserable in a houseful of Guillorys— including her Mum—she'd gone willingly, though the prospect of living with people she hardly knew frightened her. It bothered her to this day that her mum had so easily let her go.

"It's good to have you home, Miss Channing."

Was England really home? She had dual citizenship courtesy of Calvin. She'd bounced back and forth to Boston several times, finally landing the incredible job at Albright after earning an MBA at Harvard. It was only Poppa who'd tied her to England and now he was gone. But she still had Penderworth. If she stayed this time, it would mean carving out a brand-new life on her own.

* * *

Lark shook herself from an unintentional nap as the train slowed into the station at Cambridge. Begging the pardon of several passengers, she pushed the smaller of her rolling suitcases and pulled the larger down the narrow aisle. Inside the station, a security officer waved her through a gate, sparing her the indignity of trying to get herself and the cumbersome bags through the turnstile.

"Dr. Latimer!" The voice belonged to Wendi, easily recognizable from their video chats. A native of Ireland, she had flowing ginger hair that set her apart from the crowd.

"Thanks a million for meeting me. Sorry about getting in so late."

"Brilliant timing, actually. Gave me a chance to meet my boyfriend for lunch. Are you hungry?"

"No, I grabbed a bite at King's Cross."

Wendi took the larger bag and wove through the passenger pickup zone to a two-door hatchback parked haphazardly on the sidewalk.

As a clinical research manager for Gipson Pharmaceuticals, Lark was accustomed to getting the red carpet treatment whenever she arrived onsite to conduct a review of a drug trial. Millions of dollars in clinical contracts were at stake. Lark had designed the study, a Phase II trial for Flexxene, a daily transdermal patch aimed at reducing pain and stiffness from arthritis. It was up to her to determine if the contractor—in this case PharmaStat—had followed protocols to the letter. Did all the participants meet the eligibility criteria? Was the patch applied properly? Were the results recorded accurately?

Most trials she could monitor from the comfort of her office, where she'd review patient records and interview clinical staff by phone. Site visits were scheduled at random as an extra layer of validation. This particular review was for-cause—the Cambridge trial had gone horribly off the rails, landing three subjects in the emergency room with heart palpitations, and generating a ton of bad press for Gipson. A real *clusterfuck*, as Channing called it.

"How's the mood at PharmaStat?" she asked.

"To tell you the truth, we're all paranoid. Shane's convinced they'll sack the lot of us."

"And Dr. Batra?"

"Angry, frustrated. Everyone runs the other direction when they see her coming."

If anyone had reason to worry, it was Niya Batra, director of PharmaStat's Cambridge facility. Minor breaches in protocol were of little consequence…small omissions in a patient's history or a slight deviation in a treatment schedule. Those things happened everywhere, the exception, not the rule. But something had gone seriously haywire in Cambridge, endangering development of a very promising drug. Though Gipson had suspended the trial, the lab team remained confident Flexxene was safe. These aberrant results raised serious questions about PharmaStat's compliance with protocols. Lark was here to get to the bottom of what had gone wrong.

"Office or flat?" Wendi asked. "Though I should warn you, there's never anyone at the office on Friday afternoon."

"I should at least pick up my car."

"Right, it's in the garage at the Science Park." Young and physically fit, Wendi easily hoisted the bags into the hatch as Lark waited by the passenger door, which she presumed was locked. "That's me," Wendi said gently. "We drive on the left, remember?"

"Of course you do. I'm an idiot." Lark hurried to the other side. "By the time I get that fixed in my head again, I'll be back in Boston. For what it's worth, I do fine once I get behind the wheel. But I always forget which side I'm supposed to get in on, and then I have to crawl over the gearshift because I'm too embarrassed to get out and walk around."

Wendi laughed politely, as would anyone when the boss made a joke.

The boss. It was weird to think of herself that way, but until these anomalous results were resolved, everyone at PharmaStat would be kissing her butt.

"Wendi, about Dr. Batra...I know you might feel uncomfortable criticizing how she runs PharmaStat. But if there's something you think we should know—even something minor—don't hesitate to come forward. Same with Dr. Martin."

Dr. Jermaine Martin was the facility's deputy director. Along with Batra, he shared oversight of all trials.

Wendi cast a wary look. "Is Gipson absolutely sure this was a cock-up? Say we did everything right and it turns out the drug really causes heart problems?"

"That's exactly what I'm here to find out." Not the heart palpitations part—Gipson labs had provided strong proof that Flexxene hadn't caused those. Lark needed only to document that PharmaStat had followed the trial's protocols, particularly that they'd screened study subjects to rule out a history of heart problems. The aberrations could then be written off to coincidence, with the otherwise encouraging trial results validated.

PharmaStat occupied a four-story glass and steel building amid the sprawling campus of Cambridge Science Park. This was Lark's first site visit since last year's renovations, which followed a major break-in and burglary. Now the building was ultra-secure. Even the parking garage was a fortress, with keycard entry and surveillance cameras.

Wendi squeezed into a narrow space beside a silver BMW convertible. "Can't believe Shane's still here on a Friday afternoon. That's his new baby."

Shane Forster drove a pretty fancy car for someone on an entry-level salary, Lark mused. It was a cynical leap to suppose that Shane, the other research assistant assigned to the Flexxene team, might be taking bribes to tank Gipson's trials to benefit a competitor. How he could have caused three patients known only by their ID numbers to suffer identical life-threatening symptoms within a few days of each other…she hadn't exactly worked that out. Enough with the conspiracy theories.

Nearby was a row of tiny white hatchbacks bearing the PharmaStat emblem on the bumper. "Let me guess—one of those shoeboxes over there is mine."

"Afraid so." Wendi tapped a key fob that flashed the lights and opened the hatch on the closest one, a Skoda. "Here, this is your key…and the one to your flat as well. You remember how to get there?"

"In my sleep." They transferred the suitcases but Lark held onto her backpack. "I'd like to go upstairs first if that's okay. That way I can get the lay of the land and hit the ground running first thing Monday morning."

"Sure thing." At the elevator, Wendi swiped her employee ID badge again and entered a four-digit code on a keypad. "You'd think we kept the Crown Jewels in here."

"Hunh…I bet the pharmaceutical patents in this building are worth way more than the Crown Jewels."

The elevator deposited them on the fourth floor. Lark recognized the tweedy green carpet and pale yellow walls as PharmaStat's branded look, the same in its facilities all over the world.

"That's us over there, the plebes," Wendi said, nodding toward a roomful of cubicles. "My cubby is second on the right if you need me for anything. Shane's in the next one."

Lark followed her down a hall lined with private offices, only one of which was open. Inside, Dr. Martin sat at his desk perusing a stack of folders. A native of Ghana, he was a valuable conduit to Cambridge's black community.

"Dr. Martin, great to see you again."

"Dr. Latimer!" His face lit with a bright smile as he rose to greet her. "I was hoping Gipson would send you. It's been too long…though I often feel you sitting on my shoulder."

"Yep, that's me." She'd worked with him the year before during a random review and thought him both friendly and professional. It was surprising in fact that he hadn't been lured away to a more prestigious job. "Don't let me disturb you. I'm just checking in. Looks like I'll be here three or four weeks."

"Wonderful. We'll have lunch."

It was connecting with smart, interesting people like Dr. Martin that made her appreciate the cultural opportunities she enjoyed with Gipson. She'd choose world travel for research over the demands of a busy hospital any day of the week.

Wendi proceeded down the hall and swiped her card yet again to enter an empty office.

"And this is you. Once you activate your badge, mine won't work on this door anymore. Totally private, completely secure."

The executive office had a desk and credenza, a desktop computer, and a pair of matching armchairs opposite the desk. A glass wall overlooked a man-made pond with a fountain in the center.

"Not too shabby. It's a nice atmosphere for patient interviews."

Wendi removed an envelope from the desk drawer and laid out several items. "Security badge, network credentials, parking chit. You'll have to meet visitors downstairs to sign them in and out."

Lark knew the drill. It was the same in Munich, Geneva, Cape Town…all places where she'd traveled to conduct onsite trial reviews. She tugged on a locked file cabinet. "And I take it these are the patient files."

"Everything you requested. Dr. Batra will meet you Monday morning with the key."

"Wendi, I'm really glad you and Shane are on the Flexxene team. Trust me, I've worked with research assistants all over the world. You two have been on top of things since day one." Admittedly, she said that to virtually everyone as a way to set expectations. "Looks like I'm all set. You ought to sneak out early like everyone else."

"Thanks, I will…if you're sure it's okay. Just ring me if there's anything else you need."

Lark stopped her at the door with a hand to her forearm. "What I said about Dr. Batra and Dr. Martin…let's keep that between us, okay? I don't want to start any wild rumors about either of them being under the microscope. Everyone's under the microscope this time."

"Of course."

Alone in her new office, Lark shook off fatigue long enough to log onto the network and activate her badge. Then she sent a text from her phone: *I'm here! Name the pub.*

* * *

Channing awoke to the sound of gravel crunching beneath the tires, knowing at once they'd arrived at Penderworth Manor, the Hughes family home for five generations. Her last recollection was a grazing cow herd near Heronsgate, which meant she'd been asleep for over an hour. Little wonder, since she'd barely napped on the plane.

Cecil stopped in front of the main entrance to the manor house, a resplendent two-story structure of Cotswold stone with steep rooflines and four chimneys. "Welcome home, dear one."

"Look at this garden, Cecil. You've outdone yourself." Flower beds brimming with tulips surrounded the ornamental cypress trees on both sides of the columned entry.

He beamed with obvious pride as he held her door and offered a hand to help her exit. "Run along and say hello to Maisie. I'll take the luggage up to your room."

The heavy wooden door was the eighteenth-century original, varnished to a deep burgundy shine and appointed with worn bronze fixtures. She pushed it open and stepped into the great hall, an imposing room dominated by a staircase covered in worn red carpet. Stately portraits of her ancestors in gilded frames—including one of her late father wearing the uniform of the Royal Air Force—were hung on the far wall. It was the stern likeness of her grandfather, with his bushy eyebrows and handlebar mustache, that stirred her most. She'd miss him more than ever here in the halls of Penderworth.

"Miss Channing!" Maisie, wearing a gray summer smock with a white apron, stood in the kitchen archway with her arms spread wide. "Come here, luv."

"Oh, Maisie. I'm so happy to be home." As she returned the robust hug, the first tears of the day broke through, a natural drain of her anguish and tension. In that moment, it was clear that a few weeks at Penderworth were exactly what she needed for revival. The business of closing out Poppa's estate would keep her mind busy, while the warmth of Maisie and Cecil would help heal her heart. By autumn, she'd be ready for her next challenge…a return to the States or perhaps a new job in London.

"You look bone-tired, child. Get yourself upstairs for a proper nap."

Channing trudged slowly up the stairs to the second floor. The first room they passed was her grandfather's study, where she paused in the doorway. For the spring, his favorite reading chair had been moved from its usual place beside the hearth to a window overlooking the River Cam. It would remain there, she decided, commemorating this room to his memory.

As if reading her thoughts, Maisie murmured, "You mustn't dwell on it, luv. It was peaceful…like he'd dozed off in the middle of a good book."

The study, with two walls of built-in bookcases, reminded her that settling Poppa's estate would involve much more than receiving whatever remained of his deeds and accounts. As his only heir, she also was tasked with the disposition of his personal possessions. A renowned economist who'd taught more than forty years at the University of Cambridge, his trove of papers would be daunting.

"Maisie, are they still going ahead with the dedication tomorrow? I thought they might wait until we'd assembled his papers."

"They're quite determined. Miss Cross assures me the economics department has taken care of all the arrangements."

In a campus ceremony tomorrow, the university was naming its economics library in her grandfather's honor. It was yet another surprising tribute. Following his death, her plans for a small memorial service were upended by the university's request for a dignitary's funeral at the Trinity College Chapel on campus, with the Earl of Alanford delivering the eulogy. Mourners had numbered in the hundreds, including students and faculty from Cambridge and several politicians who'd served with Poppa in Parliament during the Thatcher years. Channing had found herself impressed by the whole display, having never grasped the full scale of esteem for her grandfather's scholarly and political contributions.

"Also Miss Channing, Lord Alanford asked to buy a round at the Crown and Punchbowl after the ceremony for some of your grandfather's close associates. He said to tell you Lord Teasely would be happy to collect you, and that he's most delighted to have you back in England for a while. Shall I tell him you'll attend?"

Lord Teasely was Kenneth Hargreaves, the earl's only son and Channing's closest chum from school. Though she was always glad to see him, she wasn't eager to surround herself with a pub full of stodgy old men—she'd had enough of that at the wake. But there was no polite way to say no. "Sure, that would be lovely."

"Listen to me go on. You must be exhausted from your trip."

They continued to her bedroom in the front corner of the house above the kitchen. Channing had chosen this room as a child so she could watch the drive for Poppa. His returning car was the signal to tuck in her blouse, turn off the music and put away whatever else amused her. A strict disciplinarian, he believed free time should be used for intellectual pursuits.

"I can unpack for you if you like. Shall I turn down your bed?"

"What I'd really love is a hot bath."

"Very well, I'll draw it. You make yourself at home, dear."

There was something almost magical about her childhood bedroom. When she'd first returned to England as a child, terrified and lonely, the brass canopy bed had been her sanctuary. Inside its sheer blue curtains, there was no end to where her imagination could take her. Sharing tea with make-believe playmates, guiding a ship upon a turbulent sea...even picnicking with her mum on the beach at Cape Cod.

How many times had she fantasized about sharing this magnificent bed with Payton? Yet her gut had somehow known Payton would never see this room.

CHAPTER FOUR

Lark wasn't much of a beer drinker back in Boston but she liked the occasional bitter draft in a proper pub. Admittedly it had more to do with the pub experience than the drink itself. How could anyone sit on a bench that held a century's worth of memories of mates popping in for a pint, and not feel nostalgic for that sort of metaphysical kinship?

"Something to eat?"

"Maybe in a bit," she told the bartender, who'd come around to collect a couple of glasses from the next table. She'd made the mistake of not clarifying in her invitation whether they were meeting for lunch or just a drink. It would be another day or two before her stomach adjusted to the time change. In the meantime, she found herself hungry all the time.

"Lark!" A middle-aged woman of Indian descent waved from the doorway, her broad smile rimmed with deep red lipstick that complemented her golden brown skin. Dr. Niya Batra, the woman whose work she'd been sent to review.

Lark jumped to her feet for a hug. "It's so good to see you. I can't believe it's been a year already since you were in Boston."

Oxford-educated with a stint at the World Health Organization in Geneva, Niya was more than a friend to Lark— she was a personal hero for having broken the glass ceiling at one of the world's major pharmaceutical testing centers. They got together as often as their schedules allowed, whether in Cambridge, in Boston, or at research conferences in the US and Europe.

"I'm so glad it's you, Lark. That last fellow they sent… Robert, Rob…not much in the personality department. And he couldn't hold his beer like you." They shared a laugh at her Gipson coworker's expense. "I was so sorry to hear about your mother. I know she was difficult sometimes, but she was still your mother. You're allowed to grieve."

"Thanks. I've been going through her things with Roger. They lived together for fourteen years. It helps the process." She blinked back sudden tears, her guilty response to all the wounds her mother's passing had left forever unhealed.

There was considerable irony in Niya's compassion and understanding. She'd always had kind words for Lark's mother after joining them for a family dinner back when Lark and Bess shared a home. Little did she know that Estelle Latimer distrusted dark-skinned foreigners even more than she did Jews like Bess.

"You look terrific, Niya. Working out?"

"I've been walking miles and miles on end since this awful mess started. It's how I cope with stress. And also chasing my new granddaughter around. She went from crawling to running overnight." Niya paused to order a white wine and accepted a food menu. "We're having lunch, yes?"

"I was hoping you'd say that. I'm starving." When the bartender left with their order, Lark took another swig of beer and drummed her fingers nervously.

She appreciated the optics of how their friendship might call her objectivity into question, since her work occasionally required her to review projects Niya directed. One of the VPs at Gipson told her since their bosses played golf together, she needn't worry too much about a conflict of interest. If anything, Lark felt it made her scrutinize the Cambridge trials even more. "Wendi Doolan picked me up yesterday and I tried to get her to dish on her bosses. That would be you and Jermaine." She raised her glass to touch Niya's. "She told me everyone's paranoid about getting sacked."

"Can you blame them?" The smile faded and her voice grew serious. "I'd be lying if I said I wasn't worried. Seven years at PharmaStat and I've never had such a case as this one. The executive board is extremely unhappy with me for breaking the blind."

"I read your report. What you did took a lot of guts. It was an awful position to be in."

Like most trials, the Flexxene study had employed a double-blind experimental design, meaning neither patients nor clinicians knew who was getting the skin patch with Flexxene versus the placebo, a patch that contained no medicine at all. Blind studies ensured that psychological factors and differential treatment didn't influence clinical outcomes. "Breaking the blind" meant unsealing the record to see what group the patient was in. It wasn't done lightly, usually only in life-threatening emergencies.

"I still can't believe so much went wrong, Lark. What are the chances?"

"Small but not impossible. People get heart palpitations all the time for lots of different reasons. Obviously it was just a fluke that you got three cases, bam-bam-bam."

"Too bad those vulture reporters don't believe in coincidence. You have no idea what it's like to see your picture in the tabloids. 'Mad scientist,' they called me. I'd love to know who leaked our data."

The Cambridge trial had thirty-six active subjects, all with osteoarthritis but otherwise healthy. After fourteen months without incident, it was indeed remarkable that three had suffered similar cardiac irregularities across a span of only eight days. When the first two patients presented at the emergency department, attending physicians broke the blind and found that both were getting the actual drug, not the placebo. Fears spread quickly that Flexxene was the culprit. Gipson's scientists vehemently disagreed, arguing that the drug's active ingredients weren't at all linked to cardiac function. That conclusion was bolstered when Niya, out of an abundance of caution, unsealed the record of the third emergency patient the following week to find that he was in the placebo group. The evidence came too late though, since news of possible adverse effects created public hysteria about pharmaceutical companies endangering patients for profit.

Gipson had no choice but to suspend the trial and send Lark to investigate. While a Phase II trial could survive the loss of thirty-six subjects, serious cardiac side effects usually derailed a drug's development. Gipson needed a reason to strike the damaging Cambridge results.

Niya swirled her wine before taking a sip. "It drives me mad that I'm not allowed to look at our own data. I just need to see for myself if we did something wrong."

"That's what I'm here for. I'd be shocked to find anything that wasn't by the book. Seriously Niya, there's no one I'd trust more than you to run a trial. We may never know exactly what happened to those patients, but my job is to prove what *didn't* happen."

"This has been so stressful. I don't even care if they fire me. I just want it to end."

"You aren't getting off that easy." Lark clasped both of her hands. "Okay, that's enough shop talk for today. I want to hear more about your granddaughter. You have pictures?"

They practically had the pub to themselves as they ate lunch and caught up. With Niya, a lapse between visits meant nothing. Their friendship always picked up the beat again as if they'd seen each other only yesterday.

"Any more news on the Bess front?" Niya asked.

"Nope, that's definitely over. We sold the house in January. Last I heard she was seeing somebody."

"Such a shame."

"I used to think so but I don't anymore." Lark had grown ambivalent about Bess Oppenheim, her college sweetheart who'd broken up with her for good after living together off and on for the last eight years. Granted, she'd asked a lot of Bess, basically to put their lives on hold while she moved back home to help care for her mother. What Lark had thought would be a brief interlude had lasted a year and a half. Still, it wasn't as if she'd had a choice. Her ma's boyfriend Roger was all but useless, and Lark's sister Chloe had small children she couldn't leave. "I don't blame Bess. She deserved a partner who'd put her first. But when Ma got worse, I felt like I had to be there with her. I thought I could fix everything between us before she died."

"I'd say you did. Your mother needed you and you came through. As far as she was concerned, you were her doctor."

"How's that for irony?" Her ma's first stroke was the main reason she'd bailed on her residency. That and her student loans, already in the six figures.

While they were talking, a group streamed in to fill the two long tables near the bar. Mostly men, older and dressed in stately black. Not at all the people Lark would expect in a working class pub on a Saturday afternoon.

Momentarily distracted, she turned back to find Niya's dark eyes narrowed with concern. "You're not your usual self, Lark. I don't suppose there's a chance you're unhappy working for Gipson?"

"Ha! I know this trick of yours—you goad me into complaining about Gipson and next thing I know you're floating another offer from PharmaStat." Lark actually was flattered by their earnest attempts to recruit her away from Gipson. She was proud of the reputation she'd cultivated as a careful, competent director of clinical studies.

"Can't blame a girl for trying." Niya checked her watch and removed her wallet from her purse. "I probably should get going. Dev's going to send out a search party soon. I told him I'd be home by three."

"I'll get the bill. Looks like our bartender's going to be busy for a while. I don't mind waiting." In fact, a few extra minutes would do her good. The bitter ale was stronger than what she was used to, and she hadn't planned on having two. "See you Monday at the office."

Waiting for a lull in business to signal the bartender, she noticed a maroon sports car squeezing into the space next to her tiny Skoda. The couple inside, a man and a woman, were distinctive through the glass, considerably younger than the others at the bar but also dressed formally for a casual pub. Discouraged perhaps by the persistent drizzle, they made no move to exit the vehicle.

There was something familiar about the woman in the passenger seat. With her reddish hair swept into an elegant updo above a knotted rope of pearls, she was as striking a woman as Lark had ever seen. Much like—in fact, quite a lot like—Channing Hughes. Make that *Lady* Channing Hughes.

* * *

Before she could go inside and put on a cheery face, Channing needed to finish her epic rant. "…and then she screwed me over again with another *Satisfactory* evaluation. Three years in a row. Why not *Superior*? Because she was paranoid someone would think she was showing favoritism. I wonder what she'd think if I referred her to my attorney for comment on why I left the company."

Kenneth Hargreaves was an unapologetic fop whose family money and pedigree assured him of a perpetual stream of marriageable women vying for the chance to produce his titled heir. He'd been Channing's best friend since childhood when they were packed off together to boarding school at Aldenham, one of Britain's most exclusive coed academies. Though mildly delinquent as teens, they'd both managed to skirt serious trouble to become respectable adults—he a solicitor like his father, and she a valuation analyst at one of the world's most respected insurance firms. Mutual friends had assumed they'd marry someday, despite their repeated insistence that they felt not a scintilla of romantic attraction.

Sitting outside the pub in Kenny's Jaguar coupe, they watched as some of Poppa's closest political associates dodged rain puddles to hurry inside. Right-wingers, the lot of them, but Channing was touched by their respect for one of their own.

Kenny offered a hit of weed from a small pipe.

"No, I said. I can't believe you haven't outgrown that. Don't they drug test at your firm?"

"Oh, be serious. You can't ask the Viscount Teasely to piss in a bottle."

"Cheeky bugger. You've always gotten away with everything." She cracked a window to allow the smoke to escape. Best not to go into a crowd of semi-dignitaries reeking of marijuana.

A handsome couple, mid-forties and less formal than the others, emerged from a white Maserati sedan. Apparently unfazed by the rain, they walked inside at a leisurely pace.

"Who are they? I remember seeing them at Poppa's funeral too." He was lanky and professorial in his jumper and sport coat with brushed leather shoes. She was on the curvy side, fetching in a tightly fitted chocolate-brown suit and silk blouse. Her hair was a vibrant blond, thick and bouncy.

"The Eastons, Spencer and Vanessa. Friends of Oliver's as well, coincidentally. They came to a party at our flat. I rather like them…though I'm shocked they were on Dad's short list for the pub since they're both Labour."

"Poppa is officially spinning."

"No, they probably got on. Spencer teaches at Cambridge too. Whereas Vanessa comes from money."

"All I know is I want to look that good in another twenty years."

"What is this fixation of yours on older women? Sounds like mummy issues."

"Please say that again after I've had a gin so I can bloody slap you."

"I believe you, Miss Hughes. Though I'm so glad you've quit your job. Now you can move back to Penderworth."

"And do what exactly? Horningsea isn't exactly a corporate hub for economists."

"No, but London is. How hard could it be to find a lover with a cozy flat in the city? It's what I did. And you with a country home, it's a perfect tradeoff." He pensively stroked his smooth chin. "Though I'll not be sending friends your way until your mood improves. Wouldn't want their heads back on a plate."

Why did everyone think she was such an arsehole? "Here's what really winds me up about Payton—she was so apologetic about not coming home with me for Poppa's funeral. She promised I'd never have to travel home alone again, that she was ready to file for divorce. Then not a week later—when I'm still grieving, mind you—she says forget it, that our relationship is over and she's not even gay. I beg to differ." She heaved a frustrated sigh, embarrassed to have been played for a fool. "If you're searching for the proper response, that would be an expression of outrage, seeing as how you're supposed to be my best friend."

"Very well, she's a horrid slag."

Women especially fell victim to Kenny's dimpled cheeks, which Channing found quite hilarious since he was as gay as a sequined hat. His long, thin face kept him from being classically handsome, but his sense of men's style more than made up for it. Always on the vanguard, he dressed impeccably and wore his thick lock of blond hair sharply parted and combed back from his forehead.

In all her years of living in Boston, no one had ever come close to being the friend Kenny was. Her secrets about Payton had walled her off from everyone.

"We probably should go in now," he said, nodding toward the pub. "Not that anyone will notice either of us. It's just another occasion for Dad to rally the Tory cause."

"I thought it strange your father invited me to this. Surely he knows I'm not a Tory."

"Always assume he has ulterior motives. This circus probably has nothing to do with you or your grandfather. I suspect he's laying the groundwork for *my* political future. That's probably why the Eastons are here—he's hedging his bets on both sides of Parliament. For whatever reason, he's convinced you ratchet up my seriousness bonafides. He's probably right, you know. Plus you're eye candy, and that makes you doubly good for my poofy reputation…which is likely to persist regardless, what with me shagging Oliver and all. We can skip this little soirée if the idea of being my afternoon whore offends you."

She blew out a miserable sigh. "I suppose I can be your whore for an hour or so."

"There's the spirit. It could make me prime minister someday."

"A gay nobleman as prime minister?" Channing scoffed. "It's never enough with you people."

"I'd renounce. But then I could anoint you Duchess of Horningsea." He got out and dashed around the car with an umbrella to escort her into the pub.

With Lord Alanford looking on to make introductions of both Channing and his son, she dutifully greeted each of the guests and thanked them for coming out to honor her grandfather. Yes, he'd inspired her to study economics. No, she hadn't decided on a permanent return to Penderworth. Yes, Kenneth was a longtime friend of exemplary character. The last one she even managed with a straight face.

At a tap on the shoulder, Channing turned to find the Eastons, who eagerly introduced themselves. Spencer not only worked at the university, he'd taught economics with Poppa. Vanessa though was even more interesting.

"I do capital investing here in the UK," she told Channing. "We look for inefficiencies, places where we could benefit from economies of scale, then we try to create entrepreneurial opportunities. We've had some success."

"She's being modest," Spencer added, clearly proud of his wife. "With the right touch, some of those entrepreneurs become huge corporations."

"What I wanted to say was that your grandfather's theories of labor were the basis for starting the firm. I took his class over twenty years ago."

Since Channing was already primed to like the Eastons, especially Vanessa, it pleased her immensely that they'd respected Poppa. "I'm so glad to have met you both. Thank you for honoring my grandfather by coming to the dedication."

Kenny joined her the second she found herself alone. "I've done quite enough knob polishing for one day. Grab a table. I'll fetch us a gin."

"Make mine a tea, please. I've a bottle of Poppa's cognac waiting at home. I think I'll wait and get thoroughly pissed later. You're welcome to join me."

"There's the Channing Hughes I know and love. But alas, I can't. I'm heading back to London after I drop you off. Oliver's making supper."

Turning away from the crowd that milled around the bar, she eyed a small table in the row by the window. While waiting for her tea, she obsessively checked her phone messages—another from Payton insisting she get in touch with HR. Channing had refused her calls, but what did it say about her that she hadn't blocked the texts or emails? That she was *pathetic*. If she called HR on Monday with a sob story of being homesick, Payton would leave her alone. That was what she wanted, wasn't it?

"Here's your tea," he said as he delivered a tray. "I need another moment, luv. Dad wants me to meet Smith, the Lord Justice. One can't have enough friends on the Court of Appeal."

Channing didn't mind as long as she didn't have to indulge anyone else. Penderworth was only five minutes away, practically walking distance if it weren't raining. She could always call Cecil to come for her…

"You need to let that steep for four and a half minutes," a woman's voice advised. "No more, no less."

Doubting her own ears, she timidly peered over her shoulder. Surely her trans-Atlantic seatmate hadn't randomly popped into the Crown and Punchbowl.

Yet there she sat—Dr. Lark Latimer, her quirky smile indicating she was every bit as surprised as Channing to see her there. "Did I get that right?"

Channing eyed her dubiously, ultimately deciding she didn't care if Lark's presence was coincidence or not. She was delighted.

"Why Lady Hughes...I do believe you're glad to see me."

"Oh, I am—especially if you have a car."

* * *

Lark felt conspicuous in her jeans and Patagonia rain-jacket among the sea of dreary black suits. She learned from Channing that the somber group had come from a ceremony to honor her late grandfather, apparently a bigwig at the university.

Channing looked especially elegant in a simple black dress that hugged her from hips to mid-thigh and showed a trace of her now-notorious cleavage. In her high heels, the very ones she'd worn on the plane, she towered over half the men in the room.

"Let me see if I understand this," Channing said. "You set up drug trials, hire other companies to run them, and then check their work to make sure they aren't cheating."

"Close enough."

"And you do that here in Cambridge?"

"This particular trial happens to be based at the Science Park." Recalling Channing's admonition, she resisted the urge to swirl her teabag through the pot as it steeped. "But we do them all over the world using the same protocols. It's all very scientific and methodical."

"So do you come here often?" She paused and cocked her head. "My God, I've just uttered the lamest of all pickup lines."

...which Lark wouldn't even have noticed had she not pointed it out. She was pleased by Channing's interest in her work, but it didn't strike her as flirtatious. "I get to Cambridge once or twice a year, but usually just for a few days. This one's going to take a while."

"So it's a clusterfuck after all, is it?"

"I'm afraid so."

Channing had managed a transformation overnight, from self-absorbed cynic to affable pub mate. Clearly being home in England brought out her best side.

"I'm here to look for problems," Lark went on, "all the while hoping I don't find them."

"Hmm…I would think it incredibly tedious to spend one's time searching for mistakes with no results. The joy isn't actually in the hunt, it's in the kill."

"Not the best metaphor for a drug trial. We try diligently not to kill."

"Yes, I suppose you do." A few feet away, the man who'd arrived with Channing was waving for her attention. "Excuse me a moment, would you?"

As Channing stepped away, Lark marveled again at what Fate had practically dropped in her lap. She'd squandered yesterday's opportunity to ask Channing out—she wasn't going to waste another.

"Lark Latimer, meet my oldest and dearest friend, Kenny Hargreaves."

Kenny cleared his throat and glared at Channing pointedly.

"Oh, for Christ's sake, seriously? Americans don't give a bloody damn about your silly style." She rolled her eyes dramatically. "Very well. *Doctor* Latimer, please meet my incredibly pretentious friend, the Viscount Teasely. But *do* call him Kenny…or Lord Twit, if you prefer. He's only here to collect the political blessings of my grandfather's associates. And to support me at my hour of need, of course."

"Stop saying that. It's only ninety percent true." He smiled warmly, revealing prominent dimples on both cheeks that rendered him more boy than man. And from the campy way he'd swatted at Channing's hand, Lark was almost certain he was gay. "I'm very pleased to meet you, Dr. Lark Latimer. Channing has so few friends. And yes, do call me Kenny. I only insist on that other bit from her because she finds it humiliating. She says you met on the flight?"

"That's right, about eight hours together. I guess that makes me her newest friend."

He pretended to whisper. "Then you probably know her as well as anyone. She's *deeply* shallow."

"And he's obviously an oxy*moron*."

Lark liked his dry sense of humor, inappropriate as it was for a memorial observance. Actually what she liked was the two of them playing off one another. They obviously were close, as familiar as siblings. She envied that. Her friendships with men usually fell apart once they realized she was never going to sleep with them.

"Lark has kindly offered to drop me at home while you stay and continue to debase yourself."

"Shall I remind you that Ten Actual Downing Street is at stake here? Surely that's worth fetching a few whiskeys."

He walked them outside with the umbrella and traded cheek kisses with Channing before dashing back into the pub.

"Your friend is kind of adorable, Channing."

"He knows that all too well." Folded into the cramped space, Channing shoved her raincoat into the backseat and fidgeted with the lever on the passenger seat until it loudly ratcheted as far back as it would go. "That was an absolutely hideous sound…I believe I've just broken something. A rental, I hope."

"Even better—it's a company car."

"Brilliant. I'll be sure to sell my stock." She flipped the visor's mirror and brushed her cheeks with a tissue, clearing smudges that might have been from tears at the memorial service.

Only then did Lark consider that it likely had been a difficult day for Channing as she confronted memories of her grandfather. It was a lot to deal with on the heels of a breakup and resignation from her job. Maybe it wasn't the best day to push her for a date.

"Quite the coincidence, Dr. Latimer, you being there at the pub. You aren't stalking me, are you? Not that I actually care at the moment, since you've rescued me from a rather dreadful afternoon. I couldn't have stood it another second."

"Of course it was a coincidence." Feeling defensive all of a sudden, Lark opened her texting app and handed the phone to Channing. "See? This is where my friend told me to meet her. I had nothing to do with choosing the pub. For all I know, you were stalking me."

"Easy there, I'm hardly complaining. You should have told me on the plane you were heading to Cambridge. I'd have offered you a lift from the airport."

Lark doubted that, considering Channing's sullen mood at the time. Hard to believe that was just yesterday morning. "And you should have told me you were so fancy, *Lady* Channing Hughes. I saw your driver holding that sign when I came out of customs."

Channing threw her head back and laughed. "That's just a family joke. I started calling myself Lady Hughes when I was eight years old. I also announced my intention to marry Prince William and become Queen. You see how well that worked out."

"How are you doing? Any more news from your old boss? Please tell me you haven't decided to go back to her."

"I most certainly have not. She calls, I ignore. She texts, I ignore. I suppose the nude photos will come next. Here, the drive's coming up on your right."

Lark knew from her GPS that Penderworth Lane headed toward the River Cam, which also ran through the heart of Cambridge University. The pocked pavement ended at an open iron gate flanked by two stone columns, one bearing a worn bronze marker that read Penderworth Manor 1784. Inside the wall was an impressive Georgian home right out of a PBS costume drama.

"Excuse me, Lady Not Actually Fancy. Ordinary people don't live in houses that have names. You *have* to be nobility. Are you sure there's not a lord of the manor somewhere among your ancestors?"

"Positively not. The entire house of Penderworth perished during the flu pandemic just before the First World War. Not a single surviving heir. My great-great-grandfather acquired the manor in 1923 and it's been in our family ever since." She paused with her hand on the car door, a worried look crossing her face. "I don't suppose you'd like to come in?"

Okay, so not the warmest invitation she'd ever gotten. It was entirely possible she'd misread Channing's excitement at seeing her at the pub. The charm, the disarming humor…maybe she'd poured that on to get a ride home.

"Maybe another time. You must be as jet-lagged as I am, and I bet it wasn't an easy day."

Channing pursed her lips and nodded. "Perhaps you're right. Another time then."

"Like I said, I'll be in town a few weeks if you want to grab dinner or something."

"I could probably manage that, though I'm not sure of my schedule just yet. I've several meetings next week to see about sorting my grandfather's estate."

"No worries. Come Monday, I'll be neck-deep in clinical reports. If it works out, great. If not…"

Again with her noncommittal hesitation, Channing fumbled for her phone. "Very well, suppose I give you my number."

"Here, just take mine." Lark handily produced a business card from her chest pocket. With Channing so hard to read, it made much more sense to leave the ball in her court. "Give me a call, shoot me an email…whatever. But take care of yourself first. Like I said, I'll be here a while."

It was just her luck the first woman other than Bess to really pique her interest would be emotionally unavailable at the exact moment their paths crossed. Or maybe Channing wasn't attracted to her.

Lark hardly expected a *relationship*. She was only in Cambridge for a few weeks at the most and Channing had made it plain she wasn't coming back to Boston. They were adults. Why couldn't they have a meaningless fling?

Even that wasn't happening if she couldn't manage a perfunctory invitation to come inside, Lark thought as she circled the drive and exited the gate. For all she knew, Channing had walked through that red door and tossed her card in the trash, relieved to have squirmed out of an awkward engagement.

CHAPTER FIVE

"Mum, you know bloody well I'm in England. It's four o'clock in the morning."

"That can't possibly be right." Even after nearly thirty years in America, Mum still had a marked English accent. "Irwin looked it up for me. He specifically said there was only a five-hour time difference. I was calling to catch you before dinner."

"It's five hours the other way. England is *ahead*."

Channing seethed as much as her brain would allow after being awakened from a dead sleep. It rarely occurred to Liz Guillory—she'd never get used to calling her Blumenfeld—to question her own impulses. Likely, she hadn't considered the time at all. The thought of talking to her daughter had popped into her head so she'd picked up the phone and dialed.

"What is it you want?"

"To hear about the memorial, of course. I was worried about you being there all alone again. I should be there with you."

"I'm not alone. I have Maisie and Cecil, and I spent most of the weekend with Kenny."

"I so love that boy. I can't imagine why you kids don't just get married, Channing. You two make just the sweetest couple. Plus you'd be a countess." Liz had been beating this drum from the moment she learned Kenny was heir to an earldom, having convinced herself that, as mother of a countess, she too might be given a courtesy title. "Speaking of weddings, your brother Nathan's getting married. Just the nicest girl. Her father's a periodontist. Gums. They have a vacation home in the Berkshires. Not as posh as Martha's Vineyard, but it's something."

Half dozing, Channing wasn't interested in the lives of her half-brothers, regardless of the hour. As a purely intellectual exercise, she'd once contemplated her willingness to provide either of them with a lifesaving kidney and hoped for their sake they'd never have to ask. There was a great deal of discussion over *the scientific technicalities* as to why Nicholas, Nathan's fraternal twin, wasn't the better donor. It had to do with *the birthmark on their hip*—Channing and Nathan had it, Nicholas did not. And *since it was a birthmark*, there were questions as to the viability of using *a skin graft instead of a kidney*, but then *Payton rang* to ask if she could arrange *a new rental car for Lark Latimer*.

"Channing!"

"What? I'm here...I'm listening." She'd obviously fallen asleep again and missed another critique of her love life, or lack thereof. Though Mum knew about her sexuality, Channing had not shared a word about Payton, a point for which she was exceedingly relieved. "You'll forgive my reluctance to take marriage advice from someone who stayed with Calvin Guillory for twenty-two years."

Her mother sighed dramatically. "There is that."

"Now if it's all right with you, I'd really like to go back to sleep. I have my first meeting tomorrow with Lord Alanford to go over Poppa's will."

"All right. Call me when you can talk longer. I want you to figure out how much Gary's computer company is worth. You remember Gary...Irwin's middle son, has that crooked eye? He wants to use his company for collateral at the Bank of Dad, but what good is that if he's—"

"Mum. Sleep. Later."

"Okay, okay. You get some rest. But I want to hear all about the will tomorrow. I'll have my phone on all day. We're taking the yacht down to Boca for lunch with the Solomons. Irwin and Rudy, two peas in a pod. They're—"

"Goodnight, Mum." She ended the call and drifted off with the phone still in her hand. Only moments later it rang again. "What!"

"Your grandfather's pipe collection...I was thinking you could pick out something nice for Irwin. I'd be happy to pay the post. But you mustn't send it here to the yacht because I'd like it to be a surprise. Use the Solomons' address. I've got it on a scrap of paper somewhere but you'll have to look up the zip code. Let me—"

"Mum, if you wake me again I'm going to tell Irwin what you did with his mother's zircon ring."

"Channing, that was just the most hideous piece of junk..."

* * *

Lark shook out her wet hair and shaped the curls with her fingers. Freshly cut for her trip, it would dry on its own before she got to her office. It hardly mattered how she looked, since her white lab coat rendered her practically invisible among the other doctors at PharmaStat. Being an MD had its perks.

At barely five hundred square feet, the corporate apartment had everything she needed to feel at home away from home— bed and bath, a cozy living area and a kitchenette. A pair of barstools at the counter served as her dining room, where she sipped from a pot of tea steeped for exactly four and a half minutes and poured over a tablespoon of milk.

Six days had passed without a word from Channing, leaving her disappointed but not surprised. It was silly to think she'd made any sort of impression at all. A chance meeting that had lasted no more than thirty minutes and Lark was still treating it as the highlight of her week.

Channing probably never gave it another thought, mired as she was in the emotional fallout from a broken affair, the loss of her grandfather and resigning her job. Anyone with that much going on in her life could be forgiven for ignoring social trivialities.

Over a breakfast of yogurt and muesli, she searched the web and found the obituary from three months ago of The Honourable Lord Hughes of Horningsea, given name Patrick. A professor of economics at Cambridge and a proponent of privatization, he'd served fifteen years in the House of Lords after receiving a life peerage from Margaret Thatcher in 1982. Lark didn't know much about the British system of government, but a title from the prime minister struck her as a significant honor, even if it didn't pass to his heirs.

Lord Hughes was previously married and preceded in death by both of his children, Frances Hughes Martin and Royal Air Force Wing Commander Henry Hughes, the latter apparently Channing's father. No mention of Channing's mother. Deceased, estranged or indisposed? Or perhaps the British simply ignored in-laws in obituaries.

The article confirmed that granddaughter Channing resided in Boston, which led Lark to track down her work bio. Channing T. Hughes, valuation analyst at Albright Trust, a company that insured parties undergoing mergers or acquisitions. A gorgeous color headshot, naturally. Male clients probably asked for her by name—Lark certainly would have. A graduate of Wellesley, she'd worked at Lloyd's of London before returning to Boston for an MBA at Harvard. Quite the impressive résumé, ironic considering Lark had taken one look at her voguish appearance in the airport and immediately written her off as someone who couldn't possibly be a business traveler. On the contrary, people who understood money like Channing did were the engine of the business world.

Curiosity drove her to check out Payton Crane as well. A senior client manager with a background in accounting, she too boasted a Harvard MBA. Mid-forties by her photo, but with ash-blond hair cut in an asymmetrical style more typical of women twenty years her junior. Lark conceded the hypnotic appeal of her steely expression, which oozed power and self-possession. Of course Channing would fall for a woman like that.

Enough with the cyberstalking. Finishing her tea, she scrolled through her email and found a late-night note from Bess saying that Otis, the scruffy stray they'd taken in four years ago, had gotten a clean bill of health from the vet after a stubborn ear infection. It was telling that after a relationship lasting nearly a decade, the only thing keeping them connected was a dog. What did that say about her emotional maturity?

Besides the note from Bess, there was a frequent flyer summary from British Airways and an offer of extra nights through Hilton Honors. And something spammy-looking that came in at 4:10 a.m. from an unfamiliar gmail account...*l_of_hsea*, which she very nearly deleted without even giving it a look.

Channing Hughes here, aka the Lady of Horningsea. I haven't forgotten your rain check. Supper Sunday at Penderworth?

* * *

A house with a name, Channing thought, recalling what Lark had said about Penderworth Manor. She must have found it amusing, the grandiose story of a child who'd appropriated a royal style for her identity. Lady Channing Hughes.

She'd dragged her feet all week about reaching out to Lark again. It surprised her how happy she'd been to see her in the pub. Then she'd grown uneasy, what with Kenny pointing out that she wasn't exactly the best company right now. Besides, the last thing she needed was to get involved with someone who lived in Boston. Or was it? Maybe Lark was the perfect candidate. Three or four weeks, no strings.

What would Lark make of a courtly home like Breckham Hall? Situated at the back of a vast lawn, its ivy-laced facade rose three stories above a circular cinder drive, the grass edges of which were meticulously trimmed. On the near end was a carriage house that Channing knew housed several flashy vehicles. Opposite was a covered brick walkway that connected the house to the stables.

She knew the Alanford estate well, having spent countless hours of her youth exploring its corners with Kenny. They'd forged a trail through the woods, where the property line abutted Penderworth. Though Kenny's estate was a hundred times larger at least, she'd always lorded it over him that Penderworth cut off Breckham's access to the river.

The interior of Breckham was no less impressive, with its towering ceilings, wall designs and ornate chandeliers. In a nod to its historic significance, most furnishings on the ground floor were eighteenth century antiques. House servants managed somehow to be both ubiquitous and invisible.

Sitting in a manly study adorned with gauche hunting trophies, she readied herself for the terms of Poppa's estate, executed by Kenny's father, the Seventh Earl of Alanford. Though twenty years younger than Poppa, Lord Alanford had been one of his closest friends, and his solicitor as well.

He set aside a leather binder she presumed to contain the will and pressed his hands together as if in prayer. "I believe Lord Hughes would be quite pleased with the honors bestowed since his passing. His was such a lovely memorial at Trinity... but then I've always been partial to Keats. 'Now more than ever seems it rich to die.'"

"'To cease upon the midnight with no pain,'" she replied. It was "Ode to a Nightingale," the poem she'd read during the funeral at the historic campus chapel. "Poppa had a wonderful poetry collection. His guilty pleasure, he called it. Perhaps you'd enjoy a memento."

"That would be splendid. Forgive my atrocious manners, Miss Hughes. May I offer you tea?"

"Thank you, no. Mrs. Browning is preparing lunch at Penderworth."

"Yes, of course, my dear. It was very kind of you to accommodate my schedule this morning. It's refreshing to work at home rather than in my London office."

"You're the kind one, Lord Alanford. That someone of your stature takes time for such a small matter is greatly appreciated."

"On the contrary, our families go back four generations. I was honored when Hughes asked me to sort his estate."

Pleasantries aside, Channing found it disconcerting that Lord Alanford knew more about the Hughes family accounts than she did. Poppa had always kept his finances close to the vest, maintaining that one's worth ought not be measured by accumulated wealth but by contributions to humankind. His core theory—the one for which he was most revered by conservative economists—argued that financial contentment was a disincentive to productivity, whereas a labor force that constantly strived to keep up was a perpetual engine of economic growth. He rarely splurged for personal enjoyment, other than for his comfortable life at Penderworth. That the Iron Lady herself had sought his counsel on global economics was far more meaningful to him than the luxuries other peers purchased with their wealth.

Lord Alanford cleared his throat as he opened the binder. "Very well then…let me first dispense with concerns you might have regarding Penderworth. You are to inherit the manor, which is at this moment free and clear of debt. As you know, it's a rare historic property, thus its value well exceeds the allowed amount under estate laws. I'm afraid you'll be facing a considerable tax bill."

"I assumed that would be the case." At Britain's rate of forty percent, it could be several hundred thousand pounds.

"To my beloved granddaughter, Miss Channing Trilby Hughes, I give, devise and bequeath the whole of my estate both real and personal of whatsoever kind and nature and wheresoever situate unto…"

He might as well have been reading from *Beowulf*. Virtually the only decipherable point she gathered from the legal gibberish was that Poppa had left her everything.

"…shall constitute a full and sufficient discharge."

She nodded along, for the first time taking in the fact that she now was an independently wealthy woman. Her grandfather had instilled a work ethic that was incompatible with a life of leisure, but she was glad at least to enjoy financial security while she explored new career options. "I'm honored by his generosity and the trust he's shown in me."

Lord Alanford assumed a stern paternal look. "Miss Hughes, if you don't mind my asking, how familiar are you with your grandfather's financial accounts?"

"To be honest, not very. But as you know, I've degrees in economics and business administration, and I'm a valuation analyst by profession. I've done some estimates given the market run-up of the last half-century, and the fact that Poppa lived like a miser. If I had to guess, I'd put it about—"

"Best that we…not index to the market…in this particular case," he said haltingly. "You might recall a falling out with London's Bedstek brokerage house around the time of the crash in 2008, a scandal involving inflated assets. A Tuesday, as I recall. Account managers first got wind of the problem around two in the afternoon. Those of us with Bedstek holdings acted quickly to divest before the European market closed, though the selloff continued in New York and by midnight Bedstek had collapsed."

"That was devastating. I was working in London at the time." Never had she seen Poppa so agitated. But the 2008 panic was well behind them, as the markets had recovered almost fourfold. "Heavy losses for some."

"Right…I'm afraid it all went rather toes up for Hughes." His voice had gone somber as he toyed absently with a paperclip, avoiding her eye. "Geoffrey McShane was your grandfather's broker…"

"McShane…I remember. Quite sad that was. Killed himself and wasn't found for several days, as I recall. They were good mates. Poppa took his death very hard."

"Yes. A hunting rifle, they said." He glanced up nervously and added, "Phone records seem to suggest he took his life shortly after your grandfather's call. As a consequence, McShane never followed through on executing the sale."

Which meant everything Poppa had invested with Bedstek… "You're saying he lost a lot of money."

"What I'm saying…" Lord Alanford's contorted face made him look as if he were passing a kidney stone. "Hughes had been quite disturbed by the market's volatility over the summer. He'd asked McShane to aggregate his assets at Bedstek and advise him on a more conservative distribution."

"And the collapse at Bedstek…"

"Wiped out the bulk of his portfolio, I'm afraid. More than thirty million pounds at the time."

Thirty million pounds.

Wiped out.

Thirty million pounds wiped out.

Channing stared blankly and forced herself through a mental checklist to verify that she was indeed awake and this was not a dream. The room was warm and smelled of leather, and the cushioned chair felt soft to her seat.

"That can't be." No one was so foolish as to consolidate all of their financial holdings in one place, certainly not Poppa. "Surely not the entire portfolio. He held onto Penderworth… kept the Brownings on staff."

"Paying them from his own salary, it seems."

"You can't be serious."

"I'm so very sorry, Miss Hughes. It's why he continued all these years at the university instead of taking his pension. Your grandfather died with very little cash on hand, I'm afraid."

In other words, she'd inherited Penderworth and no means to sustain it. "What about the Brownings? Did he at least provide for their—"

"Oh yes, he paid into their pension accounts as required. Hughes was quite unbending when it came to his obligations."

And yet he hadn't felt obliged to prepare her for a squandered fortune and a six-figure tax bill. He'd obviously taken for granted that she'd simply sell the manor and stay in Boston. Little had he known how much Penderworth would mean to her after he was gone.

"Now darling, I know this has been most difficult to hear, and I profoundly regret that I've been the one to tell you. Marjorie and I, Lady Alanford that is, stand ready to assist you in any way we can. And Kenneth as well. You have but to ask."

How to comprehend the incomprehensible? In a matter of moments, she'd gone from the fringes of British nobility to a pasteboard bed on the streets of London. Not only that, she'd walked off a good-paying job without so much as a penny severance, thinking she'd have months to sort herself. No references, no prospects.

It could hardly be a coincidence that she'd been gutted twice by those she trusted. First Payton and now Poppa—the two people she'd loved most.

CHAPTER SIX

Lark scribbled some final notes in the margins of her form while Subject 17 quietly watched. *It's why they call them patients,* she mused. This was her third interview of the day, bringing the first week's count to nine. Sixteen still to go, since she didn't need to interview the whole placebo group, just the one who'd had the cardiac complaints.

So far there were no red flags, but Lark wasn't yet sure what she was looking for. She'd know more once she talked to the three subjects whose medical emergencies had sent the trial into a tailspin.

Mrs. Browning was typical of most subjects in the Flexxene trial—senior and arthritic, but otherwise in good health. The medical history she provided today echoed the one given prior to being selected for the trial, with only slight deviations that could be chalked up to faulty recall. She met all of the study's eligibility criteria and had faithfully followed the treatment regimen, which consisted of weekly visits to the clinic at Shire Hospital for evaluation, and to pick up her packet of seven skin patches.

For thirty-four years, Mrs. Browning and her husband had been domestic workers in a private household. Diagnosed with degenerative arthritis three years ago, she'd followed the usual course of medications and therapies for a year with little relief from the stiffness and pain. The couple had hoped to retire soon and move closer to her brother in a small community in Suffolk, but the family they worked for needed them now more than ever, she said.

Lark resisted telling her that her health and well-being were more important than duty to her employer, especially at her age. It wasn't her place to second-guess anyone's personal judgment, and she technically wasn't qualified to give medical advice.

"I'm really sorry this is taking so long," she said. "We'll be finished soon."

"I don't mind so much. It's nice to get out of the house now and again," Mrs. Browning replied. "Besides, my husband—he's waiting in the car—he told me to take my time so he could finish his book. It gets him out of trimming the shrubs."

Lark's executive office at PharmaStat was a huge improvement over interview facilities in some clinics, where she often was relegated to a glorified broom closet. In her experience, a formal office setting conveyed professionalism and made study subjects more forthcoming. Plus Wendi always stopped in to offer tea to her guests, allowing her to test Channing's theory that there was but one proper way to prepare it. Mrs. Browning was a "milk first" disciple, but she also took one cube of sugar. Perhaps if they'd had biscuits…

Lark found herself more engaged than usual in this particular interview for the simple reason that Mrs. Browning reminded her of her mother, at least in appearance. At sixty-six, she was slightly built with short wavy hair the color of pewter. The similarities ended there however, as Mrs. Browning hardly seemed the sort to hurl dishes across the room the way Ma had.

"I saw the stories in the newspaper. Terribly frightening. They said some who were taking the drug nearly died."

"It was never as serious as the papers made it out to be, and there's no indication at all that our drug was responsible. Unfortunately, the hysteria caused a lot of needless concern."

"Of course, my doctor explained all that. But what would the red tops be without their sensational scandals?"

"Red tops?"

"The gossipy tabloids. The top part is red so it jumps out at you."

Given the controversy, Gipson had felt an obligation to inform patients of their group status once the trial was suspended. Mrs. Browning had indeed gotten the Flexxene patch, and as hoped, had reported far less joint stiffness and pain relative to those in the placebo group.

"Just to be absolutely clear, there's no evidence at all that Flexxene caused anyone harm. People get heart palpitations all the time for a variety of reasons. But we'll continue to research the question to confirm our drug is safe."

"That's a relief. Not that I was terribly worried, mind you. Whatever magical potion you're putting in that little patch, I found it most helpful."

"I'll be sure to let the company know you felt the drug was working as intended. I'm very sorry you weren't able to continue."

"Bit of hard cheese, it was." She drew in a breath and straightened her posture, a defiant gesture. "I managed before...I suppose I'll manage again."

Lark offered a hand to help her stand, noticing bone spurs in her fingers that probably caused her a lot of pain. Such suffering was hard to watch, especially as it reminded her of Ma's struggles after her stroke.

Mrs. Browning hobbled as they walked together toward the elevator, a classic display of arthritic stiffness. "As the old saying goes, it was nice while it lasted. At least I can take comfort in knowing there might be something on the horizon once you get it sorted."

"Believe me, Gipson is doing all it can to get this drug to the folks who need it, Mrs. Browning. I'm very hopeful you'll benefit from it someday soon."

Moments such as these made her feel better about the agonizing decision to skip her residency and take the job at

Gipson. Her work here would touch far more people who needed relief.

* * *

"I'd forgotten how much it bloody rains here," Channing grumbled, accepting Kenny's handkerchief to wipe her face and arms. "It has a name, you know…a seasonal disorder of some sort. Seriously, there's an actual psychological diagnosis for people who want to kill themselves because it's always bloody raining."

"Be honest, you missed this."

"Like toe fungus."

During a stroll through the garden, they'd taken shelter from a sudden shower in the gazebo. The warped wooden floor, mildewed lattice and rusty wrought-iron chairs were haunting evidence of Poppa's financial hardship. Such clues had been hiding in plain sight for nearly a decade—like the worn carpets and stained wallpaper—little things Channing had written off to his eccentric frugality.

"The truth, Kenny. Did you know?"

"Of course not. Would I have been your friend if I'd known you were penniless?"

Her flailing kick missed him, as she knew it would. She was touched that he'd dropped everything and driven from London when she'd called him with the news. "I'm delighted that my utter collapse amuses you so."

"Don't be so dramatic." He dragged a bench closer and perched on the edge with his legs apart, an unusually masculine pose for him. "Just to clarify…this is about the estate, right? You aren't still whingeing over that despicable Payton creature."

"So that was whingeing, was it? Not that you'd know this, but broken hearts take time to heal. On top of that, I'm about to lose my family home, and I have to walk in there and tell the Brownings that after thirty-odd years of faithful service, it's time they packed their kit and found a new place to live. And if all of that is not miserable enough, I don't even have a bloody job."

She glared at him pointedly. "I'm sorry, was I being dramatic again?"

He hopped to his feet and began to pace. After three laps across the floor he struck a theatrical pose, one hand pointing aimlessly and the other in his pocket. "Channing, I have this amazing idea. Hear me out."

"Good, as long as it involves suing the knickers off everyone who made a killing at Bedstek before driving the company into the ground."

"Actually, my idea is a bit more old-fashioned. It solves your problems…and several of mine as well." He drew a deep breath and blew it out loudly. "All right then. I think you and I should get married."

"Ha!" She could always count on Kenny for a good— "Bloody hell, the one time in your life you aren't joking and it's to say something utterly absurd?"

"Come on, it's brilliant. I'd move my belongings into Penderworth—a separate bedroom, of course—and assume all financial responsibility for the manor. Best of all, you'd hardly see me because during the week I'd be in London at Oliver's."

"And why on earth would you do that?"

"Yes, well…there's the tricky part. What I need… obviously…"

"Oh, don't even."

"…is an heir. A male heir, to be precise."

Against all her will, Channing quickly extrapolated what that actually meant, the mental vision of which might take her years to scrub. "You are bloody starkers."

"I am bloody *serious*. Oliver and I are dying to have children. Do you realize what happens if I should keel over without an heir? The House of Alanford passes on to Finn McNulty and his family of Irish fishermen."

"Oh, don't be such a snob."

"I'm not being a snob. They are a criminal enterprise, Channing, the lot of them. Ask anyone in Galway how to get a boatload of drugs into Reykjavik—Finn McNulty and his boys do it once a month at least."

"Says the biggest stoner in Horningsea."

"I couldn't stand it if a bunch of hoodlums ended up in Breckham Hall."

"What could you possibly care? You'll be dead and gone."

"But meanwhile I live my whole bloody life knowing my legacy is to be the man who brought the Irish mafia to Horningsea. That's the life you want for me?"

His plea held a genuine tone of anguish that surprised her.

"Marrying you would be an utter farce. The whole world would see right through it in an instant."

"And why should I bloody care? Anyone who knows me can see that I'm over a fucking barrel as it is. It's not as if we have to be Victoria and Albert—we just have to be legal. And we wouldn't have to…"

She slapped her hands over her ears. "I *must not* hear this."

"Come on, they practically grow the little buggers in a petri dish." He returned to his chair sporting an ornery smile. "Plus you'd be a countess, a legitimate one."

"A countess without an actual life. Besides, what about you and Oliver? I thought you were going to get married."

"We're prepared to sacrifice. Children are important to us."

"And suppose I were to fall in love with someone and want a family of my own? In the eyes of the Crown, any children I had would be yours."

"It wouldn't have to be forever. People get divorced all the time."

It was clear he'd thought about this quite a lot. That didn't make it any less insane.

"Look at it this way, Channing. You could have the experience of motherhood without actually having to be a mum. Pop it out, hand it over and go your merry way."

"Right, what's a little gestation slavery between friends?"

"And you say I'm a drama queen. Since when have you ever wanted children of your own?"

"I'll have you know I've actually considered it quite seriously, thank you very much." In fact, she'd once floated the idea of having a child with Payton. Granted, it wasn't met with enthusiasm, but she'd mused that Payton might someday warm to the idea. "I'm hardly sweating the biological clock, you know. Theoretically I probably have twelve or fifteen years to find a proper partner with whom I could share the role of parenting. Though it's more likely I'll stuff the lot of you and go it alone."

"Are you insinuating that you don't actually love me?"

Ironically, she did. "You really have gone mad, you know."

"Does that mean you'll at least think about it?"

"It means I should have my bloody head examined just for buzzing you through the gate." So much for getting her problems off her chest. This was all her fault for being impetuous, for storming out of Albright without securing a new job. If only Poppa had told her the Hughes estate was worthless. Could she even find decent work in London? All her business connections were back in Boston. Plus that bloody noncompete clause in her contract that prohibited her from going to work for a similar firm. "Speaking of Boston—"

"Were we?"

"We were about to. My friend Lark…you remember, the woman at the pub who was on my plane. She's coming by on Sunday for supper. Suppose you and Oliver join us before you go back to the city."

"A date already. Smashing. Except do *not* go getting involved with someone else from Boston. You live here now."

"This is not a date. It's supper with friends…and you, of course."

Besides, she'd worked out the logistics—three weeks, no strings. What better way to get Payton out of her life once and for all than to move on? Lark could help her with that. It didn't matter that she lived in Boston. Channing had no intention of going back to Boston except to clear out her flat, but there was no reason not to take advantage of Lark's time in England.

"She's a lesbian, right? And she's quite the fit bird from what I saw. I suppose you could do a great deal worse." He covered his mouth to cough, simultaneously mumbling, "Payton."

"Such a wanker, you are. You never even met Payton." Kenny had always been a world-class meddler. To head off his conjectures, she dismissed Lark as reasonably attractive but hardly stunning, smart but probably not brilliant, a doctor in name only who'd left before completing her training. "She's all right…though not someone I'd normally notice. I asked her for supper because she expressed an interest in seeing Penderworth. Some consider that appropriate social behavior. Really, you should try it sometime."

"There's nothing socially inappropriate about a good shag."

"Give it a rest already. She's not my type."

"So not a married closet queen, eh?"

On the edge of losing her temper, she shot back, "Payton Crane might have been a 'horrid slag,' as you called her, but our relationship was special to me. Her emotions ran very deep, something you couldn't possibly understand."

"Fine, but if you're going to bend my ear about all the despicable ways that woman fucked you over for the past two years, the least you can do is allow me to detest her."

Channing closed her eyes and sighed, scolding herself for treating Kenny the way she'd treated everyone of late. This wasn't even about Payton. She was arguing with herself over what to do about Lark's attention. It made her feel good for now, but what about later if Lark wanted more than she could give? "By all means, detest her. But please just sod it over Lark. I don't want her to get the wrong idea."

Kenny shrugged, a final surrender to her objections. "She seemed nice."

"She is nice. And she rather liked you, though God knows why."

* * *

Robin Saunders, read the phone display. Channing knew her as administrative assistant to Mitch Medrano, the charismatic CEO of Albright Trust. Robin had left a message earlier to say she'd call back at precisely eight p.m. BST, which was three in the afternoon in Boston.

"This is Channing Hughes."

"Please hold for Mr. Medrano."

She'd been dodging this call all week, convinced that nothing good could come from an exit interview with Mitch, especially if his suspicions led him to ask about Payton. Or maybe he simply wanted to be sure she hadn't absconded with competitive intelligence. Walking off her job without notice was admittedly unprofessional but she'd hardly left them in a lurch. Her desk was clear already, all of her projects handed off in preparation for the extended leave of absence she'd taken so she could tend to matters of her grandfather's estate.

"Channing, how are you? Belinda and I were quite pleased to read in the *Financial Times* about your grandfather's memorial at the library. Such an accomplished man. Did I ever tell you that we used his text in my economics class at Yale?"

She genuinely liked Mitch, and his wife too. For someone rightly considered the corporate elite, he was down-to-earth, helping to foster a family atmosphere in the office. While Payton had been almost paranoid about Mitch discovering their affair, Channing liked to think he'd have been sympathetic to their situation. It was plain that Payton was trapped in her marriage because society had for so long deemed it the only relationship worthy of recognition.

But Mitch couldn't possibly have known of their affair because it was the best kept secret in Boston. Two lovers had never been so discreet.

"Channing, your resignation took us all completely by surprise. I couldn't imagine what happened to bring that about so suddenly. Was it something to do with a client? I know some of those guys are Neanderthals still stuck in the 1950s. Please tell me you didn't have to deal with that. I don't care how big their contract is, Albright doesn't put up with that kind of garbage. All you have to do is bring it to us."

"No, it was nothing like that. Truly, I apologize for the abruptness of it all. To be honest, it surprised me as well. I thought with my extended leave already scheduled—"

"And then Belinda wondered if it involved someone here at the office. We don't sweep that sort of thing under the rug either, Channing. Human resources takes these issues very seriously."

A sickening mix of panic and embarrassment triggered a warm shudder. His cryptic musings hinted that he might know about her relationship with Payton after all. If so, then HR and legal had probably huddled with their knickers in a knot and insisted he call her for assurances that she wouldn't sue the company for sexual harassment. The thought had never seriously crossed her mind. Yes, her career had suffered from the affair—mostly because she'd willingly passed up the chance to apply for a promotion that likely was hers for the asking. Overnight travel for client meetings was her only chance to be with Payton without the stress of someone finding out.

"I spoke with Payton. She said you were very close to your grandfather, that he was your only family in England. So of course it makes perfect sense that you're still struggling with his loss, maybe feeling homesick. I can see how that might have snuck up on you the day you left. It's just that you're not the kind to do something rash."

Was he having her on? Like Payton, Mitch sounded very much as if he wanted her to confirm that she'd left for personal reasons unrelated to Albright. Apparently that was the company line—get this matter closed as soon as possible. Homesickness was as good a reason as any, she decided, since she had no desire to drag her own name through the mud with a salacious exposé. "That's exactly it, Mitch. I've been feeling out of sorts since Poppa died, a longing for the family home, if you will. It overwhelmed me all of a sudden."

"I understand completely, believe me." His voice took on a fresh enthusiasm that sounded like relief. "I went through something similar last year when Pop died. Rest in peace."

She envisioned him genuflecting, good Catholic that he was.

"It helped me a lot to feel like I had a family here at Albright. What I'm saying is this—I'd like you to reconsider, Channing. I get that you're feeling overwhelmed. By all means take as much time as you need. The whole summer if necessary. But then come on back. We're your family now, all of us at Albright. We've got a busy calendar this fall for mergers." He then lowered his voice. "Just between us, I don't think Boyd Womack can handle all these clients. Sometimes I think Payton threw him into the deep end of the pool just to see if he'd drown." He named several projects their team had been working on, and even mentioned that he was counting on both her and Payton to close the Grandover deal by October.

He honestly didn't have a clue why she'd left.

"What I'm saying is you should take some time to get your bearings. Don't be afraid to pick up the phone if there's anything we can do to help. I'll need to run all this by the board, so it could take a while for HR to put together a formal package. But the bottom line is you belong here at Albright. In fact, I'm looking for you to take over the Eastern region. Senior client manager. Will you think about it at least?"

Head up the Eastern region? That was Payton's job.

Was there such a thing as mental whiplash? She'd climbed out of bed this morning moderately wealthy only to learn she was broke. But not to worry, because she could rent out her uterus to her gay best friend and become a countess. Now Albright was riding in on a white horse to save her from financial collapse—by giving her Payton's job.

So what the hell did that mean for Payton?

CHAPTER SEVEN

Penderworth was as fascinating on the inside as it had appeared to Lark from the driveway. Not a royal mansion by any means, but grand just the same. Though to hear Channing tell it, it was quite ordinary despite its historic designation as a manor home.

The guided tour had so far been a history lesson, from the craftsman masonry and woodwork to the rugged period pieces blended among more modern furnishings. Very few fine antiques—just old stuff. On the upper floor were four cavernous bedrooms, one of them converted to a study. All had high ceilings with crown molding and crystal chandeliers, and large casement windows. Channing's room had a private bath, a renovation from twenty years ago. The older lavatory, with its claw-foot tub and marble top basin, was off the main hallway. Though far from lavish, it was a splendid home for a family, certainly more opulent than Channing was willing to admit. Penderworth was a palace compared to the dilapidated row house in Mattapan where Lark had grown up.

Lark paused at the top of the stairs to envision life at Penderworth more than two centuries ago, before electricity and running water. The eyes of the manor's earliest occupants followed their movements from imposing oil portraits that lined the second-floor hallway. All covering cracks in the walls, Channing had said.

"Channing, I can't believe you might lose all this after having it in your family for so long."

"I'm sure it never occurred to Poppa that I might someday want to live here, or he'd have told me about his portfolio. I'd made a life for myself in Boston, and for all he knew I was happy there. For all *I* knew, as well."

The Channing Hughes enigma again, revealing yet another permutation of her complex persona. Gone for now was the angry brooder with the sardonic swagger. This Channing was coming to grips with her vulnerability.

At first glance, the invitation to tour was Channing honoring a rain check, repaying a favor for the ride home from the pub. Or maybe she'd felt compelled to demonstrate, as she had on the plane, that she was capable of being polite. Surely she knew that good manners displayed only as social pleasantries didn't strictly require follow-through.

Or maybe Channing actually liked her well enough to extend herself, something Lark had begun to doubt until she got the invitation.

"I checked you out online, Lady Hughes. I know…it's kind of stalker-ish. But trust me, everyone who meets you does the same thing. You have a way of sticking in people's heads. And unless you've fudged your work bio, you're still holding a pretty decent hand." To say nothing of the fact that women who knew how to present themselves in a world where appearances mattered could usually write their own ticket. "This is a temporary setback, nothing more."

She kept her voice down, since Channing said she hadn't yet told the domestic couple in her employ that the dwindled estate would soon force them into retirement. Her concern for their welfare was poignant.

Channing nudged her to start back down the stairs. "That should be a comfort to us when we're all sleeping rough, with our pitiful signs and tin cups. Best watch your step here…I'm fairly certain the insurance has lapsed."

"If I were litigious, I'd have sued you already for destroying my company car."

"Point taken, Dr. Latimer."

"I bet this is a great house for parties."

"Perhaps for the Penderworths. We weren't the partying sort, Poppa and I. Most of his closest associates had *real* money, if you know what I mean. Like Kenny's dad, the Earl of Alanford. A party here would be like a social welfare visit for them. Speaking of Kenny, my silly *viscount* friend…he's joining us for supper with his boyfriend Oliver. Hope you don't mind. He's really quite harmless."

"He's really quite hilarious."

She'd genuinely enjoyed their banter at the pub. And while she appreciated Channing sharing her friends, she wondered if Channing had invited the guys as a buffer, a way to keep her in the friend zone. Which was disappointing. But also fine. Best not to get the wrong idea.

Their tour wrapped up downstairs in the great hall before another row of gilded portraits, where Channing shared a bit of history on the Hughes family. Great-great-grandfather Samuel had launched the family business in 1910, a small textile company that grew rapidly with a contract for the half-million military uniforms needed in the First World War.

"Little did our defense ministers realize the khaki dye they demanded had to be smuggled in from Germany."

"So you're descended from scofflaws."

"Oh no, I'm a Hughes."

Lark sighed loudly. "I refuse to laugh at slapstick humor."

Channing grinned, exposing a slight upper snaggletooth Lark hadn't noticed before. "Speaking of slapstick, Kenny was quite impressed to hear that I'd actually made a friend, meaning you of course. Though I can't imagine why. I'm not a monster… despite what you might have seen of me on the plane."

"We all have our bad days." Hearing Channing relegate her to the friend zone was deflating at first—she wanted Channing to find her fascinating—but there was something to be said for making it onto what was probably a very short list. "I'm a sucker for anyone who tosses her drink at a creep. If you're going to be a monster, be a righteous one."

Channing guided her down the line where they eventually reached a portrait done in the Dutch Masters style, a brightly-lit mustachioed face against a dark background. She stood back and folded her arms as if studying it anew. "This was Poppa, my grandfather...painted thirty-odd years ago before I was born. He never seemed to age but for the gray. Cheeky looking, wasn't he?"

Lark had to agree. "A white beard and he'd be Santa Claus."

Channing lingered as if paying homage, her eyes glassy with tears.

"You miss him."

"Very much. I'd have liked the chance to say goodbye."

"For what it's worth, goodbyes aren't always what they're cracked up to be. Especially long ones." She briefly described her mother's lingering deterioration from diabetes and a series of strokes, frankly admitting the most trying part of the ordeal was Ma's angry disposition.

"Seven years. That's so dreadfully sad. I suppose I should feel lucky Poppa didn't suffer."

"You're allowed to feel any way you want." Lark regretted that her reflections on Ma had shifted the spotlight away from Channing and onto herself. "I bet you and your Poppa made quite a pair."

"Mum sent me back here to live at eight years old. Poppa and I were rightly terrified of one another but we somehow muddled through. He was quite important then, a member of Parliament, economic advisor to Thatcher. Very proper. Whereas I had an embarrassing knack for finding trouble."

"Why doesn't that surprise me?"

"Nothing too awful. But when I found it, it was usually because Kenny lifted the rock and showed me where it was."

They wrapped up the portrait tour with Channing's father, a handsome air force officer killed in the First Gulf War when she was just a toddler. And Aunt Frances, who'd suffered from depression and taken her own life shortly after a miscarriage. It was a lot of tragedy for one family, despite the fortune they'd enjoyed. And now Channing was last of the line.

"Any chance your portrait gets added to—"

"Excuse me, Miss Channing. Shall I bring tea?"

Lark pivoted toward the familiar voice and found herself face-to-face with none other than Subject 17, Maisie Browning. A flicker of recognition flashed in the woman's eyes, but then she fixed her gaze firmly on Channing. Clearly she was anxious, perhaps that Lark would give away something learned in the interview. She recalled that Mrs. Browning hadn't told her employer of her wish to retire. It was possible she'd also hidden the extent of her ailment.

Channing said, "There you are. Cecil said you were feeling a bit under the weather. Are you better?"

"Yes, thank you. Nothing of concern."

"I say we pass on the tea since Kenny should be here any moment for supper. Unless of course"—she addressed Lark—"my guest would like to show off her tea skills."

"No, thank you. But I've been practicing at home. Four and a half minutes, no swishing the tea bag, milk first."

"I had a clue you were very bright. Lark, please allow me to introduce someone I consider part of my family." With obvious affection, Channing wrapped an arm around the housekeeper's shoulder. "This is Maisie Browning. She and her husband Cecil—he's the gentleman you saw waiting for me at the airport—they've worked for the Hughes family here at Penderworth for…"

"Thirty-four years. I was the first to hold you the night you were born."

"I remember it well. Your hands were cold," Channing teased. "Maisie, please meet my new friend from Boston, Dr. Lark Latimer. Lark came to my rescue on the plane when I found myself on the receiving end of someone's misguided attentions. By incredible coincidence we ran into each other last week at the Crown and Punchbowl. She's in Cambridge for a few weeks working on a project for her company."

"I do clinical research for Gipson Pharmaceuticals," she said formally, signaling her willingness to play along. Confidentiality was everything in the medical world. "Something in your kitchen smells wonderful."

"That's my shepherd's pie."

"It's Kenny's favorite," Channing added, making a gagging gesture behind Mrs. Browning's back. "Everyone spoils that lad. It's no wonder he's such a pill."

Maisie's eyes darted toward the front window and she smiled. "There's Lord Teasely now. I'll set supper out, you can help yourself whenever you like."

Lark winced to see Maisie hobbling back toward the kitchen, her arthritis an obvious burden on this rainy day. The sooner Channing and the Brownings had a heart-to-heart talk about the future of Penderworth, the better off they all would be.

* * *

"...I thought I'd bloody died and gone to hell," Kenny wailed. "There I was, standing in the office of a senior partner confessing not only to the fact that I was gay, but also that by some mortifying coincidence I happened to be bonking the man our client was suing for millions." He tipped his head toward his boyfriend Oliver. "Plemmons was absolutely gobsmacked. You'd have thought I was shagging his mum."

Oliver made a *Who, me?* face and shrugged. In contrast to Kenny's crisp oxford shirt and slacks, Oliver wore the uniform of a tech hipster—jeans and a plain black T-shirt with a hoodie. His shaving schedule was bimonthly at best. He cleared his throat and spoke directly to Lark, "So you won't think I'm a prat, his client wasn't suing me personally. It was a patent case involving one of our products. I merely represented our technology interests. We eventually settled by merging with their company and firing all the solicitors."

"A man after my own heart," Channing said. "Albright insures companies through mergers and acquisitions. My job was to figure out how much capital they stood to lose if it all suddenly went pear-shaped."

Finally, an explanation of Channing's work that Lark actually understood.

"Kenny says you resigned. Where do you go from here?" Oliver asked.

They were sitting in what Channing called the breakfast room, an informal dining area off the kitchen where the family took most of its meals. Channing had insisted on swapping seats with Lark so she'd have a clear line of sight to the back door, which led out to what had once been the carriage house. The Brownings kept a modest apartment there, she explained. Best they not slip in unnoticed and overhear the news that the estate was virtually worthless. Or catch Kenny and Oliver in a kiss. Or learn that Channing had left her job after a dismal affair with a married woman.

"I've not decided what to do next. Believe it or not, I received a call on Friday afternoon from my old boss, the CEO at Albright. He practically begged me to return. Naturally my first instinct was to decline, but before I could get that out of my mouth he offered me a significant promotion that would pay a great deal more money. Under the circumstances, I'm considering it quite seriously."

Up to now, Lark had let the others do most of the talking, intimidated somewhat by their sharp-witted exchanges and shared history. This particular bit of news however hit her right where she lived. "So there's a chance you'd come back to Boston? I'd vote for that."

"It's definitely on my list of possibilities. Though one of the best things about being here in England is having a support system…such as it is." She tipped her head toward Kenny and shrugged. "The worst thing about Boston was living in seclusion. My mum moved to Florida, but she didn't count anyway. I used to have loads of mates, women from Wellesley, from Harvard. Including one or two I'd dated for a while. But then Payton came along and I lost touch with all of them. Apparently if you turn down enough invites, people stop asking."

Lark waved her arms. "Hello…there's also me. You never know when you're going to need someone to swoop in and help chase off the bar creeps."

Kenny cleared his throat and addressed Channing pointedly. "I don't like this at all, Channing. Please promise me you won't end up back with that dreadful woman again. Certainly not because you need money. I'll write you a bloody check myself."

"And all I have to do is what, sire?"

The question hung in the air for several seconds until Oliver snorted. Clearly the three of them were in on the same joke.

"In the twenty years I've known you, Kenny, I've lost count of the outrageous ideas that come from that head of yours. But that one far and away was your crowning achievement."

With a hand to his mouth to stifle a laugh, Oliver said, "Come on, you have to admit the idea is rather resourceful."

Lark whipped her head from side to side trying to follow the cryptic conversation. "What's resourceful? Did I miss something?"

Channing ignored her question, fixing a scowl on Oliver. "Where *I'm* the resource. Or rather, my womb is."

"Will someone kindly let me in on this joke?"

"Kenny has this brilliant idea that he and I should get married. If he dies without an heir, you see, one of his Irish mafia relatives becomes Earl of Alanford. If I say yes, he's promised to move into Penderworth and throw a fat wad of his father's cash around to make it worthy of a viscount until the earl kicks over and hands him Breckham Hall." In an aside, she added, "He's only sixty-one, which means I could be stuck with Kenny for forty years. In return, all I have to do is bear him a child—a male child, since our archaic laws say only those with goolies can inherit earldoms. With my luck I'd pop out an entire field hockey team before I ever got one with a handle."

"No way!" Lark's laugh died as she took in the three serious faces. "You can't possibly be considering that. Isn't there some kind of law against sham marriages? You'd have to actually live as a married couple, right? Wait, does Channing get beheaded if she can't get pregnant?"

"An excellent question!"

Kenny shifted uncomfortably. "Probably not."

"It's hard scrubbing blood out of the flagstones," Oliver added.

Channing shook her finger at Oliver. "You put him up to this, didn't you? He told me you were the one who wanted kids. A dozen of them. Who in their right mind seriously thinks Kenny Hargreaves should be allowed to reproduce?"

The back door opened to Cecil, who entered the breakfast room without a word and began clearing the table.

Channing made a slicing motion across her throat to quiet the conversation. "Is Maisie ill again?"

"A wee bit tired is all, Miss Channing. I thought I'd give her a rest."

"Don't worry yourself, Cecil. Out of gratitude for the delicious shepherd's pie, Lord Teasely said he'd be more than happy to tidy up. His personal tribute to Maisie."

"Of course I did. It's only polite...but Channing refused my generous offer, as usual. She was worried I might break something, given my incredible clumsiness."

"*Wanker*," she mouthed as Cecil left through the door he'd entered.

Lark stood to collect Oliver's bowl and her own, amused to think the Brownings could possibly be oblivious to the fact that Kenny and Oliver were lovers. Channing was a different matter, but surely they'd seen clues when she was growing up. "I don't mind doing this while you guys finish your family planning session. I'm afraid it will give me bad dreams."

Channing shooed her away. "Sit, I'll do it."

"Change of subject then," Kenny announced. "Come with us next weekend to Amsterdam Pride. We're taking the overnight ferry from Harwich on Friday. The Canal Parade is Saturday on the Prinsengracht. We'll be back on the ferry by ten and home by Sunday noon. We booked an extra cabin for Ryan and Ali but they can't make it."

The Pride festival in the Dutch capital was one of the grandest in the world, the sort of event on Lark's evolving bucket list. But Kenny was shouting toward the kitchen where Channing had gone with the dishes, his invitation clearly meant for her.

"That all depends. I refuse to be crammed into that pill box you call a backseat all the way to Amsterdam and back."

"We'll take my Peugeot," Oliver said.

"And I'm not coming unless Lark comes too. Last time I went with you to London, I had to find my own way home."

All eyes were suddenly on Lark, who could barely think beyond the fact that saying yes meant sharing a cabin overnight with Channing. "I'm in."

* * *

Having walked her guests out to the parking circle, Channing leaned into the Skoda to brush Lark's cheek with a kiss. "So glad you could come. Let's have dinner this week. I'll call."

She'd have liked the chance to linger with Lark over another cup of tea but Kenny and Oliver had shown no inclination to leave. Plainly, they were hanging around to see Lark on her way.

Straddling a puddle in the driveway, Kenny folded his arms as the tiny hatchback disappeared through the gate. "I found her rather interesting. Not many Americans get our sense of humor."

"She not only gets it, she gives it back as well."

Oliver lit a cigarette and blew the smoke away from where they were clustered. "I've never seen eyes that were actually gold. Wonder what her ancestry is."

"Swiss and Irish," Channing said. "I asked. She did one of those saliva tests because her mum wasn't sure who her father was." Lark had confided that her mother was only seventeen when she was born—and that she had a half-sister who was two years older. It was nothing short of remarkable that she'd gotten through something as challenging as medical school with so little family support.

"You fancy her, yes?" Oliver asked.

"I barely know her."

"She fancies you, I think."

Only days ago, she'd deflected Kenny's musings with glib remarks about Lark so as not to subject herself to his withering judgment over something that was hardly of consequence. A possible return to Boston cast her trivial flirtation with Lark in a different light. It wasn't a conscious shift in her thinking, just a sudden realization that she'd reimagined Lark as more than a temporary fling.

Kenny waved away Oliver's cigarette smoke, crinkling his nose in disgust. "I wanted to like her, truly I did."

Channing recognized his parry—he'd thrown that out there to bait her into asking him why he hadn't…the annoying prick. "Do tell, Lord Twit. Why can't you like her?"

"Because I can't have her luring you back to Boston."

"Albright is the one luring me back to Boston. A promotion and a raise, remember? And unlike some people, they aren't asking for my firstborn in return."

"A totally unfair characterization. My offer is to help you, not to hire you. I only mean to make my child's life a pleasant one. How fortunate that yours would be more pleasant as well. Are you seriously going to give up Penderworth without a whimper?" He failed to watch his step and sloshed through a puddle. "Blimey, have you not heard of drainage? I'm sending Gerald around tomorrow to level your drive."

Channing stifled a laugh at his wet feet. "I don't advise that. If Cecil catches someone nosing around the yard, he's apt to level his arse."

"Penderworth is in serious need of attention, Channing. At least hire a maintenance crew before it falls to ruin."

"There's a lot wants doing." It was especially dreary compared to the meticulous Breckham Hall. She couldn't even begin repairs until she'd had a talk to nudge the Brownings out. "I'll hire out for the basics once I've spoken to an agent about what's absolutely necessary to get it ready for sale."

"You can't sell this place. It's your birthright. It's your home, your father's home. Think of all our memories here. How can you think of abandoning it like it means nothing?"

"What do I need of this house, Kenny? It's not as if I can waltz into the economics department at Cambridge and take Poppa's place. And don't say it—I didn't go to university for six years to whelp a litter of children for the future Earl of Alanford. I enjoy my work and I'm quite good at it."

Oliver stopped him from kicking off his wet shoes by the door. "We should get along back to London, my lord. Traffic on the A10 will be wretched tonight."

"Very well...thank you for your hospitality, Lady Hughes. We must do this again." With a despondent sigh he added, "Many, many more times, I hope."

His sincerity touched her, reminding her that she loved him deeply despite his many foibles. His concern over her emotional attachment to Penderworth struck her as genuine, regardless of his self-serving motivations. It was entirely possible he was the one still attached to the manor, as it had been a haven when battles with his father over his developing sexuality had made him dread going home. They'd shared many memories here, most of them grand.

"We'll have her to the flat in London," Oliver said, stroking Kenny's arm lovingly as he steered him toward the car.

"Kenny, wait." Overcome with emotion, Channing rushed to give him a hug, burying her face against his starched collar. "Now that Poppa's gone, you and the Brownings are the only reason I care about England at all. I can't imagine what I'd do if you weren't my friend."

"All the more reason not to fall for someone who lives in Boston. If you want company, there's a woman I know in London, someone in our office."

Oliver shook his head. "Here he goes again."

"Admit it, Channing. You deserve to hook up with someone decent for a change."

"Funny, I was just saying the same thing to Oliver."

Kenny paid no mind to the insult. "Darcey Jensen, she works with me. Mid-twenties, a paralegal. Very pretty, if you go for that perpetual Nordic frown. If you hadn't been so quick to insist on Lark coming to Amsterdam, I'm sure Darcey would have been happy to join us."

"Oh, and that wouldn't have been rude at all. 'Come along to Amsterdam. Not you, Lark. He meant Darcey.'"

"So that's all then. You invited her along because you didn't want to be rude."

"I never said that."

"But she's not your type. You *did* say that."

Kenny was a crafty bugger, usually up to something. That made his smug expression suspect. Either he was celebrating having trapped her into going out with his paralegal friend or admitting Lark was on her radar. It was no use trying to deflect.

"If it's all the same to you, I'd prefer to choose my own women."

"Fine, but she is *not* luring you back to Boston."

CHAPTER EIGHT

Lark perched on the arm of the sofa in Niya's office looking past her to the drab building next door. "How is it that you're the freaking director of Cambridge PharmaStat and you have the crappiest view in the whole building? Whereas I'm basically a migrant worker and my office looks out on the lake."

"I actually prefer being out of the bustle," Niya replied matter-of-factly. "But don't tell Dr. Martin I said that. He got an offer from Pfizer last year and used it as leverage to make petty demands. A corner office, a parking space next to the elevator. And the new woman at reception? Florence Martin, his daughter-in-law."

In Lark's view, Dr. Martin had always been polite and respectful. While she couldn't blame him for playing hardball to pick up a few extra perks, the fact that he'd demanded Niya's corner office rubbed her the wrong way. It was an unnecessary display of dominance, sexist at its core.

"Never mind my office. I want to know what popped up on your calendar that you found more important than meeting my granddaughter." As Lark described the historic manor house, Niya cut her off. "I'm more interested in the who, not the what. This is the woman you met on the plane?"

"Yeah, I'm not sure what there is to tell. I'm feeling it but I don't know if she is. She's friendly, she's funny. But she's also coming down off a two-year relationship where the other woman basically treated her like crap. Everything looks new and shiny when you're on the rebound. Then it wears off and you realize it was just a pleasant distraction."

She decided not to mention running into one of their study subjects at Penderworth. There was no legitimate reason to share details of Maisie Browning's home life.

"A couple of her friends were there too. One of them's a viscount, plus his boyfriend. I felt like that Nick guy from the *The Great Gatsby*, the one who tagged along to all the glamorous parties and told us how interesting everyone was."

She also didn't mention Channing's crumbled inheritance, nor Kenny's stunning proposition that she marry him and give him an heir. Like most medical professionals, Niya was accepting of the LGBT community, but the notion of a sham family might have offended her old-fashioned sensibilities.

"I'm going with them next weekend to the Pride parade in Amsterdam. They do it on one of the canals with a bunch of floats."

"Ha! All my efforts to recruit you to PharmaStat... I was using the wrong bait."

"Except Channing now says she might go back to Boston. Wouldn't that be just my luck? I fall in love with someone from Cambridge and take a job here so I can be close to her. Then she goes back to work in Boston. I think I'll stay put till the storm passes."

"I've been thinking about my future too, especially with this Flexxene business," Niya said, her voice taking a serious turn. "Dev and I talked about it over the weekend. My husband... he's just the sweetest, kindest man in the world. It breaks his heart to see me so stressed over this job. 'Stop worrying about the higher-ups in Geneva,' he says. If I'm forced to resign, he's agreed to sell the bottle shops and newsstands, all of them. We'll quit the rat race and buy a cottage in Portugal ten years earlier than we planned. Pretty sure we can afford it."

"Niya, you're at the pinnacle of your career. There's no way I'm letting you take the fall for something that wasn't your fault. You did nothing wrong. Relax and let me do my job."

"Yes, do your job. But no matter how this turns out, I'm at peace with it. Dr. Martin may be an arse, but he's more than capable of taking over as director. And Dev and I would be happy in Portugal. What else matters in life?"

Frustrated and sad, Lark returned to her office to prepare for her next interview. There was little doubt PharmaStat would want a scapegoat and Niya was there for the taking, especially if she refused to fight back. They wouldn't blink twice at throwing her under the bus, no matter her impeccable record.

* * *

"Bugger all!" Channing bounced her pen off her grandfather's desk and groaned. Four months—that was how far she could stretch Poppa's remaining cash. After that she'd have to tap her savings to keep Penderworth running until it sold.

That wasn't even the worst of it. Much of the profit she might have anticipated from the eventual sale would be eaten up in advance by all the repairs necessary to make a drafty, rundown manor house attractive to a potential buyer. Just to break even, she had less than a year to close the sale and pay off the tax debt. Longer than that and the inheritance might actually cost her money.

Her first step had to be a sit-down with Cecil and Maisie, something she dreaded. Suppose they'd planned to live out their retirement in the carriage house they'd called home for more than three decades? It was a reasonable assumption given their devoted service and the familial bond, especially if Poppa had kept his withering financial status from them as well.

She could always marry Kenny…

"Christ!" It was bloody bonkers, as was talking aloud when she was the only one around.

Her cell phone lit up with another call from Robin Saunders, Mitch's admin. He'd promised to call back once the HR department put together a salary and benefits package for her potential return. If he had her in mind to head up the Eastern region, he probably intended to promote Payton to VP for mergers. She'd been angling for that job for as long as Channing could remember.

Practically speaking, Mitch's offer was infinitely preferable to life as a broodmare for a couple of gay men, one of them incorrigible. The idea of returning to Albright had grown on her, especially given her new financial urgency. Plus there was that other upside to going back to Boston that she hadn't considered a week ago—Lark Latimer.

"This is Channing Hughes."

"Please hold."

She wouldn't enjoy facing Payton in the office, but she'd see less of her if Payton moved up to the executive level. Plus the challenge of heading up the Eastern region would make her job interesting again. Gradually all the water would pass under the bridge and their affair would be ancient history, an awkward but irrelevant memory.

Mitch was taking his sweet time picking up the call. If she were to return to Albright, her first order of business would be a chat with someone in corporate communications about their choice of "hold" music. New Age piano wasn't new anymore. There were better ways to—

"Channing, it's me…please don't hang up."

The shock of hearing Payton's voice manifested as pins and needles down her spine.

"Don't blame Robin. I didn't know how else to reach you since you won't take my calls and you ignore my texts and emails. It's urgent that we talk."

Channing hated the exhilaration that overtook her will to cut Payton off.

"I can't believe you walked out without a single word of explanation. How could you be so unprofessional? Do you have any idea of the rumors you set off?"

"What, that I stole client files and went to AIG? I didn't." Payton knew very well her employment contract at Albright prevented her from going to work for a similar company for five years. "Would you rather I'd told them the truth, that you dumped me after a two-year affair and promoted Boyd so you wouldn't have to travel with me anymore? He's not competent to handle client negotiations and you know it."

Payton sighed heavily. "What choice did I have? The two of us continuing to travel together was out of the question."

"Why is that? I never once let our relationship affect my job, unlike you. Did you honestly think I'd keep working at Albright knowing I was never going to get a superior evaluation out of you because you were paranoid people might think you were showing favoritism? That's worth thousands of dollars a year, Payton. How much more did you expect me to sacrifice?"

"It was perfectly within your rights to leave Albright, but the issue here is how you did it. You deliberately walked out without explanation because you wanted to dump this mess in my lap. All I'm asking is that you clear it up, that you contact HR and make it absolutely clear this was about your own issues with going back to England, and stop all this—what is it you call it—chin wagging."

"Fall on my sword again for you. That's what you always expect from me."

Drumming her fingers on the desk, Channing stewed. The angry side of her wanted to hang up, but she'd never stopped wanting Payton to say a few magic words to make everything all right. She didn't need to hear her grovel, nor did she want Payton back. All she wanted was not to feel like a fool for thinking Payton had truly loved her.

"Robin says you talked with Mitch on Monday. Knowing him, he tried to talk you out of leaving."

So Payton wasn't aware of Mitch's offer that she take over the Eastern region, which possibly meant she knew nothing about her impending promotion to VP. Unless Albright had other plans. Surely they weren't considering letting go of someone with her experience.

"If Mitch wants your input, Payton, I'm sure he'll loop you in."

Payton's voice lowered, a stark reminder of how sneaky they used to be when others milled about. "Channing, please…"

"Please? What more could you possibly want from me, Payton? I offered you everything I had."

"And I treated you horribly. This is all my fault and I'm sorry."

"Great, so *now* I get an apology. I'll put it in the drawer where I keep the rest of my useless junk." She too lowered her voice on the off-chance the Brownings had returned from their afternoon errands. Voices carried in the cavernous manor. "You had two years to untangle your life. 'Ben, I want a divorce.' Five words. Five bloody words. If you'd loved me half as much as you claimed, you'd have been bursting to get yourself free."

"You make it sound like a choice between the chef's salad or the chowder. Leaving Ben would have cost me everything, Channing. Kathleen's pregnant. What if she'd cut me off from my grandchild? I couldn't bring myself to do it. I never meant to hurt you. I don't know what else to say."

"Then why the bloody hell did you call?"

Since the first text she'd picked up on the plane, Channing had imagined herself unloading on Payton if she dared pick up her call. She'd seize the moral high ground, punish her with pugilistic jabs to her character. It was her turn to have the last word.

"Channing, this whole situation is impossible." The hitch in Payton's breath was familiar—she was trying not to cry. "You can't come back. Too many people are asking questions. My own secretary told me she'd heard you were having an affair. The moment you come through that door, they'll see it all over our faces. You know what happens then—HR will go back through our every move wondering if we put our relationship above the company."

"Wha—" Payton had always been paranoid but this was over the top. "There's no bloody end to your nerve, is there? It's not enough that you deliberately wasted two years of my life, now you have to muck up the rest. What gives you the right to decide where I work?"

"Nothing." She sniffed loudly. "That's why all I have left is to beg."

Channing's impulse to lash out again sputtered as she envisioned the pitiful sight of Payton trying to hold herself together. How many times had she crumbled at those tears?

"Bollocks," she muttered, more to herself than to Payton. "You aren't the only one in trouble here. I came home to the news that Poppa left me nothing but Penderworth and a tax bill. I can't ignore Mitch's offer. I need to go back to work—soon."

"It doesn't matter, Channing. If this blows up, it'll ruin both of us."

Several seconds of quiet followed, but Channing was determined to wait her out. She'd said her piece. Maybe for once, Payton would put someone else's needs first.

"Channing, I know what you're capable of. You can walk into any finance company in the world and tell them which office you want. Stay in London and I'll persuade Mitch to waive the noncompete."

"I can't believe you're doing this to me."

"I'm sorry. We were selfish and now we're paying for it."

"How is that, Payton? Where exactly is this costing you anything at all?"

Voices downstairs signaled the return of the Brownings. Any moment, Maisie would appear in the doorway to ask her preference for supper.

"I have to go."

"Please consider what—"

"For your information, I already told Mitch I'd gotten homesick, that losing Poppa got to me and I felt overwhelmed all of a sudden. That's the official story he's peddling to HR. Repeat it as often as you like." Channing ended the call.

CHAPTER NINE

This was a date. Never mind that Channing hadn't called with an invitation, hadn't made a reservation, hadn't bothered to change from her stonewashed jeans and bulky black sweater. To Lark, it still counted as a date. Especially since Channing had enveloped her in a long silent hug the moment she walked through the door of the tiny apartment.

"Let's push this closer," she said as she scooted the coffee table toward the couch where Channing sat. Her tiny space wasn't ideal for dinner guests, but Channing had insisted she hardly cared about an elaborate meal. It was the company she wanted.

Lark situated herself on a stack of throw pillows. "Hope you like chicken jalfrezi."

"Brilliant. What's a little acid reflux as long as there's wine?" Channing kicked off her tan flats, shoes so plain they could have passed for bedroom slippers.

"It's from Curry King. Everything on the menu is totally worth the aftereffects."

She noted also that absent her usual makeup Channing looked more girl than woman. There was a vulnerability about her, the same look Lark had seen in the airport lounge just before they boarded. At dinner on Sunday, Channing had predicted a tough week ahead, with difficult decisions about the estate.

"Any progress on Penderworth?"

"I've been up to my arse in spreadsheets. Kenny put me in touch with a property inspector who's advising me on what absolutely must be done versus what I should leave for the buyer. It's silly to pour money into custom renovations someone else will rip out." As they ate, Channing groused about her financial state and the issues with getting Penderworth ready to sell. "I still can't get over Poppa hiding this from me. He had to know what a headache it would be."

"I have to hand it to Ma. The best thing she ever did for us was leave all her worldly possessions to Roger. They'd been living together for fourteen years, so it wasn't like he swooped in and stole our inheritance. It wasn't worth all that much anyway. Chloe and I both were glad not to have the hassle."

"This would be maddening if I had to sort it with squabbling siblings too. It's bad enough that I feel eternally obliged to Maisie and Cecil." She blew out a frustrated breath. "That sounded cruel. They're practically family and I love them dearly."

Lark caught herself smiling at how relieved both Channing and the Brownings would be when they finally sat down for a heart-to-heart and discovered they wanted the same thing.

"Does my suffering amuse you?"

"No…I think it's sweet you worry about them. If you were half the ogre you pretend to be, you'd have no friends at all. I think your bitchy act on the plane was just that—an act."

"Underestimate me at your peril, Dr. Latimer. If you'd heard me on the phone with Payton today, you'd know what a first-class bitch I can be."

"You finally talked to Payton?" That, more than her financial issues, better explained why she'd wanted company tonight. "I never said you didn't have it in you. I thought you weren't taking her calls."

"She tricked me into answering by going through another number. She's always had a dodgy streak. I should have hung up, but no—I fell into my usual Payton trance. She knew I would."

"It's hard to imagine you being under someone else's mind control."

"We all have our weaknesses. Except mine isn't Payton, actually. It's my fatal need to have the last word, to argue with someone incessantly until they finally surrender and admit that I'm right." Wineglass in hand, she leaned back on the couch and tucked her bare feet beneath her. "And I've an amazing knack for humiliating myself. I assumed she was calling to persuade me to come back to Albright. Quite the opposite. She begged me not to. She's convinced they're all whispering about our affair since I left, that if I come back they'll notice the chill between us, soiling her pristine reputation. And mine too, I suppose. The annoying part is that she's probably right. It does me no favors if I go back to a promotion and my colleagues all think I earned it between the bedsheets."

"I don't suppose it occurred to her that *she* should be the one to leave?"

"So you're a standup comic now?"

"Come on, the woman's got a pair of *cojones*." Having studied the headshot on Albright's website, she had no trouble picturing Payton Crane working behind the scenes to manipulate Channing into doing whatever she wanted. Women didn't get to be executives by letting others push them around. "In fact, I'm willing to bet you used to like that about her."

Channing laughed softly before fixing a blank gaze at the floor. "I suppose I did. She's the woman we all want to be. Strong and smart, and she works extremely hard. And takes guff from absolutely no one. The most astonishing thing about our relationship was seeing her relinquish control. Not just sexually...she could be quite vulnerable whenever we were alone. Payton never let down her guard anywhere else. That's when I knew what we had was something extraordinary. I felt like the most privileged person on earth because I got to see her like that."

Lark could have done without Channing's reference to her sex life with Payton, since it jolted her with an irrational sense of jealousy. Nor was she especially happy to see the subtle smile, the first from Channing when she talked about Payton. Was it a pleasant memory tucked away or a longing to feel it again? Before giving in to her feelings, she needed to peel this part of Channing back and see what lay beneath it.

"How did it happen, your affair?"

Channing wagged her empty glass. "If I'm to tell that story, I'll need more wine."

* * *

She'd told no one, not even Kenny, the dramatic story of how she and Payton had fallen into each other's arms, into each other's beds. The details were deeply personal, and they carried consequences to this day.

"You must promise me you'll never repeat a word of this."

"Who do I know that cares one way or the other?"

"Perhaps Kenny and Oliver…anyone really. It must remain completely private."

"Of course." Lark refreshed their glasses and returned to the pillows on the floor.

"Before we got involved, I admired Payton so much, respected her. She's just the sort of example we need in the business world, women who prove it really can be done. She was extraordinary. And fit in that attractive older woman kind of way. I liked thinking I was looking at myself eighteen years in the future…which seems to be something I do. But it was never that sort of vibe that comes when you start to fancy someone. Do you know the one I mean?"

"Absolutely."

"We did a lot of traveling, just the two of us. Overnights for client meetings and all. Our territory was the entire eastern region. Miami, Atlanta, Philadelphia, New York, and everything in between. Albright's very big on sitting down face-to-face with clients. From the very start I saw that Payton had a fierce work ethic. On the airplane, in the taxi—her head was always working. But once we sat down to dinner in the evening, she was done for the day. All it took was that first sip of wine and it was as if she'd slithered out of her corporate skin."

The memory of those early evenings stirred a sense of nostalgia for what had been a warm mentoring relationship. Had they stayed that course, Channing likely would have been heading her own division by now. Instead she'd allowed their affair to dampen her ambition.

"I got the feeling she was starved for conversation, that she and her husband never talked. She was wicked smart, knew all about politics, books, film. She'd go on about her daughter in college, all the headaches of planning her wedding. Or her son, who played varsity basketball. I was happy just to listen, but she'd also prod me into sharing personal things. She loved hearing about Poppa and Penderworth, what it was like to grow up in England. Sometimes she'd grill me about the women I was dating. I always looked forward to our trips together."

"Sounds like you were falling in love."

"Hmm...it never felt that way. We were mates."

"Obviously something changed."

"It was Philadelphia, the Four Seasons Hotel. We were having our ritual wine and dinner in the hotel restaurant. She'd seemed out of sorts all day, distracted. I don't know why but I was anxious about it. I thought she was cross with me over something. Perhaps I'd botched the figures or said the wrong thing to our client. So I finally got up my nerve to ask what was wrong. She began crying. Not misty eyes, mind you—sobbing. Finally she blubbered out that she was pregnant."

"Whoa...I didn't see that coming."

"Nor did she. Forty-five years old, on the executive track for VP. And her youngest is a senior in high school, right? A baby is the last thing she wants."

"I have a feeling I know where this is going."

She studied Lark's expression for signs of disapproval. Many long-time Bostonians were staunch Catholics with pro-life beliefs. She'd totally forgotten Lark saying her mother had given birth to two children while in her teens.

"For Payton, it was never a question of what she'd do about it. What bothered her most was the guilt over not telling her husband." She sat up straight to push back against a possible objection. "No, imagine what's going through her head. They're Catholic as well. Not terribly devout, but still. What if Ben had come out against it? She couldn't bear to take that chance."

"Right there should have told you she couldn't be trusted to consider anyone's interests but her own." She held up a hand to head off Channing's protest. "Not that I think she was wrong, but that's a huge thing to keep from your husband."

"Obviously their marriage was no pillar of strength. Anyway, she'd already made the appointment for herself at a clinic in New Hampshire. Surgical, because it was too late for the pills by the time she realized she was pregnant. She'd planned to go alone, which I thought was tragic, so I offered to take off work and drive her. We do that for our mates, right? I booked the hotel and paid for both rooms so Ben wouldn't find out."

Channing did that quite a lot over the next two years whenever they'd tack on an extra night out of town. They couldn't bill Albright, but Payton couldn't risk it showing up on her credit card bill either. Besides the emotional damage, the affair also had cost Channing thousands and thousands of dollars, including not only the expenses for their illicit trysts, but lost salary and bonuses. That was when she thought she had the Hughes fortune at her fingertips.

"After her procedure, we sat together on a love seat in her room. Hardly talking, but she was shaking so I held her. For that moment I was the most important person in the world to her, and I relished it. I'm not even sure how it started. She turned… our lips were close…I kissed her."

Lark sat riveted to her story, hugging her knees to her chest.

"I don't know which of us was more shocked. Or more terrified, frankly. The situation called for self-control, obviously, which is never as easy as it sounds. I laid beside her all night, my arm around her. I was so overcome I could hardly sleep."

Talking about it triggered old emotions, among them a fierce sense of protectiveness. She'd taken care of Payton in so many ways.

"Over breakfast the next day we talked about it. Both of us thought it best not to pursue anything. We could have written it off to hormones and returned easily to a work relationship. Then two weeks later we flew together to Miami for another meeting. Three hours from home...I took some papers to her room after dinner. That was it. We both were absolutely electric with desire."

* * *

It was an incredibly touching story, and it gave Lark a clearer picture of the sort of person Channing was. No matter how dismissive or uncaring she tried to sound, at her core she was a nurturer. Lark had a similar streak, a trait she'd developed as a counterweight to her mother's poor parenting. It was why she'd gone to medical school in the first place, and why she'd dropped out to play caretaker.

From what Channing had told her, she too had grown up without the attention of her mother. Perhaps it made her more sensitive to the needs of others.

"That's an amazing story, Channing. The way you describe it, I can see exactly how it happened."

"Perhaps you can explain it to me," she said blithely.

"You said it yourself—you liked who you were with her. You relished feeling strong and protective, and she let you do that." It also explained why she was having such a hard time telling the Brownings about the sale of Penderworth.

"And you're not put off about what she did?"

"Speaking personally, I've always been a little conflicted over the issue, seeing as how I'm the product of an unplanned pregnancy. But I support anyone's right to choose—period."

"Just remember that you promised to keep it secret. She'd be mortified to know I'd told a soul."

"No worries, ever." In fact, she had a similar secret of her own, one she wouldn't breach on the chance that Channing might someday meet her sister. Lark had cut class in high school to go with Chloe to the women's clinic in Waltham. Even fifteen years later the memories were visceral.

"Lately I've wondered if she regrets it," Channing mused. "Maybe it got to her and I remind her of it."

For Lark, sitting through details of the affair with Payton had the unintended side effect of making their evening feel less like a date. It was almost as if there were a third person in the room. But since they were on the subject…

"Didn't it ever bother you that Payton was married?"

Several seconds of icy quiet followed, after which Channing reached for her shoes.

"No, wait. I didn't mean for that to sound judgmental… honest."

"Then why do I feel that I'm being asked to defend myself?"

"I'm sorry, you don't have to." She swallowed hard, realizing her only way out of this was some version of the truth, the gist of which probably *was* judgmental. "I was curious about how you dealt with it, is all. On the plane you said something about not deserving anyone's sympathy, that you considered yourself a home-wrecker. It must have bothered you at some level."

Her words hung interminably until Channing relaxed and tucked her feet again. In a noticeable departure from her earlier candor and ease, she was defensive, more guarded. "I wasn't proud of myself but they were her vows, not mine. She felt she'd gotten her life all wrong, that she was always meant to be with a woman. She loved her family though… That's a lot of guilt to process once you realize the life you should have had was one in which your children might never have been born. Whatever remorse I felt, it was canceled out by knowing I was giving her something she needed and not making her feel ashamed about it."

"Because you loved her."

"I certainly thought so." There was an unmistakable tinge of anger in the set of her jaw. "It's hard to look back now and not feel that I was played for a fool. Who knows if anything she ever said was true?"

"She must have loved you, Channing. A person can't fake that."

"I don't know what to believe." The tension over Lark's question had dissipated with Channing's obvious need to talk.

"Once we both realized our relationship was serious, I asked her to divorce her husband. She understood that it wasn't fair to me, but she asked me please to wait a year until her son left for university. So what did he do? The little bastard picked Boston College because he didn't want to leave home. Spoiled dolt... he can't even dress himself. So we reset the countdown. She promised to end her marriage by my thirtieth birthday or else. One way or the other I needed to get on with my life. We didn't make it that far."

That's what Bess had said when Lark's "couple of months" with Ma went on and on with no end in sight. No wonder she'd lost patience. "It's bad enough that you waited so long, but then you came away empty-handed."

"If I were being mature about it, I suppose I'd be grateful for the experience. It was good when it was good." Her slumped shoulders and sad eyes said what her words would not—Payton had broken her heart. Or maybe it was the rejection itself. There was only so much a woman of pride like Channing could take. Being prepared for the outcome wasn't the same as being ready.

"It's Payton's loss if you ask me." Lark had been hugging her knees to overcome the impulse to reach out physically to Channing. "Love's more than just the right two people finding each other. They have to find each other at exactly the right time. That's lightning in a bottle and then some."

"Mmm...it's a bit of a miracle that it happens at all."

Lark had never believed much in miracles, nor in fate if she were honest. It was pure luck that she'd missed her flight, that Jeremy had plopped her in the seat next to Channing, that Niya had suggested meeting at the Crown and Punchbowl. If what Channing said was true, she had only a tiny window in which to learn if *they* were the right people at the right time.

CHAPTER TEN

A ray of sunshine, rare of late, cast a diagonal streak across Poppa's bookcase. Dust particles floated like bubbles in a glass of champagne, causing Channing to erupt in a sneezing fit, her third of the afternoon. "I'll be so glad when we get this room cleaned out."

Maisie entered the study with another empty crate and handed her a white linen handkerchief, its corner embossed with a cursive H. "Take this, Miss Channing. It belonged to Lord Hughes."

The anticipation alone prompted Channing to sneeze again.

"Would you like me to open a window?" Toby Singleton had done the literal heavy lifting in sorting the study. A graduate student of economics at Cambridge, he was tasked with the chore of helping her collect Poppa's papers and books for archiving at the new library named in his honor. Toby was stout and ungainly, and his black-framed glasses slid down his nose at every turn of the head. His overall clumsiness made him a frightening figure atop the ladder, where he took meticulous photos of each row of books before taking them down and packing them.

"Stay where you are, Toby. I'll do it." With a grunt that was keenly unladylike, she tried to no avail to free the wooden frame from where the moisture had held it all winter.

"Let me have a go, Miss Channing. I've a trick with these stubborn brutes." Maisie pounded the casing firmly with the heels of her hands to loosen the stickiness, after which the window opened with ease. "You have to show them who's boss."

"Maisie, your hands..." Channing had never noticed the stiffened curl of her fingers, nor the bony protrusions. "Are you all right?"

"Nothing to worry about, just a touch of arthritis."

"A touch? It looks quite painful." She snatched away a crate Maisie had started to lift. "You shouldn't be doing this. Have you seen a doctor about that?"

"Aye, Miss Channing. It looks worse than it is."

Maisie was all too dismissive, Channing thought. It made sense now why she'd changed her routines in the kitchen, calling on Cecil to chop vegetables and pinch the dough for pies. "No more hauling crates for you. Toby will carry all of this to his van, right Toby?"

"Of course. Professor Lord Hughes had quite the eye for economics history," he said as he precariously waved a book from the top shelf. "He's got the entire set of *Wealth of Nations*, Adam Smith. Not first editions, mind you, but they're quite old and in excellent condition. These were practically required reading for macro theory."

"Especially in this house. My grandfather set me upon them the summer before I started university." She hadn't planned to spend this entire day in the study, nor to play such a significant role in the university's archiving. It was only when she realized Poppa had mixed his scholarly papers with his personal correspondence that she decided it would be best if she sorted those herself. But she'd had enough for one day. "Toby, what would you say to collecting all the books and taking them back to the library to finish sorting? Anything that doesn't belong I can pick up when I bring the papers. We have photos to log the contents, yes?"

"Yes, Miss Hughes."

Channing tightened her gut as he descended the ladder with his arms full, recalling her quip to Lark that the insurance had probably lapsed. She'd traded texts with Lark that morning, not for any substantive reason, but to connect after their revealing talk the night before. Their emotionally intimate conversation reminded her of the early days with Payton when they'd sit for hours shedding the layers of their inner selves, uncovering the secrets and dreams they kept from everyone else.

She regretted getting defensive over Lark's question about how she'd justified an affair with a married woman. Not only was it silly to have been offended by the obvious, it was another embarrassing display of temper, the likes of which too often had led to rash behavior. She'd be furious with herself today had she given in to her impulse and stormed out in a huff.

Lark was… Channing didn't quite have the words. She was an opportunity not to be wasted. A funny, decent, pretty woman who aroused her interests. When she'd left Lark's flat the night before, they'd shared quite a long hug, with Lark assuring her the angst over Payton would someday end with relief that it hadn't worked out. That's how it worked once people fell out of love. Then Lark has kissed her cheek and waved to her from the door as she left in an Uber.

With a crate of lecture notes in hand, she started down the stairs behind Maisie, noticing for the first time her housekeeper's halting gait as she gripped the banister. The fact that Maisie struggled so with day-to-day chores yet resisted retirement didn't bode well for the talk they needed to have. It worried her to think the Brownings might be dependent on their wages. An adult nephew was profoundly disabled, she recalled, and they helped provide for his care. What if they were devastated to learn there wasn't enough in the estate to keep them on?

They deserved better than having her dump that on them and run off to Amsterdam the next day. Sunday, when she returned—a sober conversation, after which she'd meet with Kenny's property inspector friend and set the sale process in motion. It had to be done.

* * *

With her phone set to speaker for the conference call with Gipson headquarters, Lark quietly filed a ragged fingernail. Best to let the executives argue strategies among themselves, she'd learned. She was there to provide data.

"...and I'm convinced this would all go away tomorrow if the executive board would show Dr. Batra the door. It doesn't matter at this point whose fault it is. Somebody has to take responsibility." This from Michael Dobbins, product manager for Flexxene. Not the guy Lark would want manning the lifeboats.

"We can't demand they fire their director, Mike. It's not appropriate. How would they look if they didn't stand up for their people? Besides, we've got dozens of trials in the field with PharmaStat. It wouldn't look good for us either." Wise words from Gipson's senior development officer, Kirsten Cooke, PhD. "Dr. Latimer, do you have a feel for how their CEO wants to handle this?"

Even sitting alone in her office with the door locked, Lark sat up straight to reply. "Dr. Batra seems moderately concerned, so I have to assume she's had conversations with some of the executive staff in Geneva. To my knowledge, none have visited the facility here. In fact, they seem to be keeping their distance for now. I've received no inquiries as to my findings."

"What are your findings so far?" Dobbins asked.

"I'm halfway through the subject interviews. No irregularities to date. I'm doing site visits early next week to review the clinic protocols where the cardiac issues occurred. The first two patients were at Shire, the third one at Addenbrooke." She was trying to keep an open mind so as not to bias her investigation, but it was highly unlikely two separate clinics had broken protocol in a way that would have caused identical emergencies.

Dobbins always came across as less concerned about the particulars of the trial or even her review than about his timeline for moving Flexxene along to Phase III. Industry analysts on

Wall Street believed strongly in the drug, so it was little wonder he felt pressure to get it to market as quickly as possible. "What I want to know is if there's any chance we can get back in the field in Cambridge by mid-July. If not, we need to tighten the trials in Oslo and Helsinki. We can't afford to have either of those groups dropping out at this stage, not so close to the end. Say the word and I can put a couple of girls on shoring that up this afternoon."

Dr. Cooke cleared her throat and waited a beat for a self-correction that didn't come. "Mike, please don't refer to our research staff as girls. It's demeaning. All right then, this hour seems to work for everyone. Let's schedule another update next week."

Her seamless transition to the matter of next week's call effectively cut off Mike's reply, giving her admonishment an even bigger punch. Gipson's high-ranking women had banded together last fall after a sexual harassment complaint forced the company to reckon with its culture. Ever since, they rose quickly to call out language and behavior they considered sexist or otherwise unprofessional, sparing lower-ranking staffers like Lark the risk of retaliation.

Kirsten Cooke was especially strident. Lark had taken notice of her when she joined the company four years ago. Early forties, an attractive working mom who juggled school plays and soccer games with global business responsibilities. And running marathons. Lark's relationship with Bess had been good back then, but it hadn't kept her from appreciating Dr. Cooke's appeal. Had they been frequent travel companions like Channing and Payton, she too might have fallen for the boss.

Would she have cared that there was a Mr. Cooke? She was a lot less sure of a principled answer to that after hearing Channing describe how she'd fallen for Payton.

* * *

As Toby Singleton disappeared through the gate with his van full of Poppa's books and papers, Channing spotted Cecil sweeping the gazebo. That was one of Maisie's usual chores.

Just as she'd missed the signs of decay at Penderworth due to the dwindled funds, she'd failed to notice Cecil taking on a greater share of the domestic work. She wondered how long they'd kept up the charade and how they planned to manage when Maisie's arthritis got worse.

Before she could ask Cecil for insight into Maisie's condition, her phone rang. *Liz*. What had she done now? "Hello, Mum."

"I'm so glad you answered. If I don't talk to somebody soon, I'm going to hurl myself into the ocean. Channing, I have no place to go. Literally, no place except the bowels of this dreadful boat. What the bloody hell was I thinking...coming down to this suffocating humidity to live in a floating coffin that stinks to high heaven? Raw sewage meets fish market."

A rhetorical question if she'd ever heard one. The last thing Liz wanted was an honest critique of why she'd married a man who more often than not got on her nerves. Irwin had money. Liz had never provided for herself a day in her life.

"We ha—bad—connec—Mum," she replied, moving her hand over her mouth as she spoke.

"Channing Trilby Hughes, don't think you're going to pull that one on me again. I'll call this number all night long if you hang up on me."

Channing rated the threat as Likely True. "What am I supposed to do with your problems, huh? I have my own to deal with, or have you forgotten?"

Forgotten was generous, as it assumed she'd ever understood the precariousness of Channing's situation in the first place. On the contrary, Liz behaved as if they could magically recover the Hughes fortune with a few phone calls and bank transfers like those Channing had provided when Mum was between husbands.

"I want to come to England. A month or two at Penderworth is just what I need to settle my nerves. But you know I hate to fly alone. I checked and there's a direct flight to Miami. I'll meet you there and we can go shopping in the Gables. Then we can fly back to London together. Oh, and business class is perfectly fine, it doesn't have to be first. It will be so wonderful to see Cecil and Maisie again."

"No." She'd begun pacing in the driveway. Stalking, really. Mum brought out a frantic, impatient streak.

"What do you mean no? I'm all the family you've got, Channing. Penderworth would be mine if your father hadn't died."

"You haven't heard a word I've said. There's nothing left of Poppa's estate. He lost it all in the market crash ten years ago. Thirty million pounds down the tubes. All I have is a stack of bills and a manor house that's falling apart. And the Brownings. I haven't yet settled on how to tell them I've no use for them after thirty-four years, that they're out on the street. Perhaps you can help me with that. Wait, I know…I'll go the subtle route and change the locks on their cottage like you did when Nicholas started dating that girl from Taiwan. Think they'd get the message? It's hardly as if they've done anything to earn *my* loyalty—"

An abrupt spin brought her face-to-face with Cecil, who'd brought his broom around to level the cinders in the circular drive. The fallen look on his face was as punishing as shame could ever be.

"Mum, I have to go." She pocketed her phone and went to him. "Cecil, I'm so sorry. I was being stupidly facetious. My mum…she always brings out the absolute worst in me. I love you and Maisie like family."

"I know, dear one." He accepted her hug, patting her back as if she were the one who deserved to be comforted. "Is it true what you told her about the estate, that Lord Hughes lost it all in the stock market? Maisie and I, we thought your Poppa was just sad, that he missed his loved ones and wanted Penderworth to always stay the same."

She took a deep breath, deciding Cecil deserved the truth. "No, he had no money to keep it up. Lord Alanford told me how it happened, just bad timing on a stock sale during the global crash. That's why he worked at the university until the day he died."

"The poor, poor man."

She hooked her arm through his and walked him toward the cottage. "We've so much to talk about, Cecil. I promise it's going to be all right. I'll do whatever I can to see to it. Go fetch Maisie and let's all sit down over tea and figure out how we can solve this together."

"Wait." He stopped abruptly and broke into a smile. "Does this mean we can take our pension now?"

* * *

"Have a seat, Shane. Would you like tea?" Lark had gotten an electric kettle for her office. Her tea habit was now officially out of control.

"I'm fine, thanks. Just downed an energy drink."

"Do those really work? I always assumed they gave you a temporary buzz and then you crashed back to earth with a sugar headache."

Shane was a handsome young man, clean-cut and sharply dressed in a pink Ralph Lauren shirt that retailed for around a hundred bucks. Lark knew because her curiosity had led her to look up the price online. Pretty fine rags for a research assistant living on an entry-level salary, as incongruous as his flashy BMW convertible. It was none of her business what he wore, what he drove, or that he marked time on the same Swiss watch as Gipson's CEO. What concerned her today was the kiss she'd witnessed in the parking garage between Shane and a woman who left via an emergency stairwell that exited outdoors. Around her neck was a red lanyard like those worn by employees of Haas-Seidel, a German drugmaker with offices in the building next to PharmaStat.

Lark didn't like the scenario for how those pieces might add up. All the pharmaceutical giants were in development with arthritis drugs, but competitive intelligence had Gipson out in front by twelve to sixteen months with Flexxene. A failed trial—especially one thought to endanger subjects with life-threatening side effects—could set them back long enough for one of the others to surge ahead. As farfetched as it seemed that a PharmaStat employee would sabotage a trial to give someone else the upper hand, she couldn't ignore the possibility.

"You've worked on review teams before, right Shane? Some reviews go deeper than others, especially when the results are anomalous. Like the Flexxene trial."

"I've taken part in reviews, audits, all of it...but none for Gipson. Before I say more, Dr. Batra is quite insistent that we aren't to discuss any of our projects with rival companies."

"You're absolutely correct. Confidentiality is critical to Gipson as well. In fact, we'd be very disappointed to learn that our proprietary information was shared with another company, especially one that happened to be working on a similar drug." Her office chair squeaked as she leaned back. "Speaking of other companies, I couldn't help but notice you and a very pretty lady in the parking garage on Monday. She left through one of the side exits."

He clearly was taken aback by the personal nature of her questions, but then his ears reddened and he managed a sheepish grin. "That would be Thilda Huber. She works at Haas-Seidel. But we never discuss our jobs."

"Your girlfriend?"

"Not exactly...though perhaps if I'm lucky she will be. We only met last week in the line for coffee."

It was easy enough to check if he'd exchanged prior calls or emails with Haas-Seidel from his PharmaStat phone or account. If the date held up she could rule him out—the Flexxene trial had already been suspended by then.

"I haven't discussed PharmaStat trials with her, if that's what you're asking. Though I confess that I sometimes have misgivings about all the secrecy. I'd like to think as scientists, we pursue knowledge in order to share it with the world, not to hoard so we can enrich ourselves."

So Shane was an idealist, naive but altruistic. That too could be motive for disrupting a proprietary drug trial.

"It's probably best if you keep that philosophy to yourself around here," she said jovially. "We do this to fight disease, of course, but the pharmaceutical industry is about making profits—billions of dollars in profits. I won't attempt to defend some of the exorbitant prices or how much they spend on marketing. Just be glad you don't live in the US, where there's no limit on what drugmakers can charge. Bioscience is a capitalist venture. But it's the potential for profit that drives the market to pour more money into research and development. Take away the profit and they stop investing. Take away investments and there's less money for research. Take away research and…you get the point. At the end of the day, what really matters is if we're making people's lives better or worse."

She hadn't meant to go off on a philosophical soliloquy, but it didn't hurt to underscore for Shane the human consequences of a failed drug trial that might have helped bring about a treatment for a painful disease. If he'd done something to disrupt the Flexxene trial, maybe a new perspective about the greater good would convince him to come clean.

"What was it that brought you to pharmaceutical research, Shane?"

She'd studied his résumé and found it thin for a twenty-six-year-old, owing to what appeared to be a pair of gap years bookending his university degree. There was no faulting his work however, as his performance evaluations were excellent.

"It's not what I've planned for my career, pharmaceutical trials, but it's good experience for what I'd like to do someday." Other than the brief moment of embarrassment, he didn't seem at all nervous about her line of questioning. On the contrary, he grew animated as he described his ambitions. "My goal is to go to university in America next year. Johns Hopkins in Baltimore. I'd like to get my doctorate in public health. After that, I hope to work on health policy in developing countries."

"Wow, that sounds interesting." Or totally contrived.

"Not to my dad. He'd have preferred I study engineering as he did. He's absolutely gutted that I've no interest in taking over the company. My sister, though…she wants to build the stadiums and car parks. Let her have it, I say. I'd rather do something to leave the world a better place."

So that was it—Shane came from money, enough to fund a comfortable lifestyle while he worked at an entry-level job. She'd verify his story, of course. If true, he probably had no financial motive for selling out Gipson.

The rest of her interview was dedicated to documenting Shane's role in the process, something she'd done for each staff member associated with the Flexxene trial. His duties were limited to data monitoring and scheduling. "You're saying you never actually handled any of the drug samples, is that correct? All of your work was here in the building."

"Right, except there were a couple of Mondays when Wendi asked me to deliver the packets out to the clinics. Dr. Martin jammed her up with a special report, a last-minute thing, she said. We always try to step up for one another whenever one of us gets in the weeds."

The packets he was talking about were sealed envelopes containing the prescribed treatment for a week, either Flexxene patches or the placebos. They were marked only with a subject's identification number and the participating physician. No way could the person delivering the packets know which drug was inside. "Do you recall the dates?"

"It's probably on the fleet logs. I signed out a car both times."

"If you could track that information down and email it to me, it'd be great. I'm reconstructing the timeline so we can rule out possible contamination of the contents. You verified the seals, correct?"

His eyes flickered with sudden concern. "Do you mean the individual packets? I didn't check those, actually. The boxes for each clinic were sealed with parcel tape. I presumed they were intended for clinic staff only."

It probably was nothing. There was no strict requirement in the protocols for couriers to break open the box and verify the seals on individual packets. Lark wouldn't have noticed the omission at all had Wendi not explained in great detail her process for delivery, which included removing the packets in the presence of a staff clinician and checking each seal before getting a signed receipt for the contents.

What mattered now was what Shane recovered from the fleet logs. As long as his two delivery dates didn't coincide with the medical emergencies, he was in the clear.

CHAPTER ELEVEN

"Give your bags to Oliver," Kenny said as they made their way up from the parking deck on the *Stena Hollandica*, one of two luxury "super-ferries" that serviced the route between the English port town of Harwich on the North Sea and the Hook of Holland. "We'll stow them in your cabin and meet you in the restaurant for dinner in twenty minutes."

"Hmm…probably more like eight minutes," Oliver mumbled cheekily. "And that's assuming it takes four to drop off your bags."

Channing proffered an exaggerated shudder of disgust. "Eww."

"Oversharing?"

"Exceedingly. Here's a thought. Let's skip the restaurant and have a snack in the bar with drinks. It's already half-nine."

Oliver cocked his head as he considered. "She has a point, my lord. Might we find it more pleasurable to indulge our palates with spirits?"

"Stop speaking like that," Channing snapped. "Kenny's insufferable as it is."

Absorbed in her smartphone, Lark missed the entire repartee. She'd been unusually quiet on the drive from Horningsea, fretting over an unpleasant discovery related to her office project. Channing was determined to snap her out of her agitated state, lest their entire weekend be shot.

It was her own fault Lark was disengaged, since Channing had been far too casual with the invitation. "Come with us" was for a ski trip or a clam bake, whereas "come with *me*" would have made her intentions unmistakable. They were sharing a cabin, for pity's sake.

"Excuse me, miss…do you happen to have a phone in your bag?" Channing asked.

"Silly, it's right here in my ha—" Lark stopped abruptly and made a dramatic display of turning off her phone and dropping it inside her bag. "You have a sassy mouth. Lucky for you, I like that."

"I want you to enjoy the ferry crossing. They're fun as long as you aren't hurling your lunch. Let's check out the shops." Now that Lark's hand was free, Channing hooked their elbows and began to stroll.

The shops aboard the *Hollandica* catered to a high-end crowd seeking luxury perfumes, jewelry, and electronics. A specialty clothing shop had several mannequins sporting stylish outfits, including a shimmery gold tunic she thought would look spectacular on Lark. "Look at that—it was made for you. Matches your eyes perfectly."

Lark scrunched her face. "Really? I don't think I've ever worn anything like that in my life. Not that I get a lot of invitations to the cocktail circuit."

"Who says you have to save it for parties? Wear it to lunch, to the theater. Go out and dazzle people."

"Like that black jumpsuit you wore on the plane? Put me down as dazzled, Lady Hughes. I spotted you the second you came through the door."

The Rag & Bone from Saks, one of her favorites. In fact, she'd packed it for the weekend in case they dressed for dinner aboard ship. It pleased her a lot that Lark remembered. "If you noticed, then it had the desired effect."

"So you dress to be noticed?" Lark asked.

"I dress to be happy with myself. Having the right people notice is a perk."

"Consider yourself perked." Lark hugged her arm now in a way that was charmingly possessive. "I've never had much of a fashion sense. Chloe was two years older, so I wore her hand-me-downs till I started college. It was annoying until I figured out I could call them vintage."

"I happen to think you look lovely."

Lark had called the day before to confirm the dress code for the weekend, or as she'd put it, for instructions on how to avoid looking as though she'd been purchased by the others from a street vendor. Her worn jeans and thigh-length cardigan came off as both blithe and stylish, a fashion triumph as far as Channing was concerned.

"I owe my fashion sense to my stepfather," Channing said, her voice dripping with a resentment she'd cultivated for more than twenty years. "Calvin Guillory, prick of the first order. When I was seven, I was a flower girl at his sister's wedding and I got to wear this gorgeous lavender party dress. Afterward, Mum let me wear it everywhere because I was growing so fast and she knew I wouldn't have it long. Then one day I squeezed one of those juice boxes and it squirted out red punch all over me. Calvin said that was it, he wasn't buying me any more nice dresses."

"What an ass."

"Not long after, his cousin had an engagement party. Calvin had me wear my school uniform, a tartan skirt with a green jumper. I was humiliated. When I was finally old enough to choose my own clothes, I'd ask myself if Calvin would approve. If not, then I bought it."

"That's exactly what I like about you, Channing. You don't let anybody push you around." She continued before Channing could point out the obvious, that she'd been Payton's doormat for the last two years, "You wouldn't have stayed with Payton if she'd kept stringing you along. Just like you didn't stay with

Albright. You have your line in the sand and nobody better step over it. It's your terms or nothing."

She'd not considered it that way, but Lark was right. In her own head, she'd marked her thirtieth birthday as the deadline for Payton to choose. They never got that far, but she liked to think she'd have had the courage to move on. The fact that she left Albright proved it.

"Forget I mentioned Payton, forget you mentioned your asshole stepfather. We're here to have fun."

"You're right, Dr. Latimer. Did you hear that just now?" She paused beside the duty free shop and cupped her ear. "Why, I do believe someone is calling out for us. Sounds as if he might be trapped in a gin bottle. Come, we have to save him."

She led Lark by the hand to the bar, where they secured a small table for four near a giant porthole that looked out onto the harbor.

"Sorry about my phone. I promise not to let work get in our way this weekend."

"Is it really that bad, this situation at your office?"

"It could be. I wish I'd waited to open that last email from Shane. My weekend would be a lot more fun if I didn't know how much shit was going to hit the fan on Monday. But there's nothing I can do about it before then, so I'm not going to spend another second obsessing over it. Now where's my drink?"

A gorgeous smile overtook her face, the brightest since their moment of recognition at the Crown and Punchbowl. Around her amber eyes were the creases of a thousand laughs. In the split second they connected across the table, something in Channing clicked *hard*. "You're really very pretty, you know."

The bustle around them fell away, a distant din. Their moment—an unbroken gaze filled with acknowledgment of mutual feelings—lasted only seconds before Kenny and Oliver slid boisterously into the adjacent chairs.

"Okay, who wants a Blow Job?"

* * *

Channing had a whipped cream mustache left over from her shot of Kahlúa and Bailey's, ever so tiny but enough to drive Lark to distraction. She was torn between the urge to blot it with a cocktail napkin or watch for Channing's tongue to slither out and wipe it away. Had Kenny and Oliver not been sitting there, she might have kissed it away. Surely that would have been all right—Channing had looked at her with traces of lust and told her she was pretty. Something was definitely brewing between them. It would seriously suck to be wrong about that.

The distraction finally proved too much. "You've got a little dollop…" She touched it softly with her pinky and popped it into her own mouth, earning a playful twinkle that settled it—they both were in flirt mode.

"Who wants another?" Kenny asked. "I'd be most delighted to fetch us another round."

Channing eyed him cynically. "Of course you would. You only drink these for the perverse kick of ordering them. 'Excuse me, mate. Would you mind terribly giving me a Blow Job?'"

Kenny puffed his lips and raised a finger as if to signal an important pronouncement. Then a drunken dramatic pause. "That's possibly true."

Lark had laughed along all evening at their lively banter, but she was ready now to ditch the guys. Actually she'd been ready from the moment Channing had taken her captive with that smoldering gaze. Making love to the rhythm of the North Sea had shot to the top of her bucket list.

"And you are possibly sloshed, my lord."

"I'm bloody…blooming…bladdered. But I know an ace performance when I see it. Oliver was positively ace, wasn't he?"

"He was indeed," Channing replied, offering a fist bump to Oliver, who'd won their informal contest, the quickest to down the cream-topped shot without using any hands. He'd scarfed the cream in one bite and somehow slurped the liquid contents by rolling his tongue into a straw. Four seconds flat.

"How about it, Lark? Another?"

"No thanks. I have a scary feeling one's my limit."

"But you've had two."

"That's what makes it scary." She wasn't going to dampen this night by drinking too much.

Kenny was four or five drinks ahead of everyone else, having polished off a pair at the bar and several more at the table. He took Channing's hand as he addressed her. "My darling, I noticed a jewelry shop on the lower deck, duty free. All sorts of fabulous diamonds and rubies. Probably a fair bit of polished glass too. What do you say we go pick out a ring?"

"A ring?"

"An engagement ring. Anything you want, my lovely countess."

"Oh, stop your silly nonsense. I'm not marrying you."

"Why not?" His wailing drew the attention of the three women at the next table, who'd paused their conversation to eavesdrop.

"Because you're pissed."

"I didn't mean right now. We'd have to do a proper announcement at Breckham with all the posh people. In our finest clothes, of course. I can wear my top hat! I *love* my top hat. And I look amazing in it, don't I, Ollie?"

"It really is a smashing hat."

"You can invite all of your friends," Kenny went on, gesturing toward Lark as he swayed in his seat. "All of your *friend*, I should have said."

Channing shot her a wink. "Pay him no mind. He's taking the piss out of you."

"Nooo! I was taking the piss out of you, Channing. Because you don't have friends, you have *friend*. Singular. She is your friend, isn't she? *Just* your friend, as I recall you saying."

As usual, Lark got the feeling she was the only one not in on the joke. What made this time unnerving was that Kenny didn't seem to be joking.

"Of course she's my friend. She's your friend, she's Oliver's friend."

"You said she was very nice. I think she's nice too." He looked over his shoulder at Oliver. "I'm right, am I not? Dr. Lark is very, very nice."

"Very nice." Oliver zipped his hoodie and draped Kenny's sweater across his back. "It's time we called it a night, my lord. Bid the countesses adieu."

Kenny ignored him, turning his attention back to Lark. "I told Channing you were a fit bird."

"A fit bird?"

"That means the viscount thinks you're hot," Channing said.

"You know what she said? That you weren't her type. Which is good for you, since her type apparently is an old, bitchy slag."

Channing stiffened. In a growling voice Lark hadn't heard her use before, she sternly said, "You're drunk, Lord Teasely. I strongly suggest Oliver walk you back to your cabin and put you to bed."

Not her type. It stung to know she'd said such a thing. Obviously she and Kenny had discussed her at some point, and Channing had thought it necessary to emphasize the fact that they were just friends. That explained the *friend* talk and all the *very nice* platitudes.

Kenny jerked his arm away, his odious sneer forewarning a nasty turn. "And you should also be aware that Channing only likes women who are smart."

Lark's stomach heaved, as though the ferry had dropped from the top of a giant swell. "Sounds like you guys did a full assessment."

"In fact we did. I told her I thought you were smart…that you'd have to be because you're a doctor. But she said you aren't really, so maybe not *that* smart. Dr. Lark…what's your last name again? Should I call you a doctor? Ha, that's funny. 'Call me a doctor… Okay, you're a doctor.'"

"You're such a bastard," Channing muttered viciously.

That she'd answered with an epithet instead of a denial might as well have been an admission as far as Lark was concerned, especially since her cheeks were glowing red. There was no reassuring look, no clarification that Kenny had taken her words out of context.

So she wasn't really interested…fine. That alone was awkward enough, as it meant she'd been playing her all evening, probably hoping to get laid. But why all the badmouthing her to Kenny? No wonder she'd felt out of the loop so often with their jokes—because she *was* the joke.

Lark felt a surge of indignation. She had better things to do than serve as a mascot to snooty people whose idea of fun was talking about people behind their backs. If this was the way they behaved together, she wanted no part of any of them.

Oliver implored, "Come, Lord Teasely. You promised me a cigarette."

"No! I want another Blow Job." Kenny said it again, louder the second time, eliciting another giggle from the next table. Now sloppy with both his posture and speech, he addressed Lark again while waving a dismissive hand at Channing. "Don't listen to her. *I* think you're very smart."

No way was she going to spend tomorrow with these three in Amsterdam knowing what they were really like. When they reached Holland in the morning, she'd book an immediate return trip and arrange for her own ride back to Cambridge.

"It's been a long day," she said, leafing through her wallet for a few quid to cover her part of the bar bill.

"Please don't go." Channing grasped her forearm and spoke to Oliver through gritted teeth. "Oliver's taking Kenny to bed right now."

"Blow Job, Blow Job."

Oliver pulled him to his feet. "That's enough, Kenneth. You're being a right knob head."

There was no graceful path out of the conversation for Lark. At best she'd get a thorny apology, something with a *'splain* suffix. Drunk-'splain, joke-'splain. Their fabricated excuses would only make it worse. "I'll catch you all later."

* * *

Channing had forgotten what a dick Kenny could be when he drank too much. He'd pulled a similar stunt several years ago at a Christmas party, repeating an unflattering comment she'd once made about an associate of Poppa's…that she'd rather run the till at Starbucks than take a job at his bent investment bank. Kenny's slip of the tongue had caused hard feelings between Poppa and his friend.

The lounge on Deck 9 held several rows of reclining chairs for passengers who hadn't booked a cabin. Lark was probably in one of them, hidden by the dim light. After a third pass of the ship's common areas, Channing gave up her search and retreated to the stateroom.

The interior berth was anything but stately, barely wide enough for the two single bunks that swung down from the wall on either side. A cabin steward had turned down the fresh white sheets and placed a chocolate on each pillow.

Plz come to the room, she texted, adding four different emojis saying she was sorry. Dots appeared briefly on her screen to indicate that Lark had seen it and was typing a reply, but the message never followed.

Lark had her own key. Maybe her plan was to wait until much later when she thought Channing would be asleep. As if…

"Bollocks!" She banged her hand on the door to the bath and shook it until the pain subsided. As much as she'd like to blame Kenny for this whole cock-up, he wasn't the real culprit. Those cutting remarks about Lark had come from her mouth, an elaborate dodge to avoid admitting an attraction. All because she hadn't wanted Kenny to minimize her relationship with Payton. Hadn't wanted to appear fickle. Hadn't wanted to hear his endless, self-serving advice.

She was seconds away from returning to Deck 9 to try again when the door handle turned and Lark entered. A quick search of her face yielded nothing encouraging, only a strained pursing of the lips and a deliberate effort to avoid eye contact. At least she was here.

"Lark, I'm so very sorry. What Kenny said…that's not at all what it meant."

"It's fine, obviously a misunderstanding. We're all cool." *Cool* indeed—her tone was icy with feigned civility. "I didn't realize these inside cabins were so small. Maybe I should go back up to the lounge."

"No, please stay. I'd feel simply awful if you left." She'd feel awful no matter what, since her flippant remarks had caused this mess. "You must think I'm horrid. For what it's worth, I *feel* horrid. I'm absolutely gutted to think I've hurt your feelings or disrespected you in any way. If you'll please let me, I can explain."

"No explanation necessary. It's late, we're tired. I'm just going to grab a quick shower and call it a night."

Except Channing wouldn't sleep a wink. It was painfully obvious their morning would be dreadful if they didn't put this awful mess to bed.

"It's not fine, Lark. It's upsetting. We'd been having such a lovely time and it all went to shite. If I could just…" She closed her eyes and sighed, achingly aware that her words made her sound as though she was focused more on fixing her guilt than making Lark feel better. "Never mind, I'm sorry. Needless to say, you have every right to tell me to sod off. A decent person would respect that."

Lark rummaged through her overnight bag, setting out her toiletries and a pair of navy blue pajamas exactly like the ones Channing had brought, the cushy knits British Airways had distributed to first class passengers on the flight from Boston. Entering the bathroom, she replied over her shoulder, "I never said you weren't decent. It was awkward is all, knowing you guys had been talking about me. Surprised me a little…I didn't expect it."

"Bollocks," Channing said again, this time under her breath as the door closed. A mere apology would fall dreadfully short, no matter how sincere. Had there been a florist aboard, she'd have tried her luck with a peace offering. Surely there was a fresh floral basket that said, "Forgive me, I'm a reprehensible arse."

The next twenty-two and a half minutes passed like a dinner with her mum as she waited miserably on her bunk. It was a relief at least that Lark was in for the night. If she'd intended to leave the cabin after her shower, she'd hardly do so in pajamas.

When she finally emerged from the bath, Channing wanted to smile at the sight but didn't dare. The sleeves of the oversized knits extended past her fingertips, while the legs pooled at her ankles. Lark's curly hair stood every which way from its towel drying, and her face was red from a good scrubbing.

"I know my credibility is in the toilet right now, but you look absolutely darling."

Lark checked herself in the mirror that was mounted on the back of the door. "These don't exactly fit, do they?"

"On the contrary, they're perfect." Channing gestured for Lark to sit on the other bunk. "Will you please allow me to properly apologize? Surely you'd like some explanation of that miserable debacle."

"To be honest, I'm worried that I won't. Like it, that is. My experience is that people try to explain why they did something shitty and they sometimes end up making it even worse."

"Fair enough, but I'm going to take that as a personal challenge to leave things better than they were." So Lark had decided she was shitty. Nothing like starting off deep in the hole. "I suppose I should get this bit out of the way first. It grieves me to say that despite being pissed out of his mind, Kenny actually managed a rather accurate recitation of our conversation, which it so happens took place several days *before* our dinner at Penderworth. He'd met you only once, briefly, at the Crown and Punchbowl. For that matter, I knew you only slightly better. I wish I could at least challenge his version of events, but I'm afraid I can't. To put it bluntly, I said what he said I said, every word."

"See, this is exactly why I was worried I wouldn't like it."

"Right, well…he recalled the words but he totally left out the context, which is why it sounded so horrid coming from him. He's always had a certain silliness about him, which I'd meant to avoid. I'm sure you've noticed that side of him, what with his screaming for Blow Jobs and all. When I told him you were coming for dinner, he practically had us both at the altar in a fortnight. He's not the sort of person who needs encouragement to run off on his own tangents. To quell that, I *stupidly* said you weren't my type…that I found you rather ordinary looking. But the mere fact that I said it to Kenny does not make it true."

Through the torturous recitation, Lark busied herself picking the white towel lint from her pajamas. A faint smile flashed before she said, "So I'm not *ord-nry* looking?" It was a deliberate mocking of her accent.

"Not or-di-na-ry at all," Channing replied, sounding out all the syllables. "Granted, I don't make a habit of scoring all the women I meet, but I do indeed find you pretty. In fact, you may recall I said those very words to you just this evening in the bar. I looked up and at that instant there was a certain grace about you that struck me as quite fetching."

A more genuine smile lit Lark's face this time, but still she avoided looking up. "You did say that. I also like how you say stew-pid, not stoo-pid. It's so much more emphatic....as in too stew-pid to get through medical school."

"Euunh, that." Channing clenched her teeth and hissed. "What happened is that Kenny made some crude remark about Payton being a 'closet queen,' so he had me in a mood. He then pointed out that any woman who *was* my type would have to be smart. Bearing in mind that I was attempting to thwart his impulse to meddle, I thoughtlessly replied that you were hardly a genius, since you'd not finished your medical training. It's quite clear to me that you're smart. Your company obviously trusts you to carry out complex analyses that *stew-pid* persons could not. I'm rather impressed by it if you want to know the truth."

The cabin grew increasingly claustrophobic as she waited interminably for Lark's response. The space simply wasn't large enough for the both of them if they couldn't bury this agonizing rift. As the seconds ticked by, Channing made mental plans for her retreat. She'd gather her pillow and blanket, find Oliver and get his keys to the Peugeot.

"That one hit kind of close to home," Lark finally said. "Because you were sort of right, I washed out of my residency before I ever started. I was smart enough I guess, but just barely. Everyone else was brilliant. I had to work twice as hard just to keep up, and all the pressure of having to make snap decisions and doctors grilling us constantly and trying to trip us up... I was exhausted. Another four years and I'd have thrown myself on the bonfire."

In just those few words, her indignation visibly collapsed. All the ire she'd aimed outward was now turned on herself.

"Lark, there's no shame in making whatever decision was best for you. We all should know ourselves so well."

"The problem is that I've never taken responsibility for it. It's one of those lies you tell over and over until you believe it yourself. That it's Ma's fault for not taking care of herself, for having a stroke and getting diabetes right when I was supposed to start my residency. Or my sister's fault for not stepping up to help out. Or Bess's for not wanting to move to Delaware where my residency match was. Believe me, I've got all the excuses down pat." She raised her face to blink back a welling of tears. "You're the smart one, Channing. Wellesley, Harvard. I figured you saw through it."

"There's nothing to see through. As far as I'm concerned, you're exactly who you say you are."

"And who is that?"

"You're…" Her mind raced back through the hours they'd spent together. She'd groused about Payton, about Poppa… about Kenny's absurd proposal. Had she posed even a single query of Lark? "You're someone I want to know."

Lark gaped at her dubiously and then laughed. "That was desperate."

"Yes, it appears I've quite the gift for conceit. But now it's my turn to be honest, all right? I've enjoyed my time with you, even on the plane when I wasn't strictly capable of enjoying anyone. I find you kind and compassionate. I've needed that more than usual of late, but I don't want *my* needs to be all I am to you. You deserve better." Her careless words to Kenny, her self-absorbed grumbling. And the vain assumption that Lark would say yes to anything. "If you would graciously indulge me for another few hours, I shall attempt to prove my worth starting first thing tomorrow. It's to be *your* day in Amsterdam. I want to show you the grandest time."

A candid chuckle from Lark finally drained a fair bit of the tension from the room. "I should warn you, not all of me is kind and compassionate. But if you'd like to put me on a pedestal for a day or so, who am I to be anything but accommodating?"

"So we have a deal?"

"We do…on one condition. You have to tell me the truth." She wagged a finger between them. "Is there something going on here, or am I imagining things? Either answer is okay…I just need to know so I don't make a fool of myself."

"Do you need a verbal answer…or could we maybe…" She slid from her bed to Lark's and took a fistful of wet hair. With a tug that was almost fierce, she brought Lark's mouth to hers for a decisive kiss.

Lark responded with quickening intensity, stroking…caressing…her tongue tickling Channing's lips.

Their breath came in gulps and before Channing knew it, she'd guided Lark backward on the narrow bed and fallen atop her. Her hips writhed with excitement as her hands found the bare skin of Lark's stomach beneath the loose knit top.

A flat palm pressed firmly against her chest. "Wait."

"All right." Channing sat up straight, mentally dousing herself with cold water. "What have I done now?"

"Nothing, but…" Lark squirmed until she too was sitting up. "This feels too much like makeup sex. I don't want our first time to be like that."

If anyone knew makeup sex, it was Channing. Payton had promised it implicitly each time she criticized Channing's work or spent another long holiday with her family. It always came with an undercurrent that made it feel transactional.

"We can't have that, can we?" She leaned in and planted a loud, smacking kiss just above Lark's ear. "But you have your answer about what I think is going on. Next time's up to you."

After an elongated groan to announce her suffering, she gave Lark one last peck on the lips and headed for the shower. Several seconds of icy spray cooled her body, but it was hardly enough to chill her thoughts. Lark would be in England for only two more weeks, three at the most. That was all they'd have together unless she decided to go back to Boston too.

CHAPTER TWELVE

Channing had taken her hand the moment they stepped off the light rail near city center, ostensibly to keep them from getting separated in a Pride crowd that was shoulder to shoulder in anticipation of the festivities. But then she never let go, not even after they'd shaken free.

Lark found the simple gesture exhilarating, its unspoken declaration clear to everyone whose path they crossed: *We're together.*

She had a vague idea where they were, having toured Amsterdam on a weekend holiday during a drug trial review in Munich three years ago. The Prinsengracht was one of the city's major canals, along which one could view the Anne Frank House and Westerkerk, a seventeenth-century Protestant church that held the remains of Rembrandt.

She and Channing had walked past the throngs at those landmarks to claim precious seats on the canal wall near the bridge at Berenstraat, a prime perch from which to watch the floating parade. A sparse elm tree provided only modest relief from a blistering sun. Hundreds of celebrants gradually filled in behind them, lots of them proudly wearing pink to mark their solidarity. In the distance, the flamboyant floats of the Canal Parade were approaching.

"I wonder where Kenny is right now," Channing said. They'd had a good laugh over his punishing hangover and his frivolous vow to remain sober for the remainder of his miserable life. "I've never heard him so contrite as he was at breakfast. Oliver said he was truly horrified to hear what he'd said last night."

"I forgave him after his gift of bacon."

"Technically it was I who snatched it off his plate and put it onto yours."

"But he didn't snatch it back so it still counts as a gift." His expression had been that of a scolded puppy. "I shouldn't have been so sensitive about it. You guys have the driest sense of humor. I can't always tell when you're joking about things."

"You are not to blame for our boorish behavior."

True to her word, Channing clearly was making a concerted effort to learn more about her today, asking her opinions, peppering her with questions about her family and upbringing. While Lark appreciated the gesture, it bugged her to think some of it might be contrived. She'd feel better if they could shed the specter of Channing paying penance for the night before.

After a couple of minutes sitting on the wall, Channing said, "This concrete's cold on my bum. Would you like to sit on my sweater?"

"You don't have to keep doing this. I'm fine about last night, really."

"A promise is a promise. I've been a self-centered shithead. You can't possibly say you haven't noticed. Besides, I was offering only to *share* my sweater, not to give you the whole thing. I'm not *that* charitable. You can have the sleeves, or perhaps the side with the buttons, which will make little round indentations in your bum."

"All right then, but I draw the line at having you fetch me a cup of tea, extra hot. That would be taking advantage."

Channing squirmed to her feet, gripping Lark's shoulder so as not to lose her balance and end up in the canal. "I don't suppose you'd like a biscuit with that."

"Listen to you...so kind."

She chuckled to herself as Channing disappeared through the crowd. Humor had served them well in sticky situations, starting way back with their thorny confrontation on the plane. She liked that Channing was witty, droll, and otherwise entertaining, but Lark also appreciated knowing there was a genuine solemnity underneath, that Channing cared about her feelings. Given her privileged upbringing and educational background, she really was quite down to earth with problems like everyone else.

With no sign of her return, Lark broke a promise and checked her phone for messages. While hiding out last night she'd dropped a note to Niya voicing her suspicions about Shane and asking who might be able to provide corroborating details about his relationship with the mystery woman. Niya's response, which she read hurriedly while awaiting Channing's return, was uncharacteristically angry and belligerent—she would immediately resign her directorship if Gipson continued its intrusive investigations into the personal lives of her staff.

Lark was shocked more by the tone than the message itself. This was her longtime friend basically threatening to quit if Lark continued to do her job. For the first time, she questioned her own perspective. Was her zeal to find a culprit so Niya wouldn't be held to blame getting in the way of conducting an unbiased review? It was understandable that Niya would be protective of her staff, especially if she thought Lark was going out of her way to pin the trial failure on one of them.

"Hey, did you just trick me into getting lost so you could check your phone? You promised to turn that off." Channing handed her both cups of tea and slithered back into the narrow space just in time to see the first boat of the parade, a floating homage to the Village People.

"Doing it now." She turned her eyes toward the colorful Canal Parade, though her mind was still on Niya's note.

The hundreds of partygoers who were packed along the canal and bridge sang along and swayed their arms in unison to "YMCA," an excitement they sustained for more than an hour as dozens of floats sailed past, music blaring, riders throwing candy and condoms. There were outlandish costumes, half-naked dancers. Even a fully-naked dancer painted purple from head to toe. Everyone laughing and cheering. Everyone proud.

"What's up with you?" Channing shouted. "It's supposed to be a party."

Niya's note had killed her celebratory mood. It was bad enough that Lark didn't yet know what had gone wrong with the Flexxene trial—now she stood to lose a good friend over it.

"That's it, let's get out of here." Channing tugged her to her feet and led her through the crowd until they were a block away, out of the noise and the press of people. "What's going on?"

"Remember on the plane when I said this project of mine might be a colossal clusterfuck? Turns out that was an understatement." She briefly explained her concerns about Shane, that his personal involvement with a woman who worked for a competitor might have compromised his integrity. "We're talking billions of dollars at stake for Gipson. This drug could help millions of people with crippling arthritis. We have to know what happened with this trial, or at least what didn't happen. If I don't figure it out, our drug could die in development. Years of research wasted, and millions of dollars. And now one of my best friends…instead of helping me find out what went wrong, she's actually threatening our friendship because I'm doing my job."

Channing frowned and shook her head.

"What is it?"

"You told me the other night that this friend of yours, this Dr. Batra, was already talking about resigning even before you completed your work. Don't you find it curious how eager she is to remove herself from the situation? Most people under circumstances such as these would be fighting tooth and nail for their job, if not their professional reputation. Anything else seems an admission of incompetence."

"I wouldn't go so far as to call her—" She recalled the conversation in Niya's office in which she'd laid out her response should the board ask for her resignation. Dev would sell the shops he owned and they'd retire to Portugal ten years earlier than planned. "No, there's no way Niya orchestrated a trial failure as an exit strategy. My brain can't even go there."

"That's good, because you'd be jumping to conclusions. But the seed has been planted." Channing poked her gently on the temple. "Now give it just a bit of water and see if it grows. Trust your instincts. I'm very bloody certain you're smart enough to figure this out."

Lark basked in the compliment, conspicuously aimed at smoothing over Channing's comments about not finishing her medical training. "I'm sorry I was such a downer. I shouldn't have looked at my email…then I wouldn't even know. You want to go back and see if we can catch the end of the parade?"

"No, we need to go in the opposite direction. I don't want to risk running into that naked purple guy again."

* * *

For the return trip to Harwich, they'd booked aboard the *Stena Britannica*, sister ship to the *Hollandica*. Around three in the morning, the two ships would actually pass in the night in the middle of the North Sea.

Kenny had sworn off the bar, offering instead to buy dinner for the four of them in the ship's fine dining restaurant. An excuse to wear natty duds, he said. He was indeed spiffy in his slate-gray solicitor suit and open-collared pink shirt. Even Oliver looked his best tonight, having shaved and traded his usual hoodie for a sporty jumper.

Channing especially enjoyed her favorite jumpsuit knowing Lark liked her in it.

The sudden call for fancy dress had sent Lark scrambling to the ship's store, where she'd found black leggings to go with the sparkly gold tunic that matched her hair and eyes. Channing thought it lovely, but in her hopeless condition she'd likely have thought the same of a rugby shirt. That's how it happened with her—a sudden recognition of her attraction, and the endorphins were off and running. Overnight Lark was prettier, more charming. And Channing would do anything to please her.

No doubt about it, the feeling was mutual. Beneath the table, Lark had begun tickling her calf with a bare foot. Meanwhile Channing plotted how she'd politely excuse them from the table the moment they finished eating so they could head back to their cabin to follow up on last night's kiss.

"You have to admit," Kenny said, "the Dutch really know how to throw a party. If we'd arrived on Thursday, we could have gone to the world's largest drag show. And of course the street parties took over the whole city last night. The atmosphere in Amsterdam is so 'anything goes.' Even I'd have trouble getting arrested."

"Don't listen to him," Oliver told Lark, who was eyeing Kenny dubiously. "He's been known to take the occasional toke, but otherwise he's quite between the lines."

Channing scoffed. "The occasional toke? He keeps a tin box of weed in his car. He got high at my grandfather's memorial service, for bloody's sake. And he answers to no one for it because, in case you've forgotten, he's the Viscount—"

"Please lower your voice, Channing. I'd rather not have my stateroom tossed by ship's patrol, thank you very much. And I'll have you know that I've stopped with the weed. The very day you compared me to Finn McNulty, as a matter of fact. I ditched the box at a petrol station on the A10 on my way back to London." He sighed longingly. "I thought of just leaving it in the loo. Imagine someone's joy at finding such a treasure. It was top grade stuff."

"Oh, sod off. Surely you don't expect me to believe you gave up weed because I took the piss. Since when did you ever give a fig what I thought?"

"Not only that…" Oliver poked him in the ribs. "Go on, tell her what you said today."

"Very well. Last evening—for which I've apologized strenuously—that was the last you'll see of me in such a disgraceful condition, at least for the foreseeable future. Not that I'm confessing to a particular weakness, mind you. Wine with supper is still a given, and I'll pop in for a pint when it suits me. But no more getting completely shit-faced. Such behavior is not only offensive, it's irresponsible."

Oliver added, "And we've both agreed that irresponsible is not the image either of us wants to project, especially right now."

As the waiter cleared their plates, Channing studied Kenny's demeanor. It would be just like him to set up a prank with a dramatic announcement. "Is there a punchline? 'Oh bugger all, someone give me a Blow Job!' Unless…whoa. Is this about politics? Has your father put you up for a run at parliament already?"

"He has not, at least not at the moment." There was a rare sincerity in Kenny's tone. "It's about what we discussed last weekend. Plan B, if you will. Oliver and I walked all over the city today talking about it. We've decided to look into surrogacy. There's a company in London that specializes in helping gay men become fathers."

"Wow, congratulations…I guess," Lark said, looking at her hesitantly. "That's good news, isn't it?"

"It's very good news, considering I was Plan A."

"Plan B might actually be better," Oliver said. "And I like it because it means Kenny and I can get married."

"To each other?" Her impulse to laugh was quashed when Kenny raised Oliver's hand to his lips for a sweet kiss. The feeling of freedom from being at the Pride festival lingered for all of them.

Oliver added, "We've been together three years now. Exclusive, believe it or not. Or so he says."

"I swear it on Her Majesty's handbag."

"You've always coveted that handbag," Channing replied flatly. Turning to Oliver, she said, "Obviously you feel Kenny is up to this."

The oldest among them at thirty-five, Oliver often brought wisdom to their zany discussions. "One of my greatest disappointments as a gay man was thinking I'd never have children. I'm the world's greatest uncle but it's not the same as being a dad. I want the chance to help shape another human being into someone good. I see that desire in Kenny too when he's with my nieces and nephews. And they absolutely adore him. I know he's meant for this."

That must have been quite the conversation in Amsterdam, Oliver scolding Kenny about the implications of getting drunk and how it might doom their chances for fatherhood. To his credit, Kenny had responded with uncharacteristic maturity.

"And since I've got the issue with Alanford and Breckham Hall," Kenny said, "we've agreed that it's best if I provide the little swimmers. But we'd both be listed as fathers on the birth registration, which it turns out is perfectly lawful for the purposes of inheritance. It's also our only feasible path, Lady Hughes, since you've selfishly denied me marriage and rental of your baby oven. Which I might add is sitting idle and at risk of atrophy."

She groaned. "Spare us the mental image of your little swimmers and my atrophied oven. Dr. Latimer, what do you know about surrogacy?"

"It's trending up. From a medical standpoint, there's really not much to it. IVF…it's all done in the clinic and the lab. Most of the complications are on the legal front."

"Precisely," Oliver said. "Surrogacy laws haven't kept pace with the technology. When the parents are two gay men, it can throw a real spanner in the works if the surrogate decides at the last moment she wants to keep the child. Even if the courts are inclined to side in our favor, the case still has to be litigated, which means fathers lose precious bonding time with their infants."

"That's so absurd," Lark said.

Kenny added, "Cruel is what it is. With all the stress of preparing for fatherhood and fretting over whether or not the baby will be healthy, there's this constant worry that we'll have to fight the birth mother for custody. Unless of course she's someone we could absolutely trust. Otherwise they say it strengthens our legal position to use a surrogate who has no relation to the baby."

"You're talking about a gestational carry." Lark nodded pensively. "That's what they're called. You have a sperm donor, an egg donor and a third person to carry it. In some states, the surrogate doesn't even see the baby after it's born. It's brought directly to the parents."

"Right, so we need *two* women to pull off this minor miracle of modern medicine, one of whom is the actual genetic mother." He turned to Channing. "That's why we were hoping…"

His pleading look, Oliver's pleading look…a shoe was about to drop and it was a size twelve.

"…you might be willing to make a small biological contribution."

"That would make me the mother."

"Technically yes," Oliver said. "But not legally. Like Kenny said, he and I would be the parents of record. Our names would be on the birth certificate."

Oddly that sounded even stranger than marrying Kenny and bearing him a child. "I'm confused, Oliver. Why not use an anonymous donor? Someone totally off the page who you're certain won't challenge you for custody. You draw up a business contract."

"That's an option, and we're likely to go that way if you ultimately say no. Bear in mind that we'd try to choose a woman with your qualities, someone attractive and healthy."

"Good breeding stock, so to speak," Kenny added.

"Ken-ny." Oliver admonished him with a glare that reminded Channing of her stepfather. "It would give us comfort and peace of mind to know that our child's mother was also someone of good character. We can't get that assurance from a sterile list of egg donors sorted by their physical attributes."

Kenny snorted softly. "Our luck she'd be a psychopath."

With the celebratory tenor of their table conversation now shifted to serious matters of reproductive biology and law, Lark had stopped her flirtatious foot caresses.

"Even if it's just an egg," Channing said, "it's still a lot to consider."

Kenny surprised her by taking her hand. "Channing, you know better than anyone what a cheeky bugger I can be, but please…I'm about to be serious, so brace yourself. What Oliver is saying is that we aren't looking about for volunteers. We're asking you—only you. If you decline we'll go the anonymous route, but you are our first and best choice. You're my dearest friend and it would bring me such incredible joy to look at my child every day and see you in his or her face."

"Aww." Lark made a pouty face and patted her heart. "That might be the sweetest thing I've ever heard."

Though touched by his emotional appeal, Channing felt uncomfortably cornered. "Kenny, I'm honored that you both feel that way, truly I am. But it's a mammoth decision and I have to give it serious thought. Perhaps, as Lark says, it's a straightforward medical process, but that's not what concerns me most. There would be a child to sort, a child who'll grow up at Breckham Hall less than a mile from my house, a child who'll forever be part of my life."

"Not if you don't wish to be bothered. Oliver and I are prepared to accept complete responsibility. In other words, you'd be under no obligation to provide any sort of parental support."

"It's not about what you and Oliver will do." In her mind's eye she saw herself at eight years old, boarding a plane for England to be raised by a grandfather she hardly knew. How could she forget that her own mum had bowed to pressure from Calvin and torn her from her home and family? "It's what *I'll* do. I don't know if I'm even capable of abdicating responsibility for my own child—but at the same time I can't say for certain that I won't. Before I agree to this, I have to work it out in my head. I need to know what I expect of *myself*."

As she was talking, Lark scooted her chair closer and draped an arm around her shoulder.

Channing was mortified to realize she was crying. Accepting Kenny's handkerchief, she tried to laugh it off. "Obviously I'm allergic to something in this room. Next I'll be sneezing."

Lark stood and offered a hand. "On that note…"

She let Lark wrap up the social pleasantries, drifting into the hallway where she paused at a mirror to check her red, swollen face. Kenny's emotional plea had broken the dam on her tears, but it was the memory of being sent away that had brought them so close to the surface.

"Are you all right?" Lark looped an arm through hers and steered her toward the stairs.

"Fine. For a moment there I remembered what it felt like when my own mother sent me off to live with someone else."

"You don't have it in you to do something like that, Channing. It's like Kenny pretending he's living on the edge. You talk a good game about being cold and vicious but that's all it is—talk. You could never be deliberately cruel."

"I'd like to think you're right." Though she'd had little regard for Payton's family… "Mmm."

"What's that?"

"Not fifteen minutes ago there was a foot crawling up the inside of my trousers and I couldn't wait to get out of that restaurant so I could have my way with you. Now I can't decide which I need most—three more glasses of wine or a therapist who can help me pretend I wasn't actually born until I was nineteen years old."

"Or we could pretend we walked out of the restaurant fifteen minutes ago, Lady Hughes."

That would be her first choice…but sex-as-distraction was as fundamentally contrived as makeup sex. Lark deserved better. Leave it to Kenny to throw cold water on her libido two nights in a row.

CHAPTER THIRTEEN

Foregoing the enormous breakfast buffet aboard the *Britannica*, Channing and Lark had a lie-in, waking just in time to meet the guys and drive off at the dock in Harwich. Only moments into the trip, they raised an incessant grumble until Oliver relented with a stop for tea and croissants.

Once they were fed, the ride back to Horningsea was quite pleasant. Sunny for a change, and light traffic. Best of all, Channing thought, was holding hands with Lark in the backseat. It was her clearest statement yet to her friends that Lark meant something to her—and they could sod off with opinions to the contrary.

By half-ten they made it back to Penderworth, where Lark's hatchback sat alone in the drive.

"Channing, where's your car?" Kenny asked.

"Bury St Edmunds, probably. The Brownings go to church there every Sunday. They won't be home for hours." It amused her to think of the old Mercedes as hers, seeing as how she'd driven it fewer than five times in the dozen years since Poppa had purchased it. If Cecil were willing to take it on, she'd sign it over to him when they left.

"That's a forty-minute drive. They're C of E, right? What's wrong with St Peters?"

"They've always gone to Bury's. Maisie's brother and his wife live there, and they do a big family lunch on Sunday. They've an adult son who's developmentally challenged. I've met him... he's very sweet. Turns out that's always been their retirement plan, which I only learned the other day. They're keen to move into her brother's guest cottage and help take care of Stephen. I think they'd go tomorrow if I sold the manor."

Oliver walked with Lark to her car so she could stow her small suitcase, while Kenny carried Channing's into the house. "Channing, about the other night...I'm truly sorry for being a fucking knob. I apologized to Lark again this morning while you were getting tea."

"I appreciate that. She's bloody decent, you know."

"Of course she is. I just wish she didn't live in Boston. That's me being selfish."

It was nice he realized that. She didn't need his badgering over what was already a difficult decision. "This wild idea of yours, the baby business...you *do* know that isn't going to happen, right? Don't go making any crazy assumptions to the contrary."

"I promise not to assume anything if you'll promise to give it even a tiny speck of serious consideration. Try it on for real, imagine you said yes. Then honestly think about how it feels. Ollie and I both love you to bits."

"At least that part is mutual." They shared a hug as Lark came in. "By the way, your property inspector friend is coming by on Tuesday. I'll let you know how it goes."

When Kenny left, Lark took his place in Channing's arms. "Looks like everyone's abandoned you, Lady Hughes. Would you like some company?"

"What do you think? I've been trying to get you to myself for three days. I almost woke you up in the middle of the night to ask if you'd like to play doctor."

Lark rolled her eyes and laughed. "Like I've never heard that one before." She twined her fingers through Channing's hair and urged her into a kiss. *Lips...lips...tongue...lips.* Each time Channing thought it would erupt into hungry passion, Lark withdrew to tease her.

This she hadn't expected, Lark taking the lead—though she'd said after their kiss two nights ago that the next move was up to Lark. It was having a weakening effect on her knees. She'd forgotten how good it felt to be handled by a purposeful woman who was sure of what she wanted.

"I seem to remember somebody has a big...fancy...bed." Lark punctuated each word with a kiss.

Channing found herself back on her heels against the wall with Lark straddling her thighs. As a hot mouth devoured her neck, she felt a hand climbing beneath her shirt to brush against the satin of her bra.

"Upstairs, Lady Hughes...or I'm going to have you right here."

* * *

It was a girl's bed, antique white with a brushed brass canopy. Pale blue sheers were gathered at the bottom bedposts and tied with velvet sashes. Lark couldn't help the urge to loosen them, letting the sheers waft from the summer breeze.

Channing returned to her from opening the windows. "So we can listen for the car," she explained. "But I'm not expecting them until two at the earliest."

"Good, then I won't have to compete for your attention."

"I hardly think it would be a contest."

Under Channing's watchful eye, Lark boldly stepped out of her jeans and tossed her sweater aside, leaving just her bra and panties. She'd always been satisfied with her body, even if it could have used more exercise. The look on Channing's face said that didn't matter at all.

Lark followed her to the bed, which was fitted with old-fashioned floral sheets she guessed had been softened by a thousand washes. Beginning with the drawstring on Channing's summer slacks, she initiated the ritual undressing.

Channing stepped out of the crumpled cotton and stood perfectly still while Lark released the buttons of her shirt. Underneath, a satin bra pushed her breasts together. A soft moan escaped her as she ran her tongue along the cleavage. Their nearly bare bodies touched.

She could sense Channing's waver as she fought her instinct to dominate. A part of her wanted to surrender and let her take control. Channing had always conveyed authority. This time though, the hesitation felt deliberate...as if she wanted to feel Lark's desire.

With her knee angled between soft thighs, she urged Channing backward onto the bed. At the same time she slid her hand inside the bikini briefs and clutched a fleshy hip. Still kissing, still climbing, she twisted them free and dropped them behind her.

Channing instantly opened her legs and pulled her into a warm, wet vise.

Feeling her bra leave her shoulders, she pushed off her panties as well and groped Channing's back for a clasp that would free the last layer of satin between them. Luscious breasts begged for her mouth.

"God, I love that," Channing whispered, her chest heaving upward. Her hands held Lark in place as she shivered with obvious delight.

Kneading, nipping, devouring. Anchored on one knee, Lark slid her center along a silky-smooth thigh that rose in a taut cord of muscle with each of Channing's thrusts. Her hand slithered lower...through the brush of damp curls...and into a velvety slickness.

Channing's heel dug into the back of her thigh. Jarring, lurching in a fierce rhythm of want.

Lark hovered above her, close enough to share breath as she stroked the slippery cleft. Searching, studying, memorizing. She never wanted to forget the wide eyes and open mouth as her fingers plunged inside.

As their breath quickened, so did her touch…until Channing arched her back, drew a deep breath and squeezed her eyes tightly shut.

That's it, come for me.

Channing heeded the unspoken command, twisting and writhing as spasms pulsed from her core. Her next breath was a wail of unguarded pleasure.

* * *

"I deeply regret that we didn't do this sooner, Dr. Latimer." Channing propped herself on one elbow so she could watch the trail of her fingertips as they traced the contours of Lark's nude form. "On the other hand, it creates a sense of urgency about catching up."

"Think we can do it all in one day?" They'd spent the last two hours exploring what Lark had termed their "intersecting interests."

"Perhaps, but probably not *this* day. I have to figure out how I'm going to explain you to the Brownings."

"Surely I'm not your first sleepover."

"No, that distinction belongs to Alice Markham, my first crush from boarding school. Now on her second husband, I think."

"Is it possible Cecil and Maisie already know? About you, that is. Not you and me."

"I've no idea really, but I think not. I hadn't told Poppa. He was a traditional sort, Maggie Thatcher's advisor, for bloody's sake. Some of the opinions he expressed led me to believe such news would have been unwelcome, so I never brought it up. It hardly mattered once I moved to Boston. But I'd worked it out that I'd tell him about Payton. I wanted him to know that I loved someone, and that I was loved in return."

The subject triggered an unwelcome thought of a scene she'd imagined only a few months ago—Cecil's surprised reaction when she asked him to deliver Payton's bags to her room. The Brownings might have worried quietly about their age difference, but upon seeing Channing's happiness, they'd have been glad she had someone important in her life now that Poppa was gone. At least that had been her dream.

She'd hardly had time to reimagine how she'd tell them about Lark. Perhaps it wasn't necessary. They could move to Bury's blissfully unaware. Channing would send cards, drop in for an occasional visit…there was no reason to risk their reaction, especially if she and Lark both returned to Boston.

"I don't have any expectations," Lark said. "You can hide me in the wardrobe if you like."

"An excellent suggestion, Doctor."

The sound of crunching gravel alerted them to a car in the driveway.

"That's odd…if that's the Brownings, they're home much earlier than usual." She sneaked toward the window to peek out. Indeed, they'd returned immediately after the church service instead of staying for lunch with the family. "I hope nothing's wrong. We probably should get dressed."

Lark rolled out of bed and quickly gathered her clothes. "I can shinny down the drainpipe if you like."

"That would be fun to watch actually, but it shouldn't be necessary. Sunday is their day off unless I make special arrangements. They'll probably spend the whole afternoon in their cottage."

No sooner had she spoken than the sound of footsteps echoed up the stairwell, followed by Cecil's gravelly voice. "Miss Channing?"

The bedroom door was standing open—he'd be at the landing before she could cross the room and close it. At least Lark was mostly dressed, though she was conspicuously barefoot and her hair was askew.

"Bollocks!" She kicked her undergarments under the bed and shimmied into her drawstring pants. In desperation, she grabbed the first pullover she could find from the drawer, a wool sweater that was far too warm for the day.

His voice grew louder as he topped the stairs and started toward the bedroom. "Miss Channing, I thought you'd like your luggage. We hurried home because Maisie couldn't remember if she'd turned off the kettle. Turns out she had, but it's always best to—" He stopped in the doorway, his smile fading as he looked past her into the room.

"Thank you, Cecil."

"I…" His eyes went to the floor and his face reddened. "Sorry."

As he retreated, she turned to take in what he had seen. The unmade bed, her shirt and two sets of shoes on the floor. And Lark leaning all too casually against the bedpost. "Bloody hell."

"It could have been a lot worse."

That was very true. Cecil could imagine what they'd been doing, but at least he hadn't seen them doing it.

"Given a multitude of choices, that was not how I'd have chosen to reveal myself. I can't begin to guess whose embarrassment is greater. If only I'd brought my bloody bag upstairs."

"We were otherwise occupied." Lark worked her feet into her shoes, not bothering with the laces. "Let it percolate a day or two. Maybe you'll both end up laughing about it."

Somehow she doubted it. Before they could ever get to laughing, they'd have to get past awkward and humiliated. And possibly upset.

Lark ignored her gloominess and gave her a kiss on the cheek. "I don't have a fancy canopy bed, Lady Hughes, but I've got a whole flat to myself. How about you meet me there when I get off work tomorrow?"

Channing managed a smile. "That's what matters, isn't it? All this other…it's a lot less important than how I feel about you."

"And how I feel about you."

She followed Lark downstairs and waved from the front door as she got into her car.

Cecil chose that moment to fetch something from the car, then stood almost defiantly watching Lark exit through the gate, as though he'd chased her off himself. Then he turned toward Channing, his glower an unmistakable message of contempt.

CHAPTER FOURTEEN

The narrow glass cutout in her office door allowed Lark to observe foot traffic in the hallway. Since the start of her conference call with the Gipson team, Niya had walked by four times. Maybe she wanted to apologize. Lark wasn't in the mood to get jumped on again.

She'd followed up on Shane's confirmation that he'd delivered the trial samples that precipitated the cardiac emergencies for all three subjects. Interviews with the clinical staffs at Shire and Addenbrooke hospitals confirmed his report that he'd dropped off sealed boxes without checking the contents.

While Flexxene project manager Mike Dobbins summarized where they stood, Lark's phone buzzed with a text from Channing. *Good news at work?*

Finally caught a breast. Naughty autocorrect. *Break.*

Breast works too.

As if reading over her shoulder, Dobbins said verbatim, "Please tell me there's good news from the hospitals. Were you able to confirm that all the treatment packets were delivered intact?"

"Protocols checked out. I spoke with four different nurses who signed off at least once on various deliveries of the packets. Every single one said Wendi Doolan was always meticulous about verifying the seal on each packet, but apparently she's the only one who ever does that. Everyone else—whether it's a delivery for Gipson, Pfizer, anybody—handles it like Shane did. They drop off the sealed box, get a signature and leave it for the staff to open."

Left unsaid was how much better she felt knowing Shane hadn't done anything out of the ordinary. If anyone had, arguably it was Wendi, who was guilty only of being *too* conscientious. It was hard to fault her for that.

What r u wearing?

Lark covered her mouth to smother her laugh.

"It's looking more and more like this was just a phenomenal coincidence," Dobbins said. "Three random, unrelated events affecting our study subjects. And nothing anywhere points to Flexxene being the cause. I see no reason we can't get this trial back into the field right now. Even with the hiatus, the results would be favorable for us."

Kirsten Cooke also seemed less skeptical than she'd been last week. "I tend to agree with Mike, though to be on the safe side I think we should wait for the final round of blood panels. The lab should have them within a day or two."

Blood panels were a regular part of subject monitoring, done to measure the drug's metabolites. When the three study subjects showed up in urgent care with cardiac arrhythmia, the hospital checked for enzymes that would have indicated a heart attack. Gipson had asked for additional samples for its own laboratory tests.

White coat, she tapped out, picturing Channing at the desk in her grandfather's study.

Dobbins concurred. "I'll forward those results to the group when I get them. Dr. Latimer, how many of our subjects are still onboard?"

"Twenty of twenty-seven so far. Of the seven who declined, two of them were anxious about the newspaper article. The other five were upset over being assigned to the placebo group, but I'll talk to them again if we get the go-ahead." Study participants, even those who hadn't received the drug, were promised the chance to participate in the Phase III trial, during which they were guaranteed to receive the drug.

"Excellent. Good work."

And under that?

Black skirt gray top.

Under that?

She ended her call with Gipson and contemplated whether to text Channing about her plum-colored bra and matching undies. Within seconds came a knock at the door...Niya, holding a plate covered with aluminum foil.

"What's this?"

"Nan khatai...tea biscuits. I made them." She peeled back the foil to show a mound of shortbread cookies with pistachio chips in the center. "Because olive branches are difficult to chew."

"Oh, Niya." Lark was flooded with relief that Niya had reconsidered her threatening message. They shared a brief hug. "Thank you. I know this has been stressful, but you know how for-cause reviews are. We have to turn over every little rock. I think the worst is over. Without data saying otherwise, this all gets chalked up to coincidence."

Her phone chimed with another message, which she ignored for the moment. Peace offering or not, she felt disinclined to share the personal details of her weekend. The anger in Niya's note had startled her. It would take more than a plate of cookies to restore her confidence in their friendship.

"And Shane? I hope he's not still under scrutiny. He's a fine young man."

"It's not official, but it doesn't look like we'll be pursuing that. There's no evidence of contamination." Or sabotage, a word she couldn't bring herself to use with Niya, since it would throw shade on her staff.

"I'm so glad to hear that."

Remembering the cookies, Lark asked, "Would you like tea? I bet we could make quick work of these."

"Sorry, I'm sitting in on a call with Johnson & Johnson in"—she checked her watch—"twelve minutes. Lark, I can't tell you how much I've worried these last two days. I would be devastated to lose our friendship. If I ever behave that way again, I insist you call me on it. No excuses."

"It's a deal."

It was too late in the day to try to reschedule another subject interview for this afternoon. Besides, what was the hurry? Rushing through the remaining interviews would get her recalled to Boston before she had a chance to work out where things were headed with Channing. She returned to her desk and flipped through her inbox in search of paperwork she could knock off in a couple of hours before calling it a day. Her phone chimed again to remind her of the unseen message.

How soon can we have sex again?

* * *

"Thanks, Ruth." Channing handed her favorite driver fifteen quid for a fare that would have been ten had she booked through Uber. After learning from Ruth last summer how little the company's drivers earned, she scheduled her rides off-book whenever possible.

"I can do a pickup later if you like. Hugo's home to watch the kids. Just tell me what time."

"With any luck at all, I won't need a pickup until tomorrow."

In addition to toiletries and a change of clothes, her overnight bag held a vintage bottle of cabernet from Poppa's small collection. For later…lying around in bed naked later.

My place 30 minutes.

Lark's reply had caught her unexpected. She'd meant only to taunt, thinking Lark would be chained to her desk for several more hours. Instead it set off a scramble for both of them to get here.

Resisting a casual encounter during the ferry crossing had paid off with lovemaking that was both exciting and meaningful. Just as Lark had voiced reservations about "makeup sex,"

Channing had never been all that keen on sex for sex's sake, certainly not when she felt a hint of promise for more. After Penderworth, she was convinced their attraction was more than physical. Lark stirred her thoroughly. She had an intriguing balance of strength and vulnerability that let Channing feel it was safe to unveil those same parts of herself.

The sex itself—brilliant. Lark's assertiveness made her realize how weary she'd grown of the stale dynamic with Payton, who responded to seduction but rarely initiated sex. It felt good to be desired.

As she scanned the park for the familiar white company car, a horn tooted behind her. Lark waved her aside and pulled into the space. As advertised, she unfolded from the car dressed in a tight black skirt and summery gray sweater with three-quarter-length sleeves. The biggest surprise were the black heels, not exactly towering but easily the highest Channing had seen her wear. It was quite the sexy combo.

Arms folded, foot tapping, Channing said, "Excuse me, miss…I'm supposed to be meeting someone. I was told she's rather *ord-nry* looking. Have you seen anyone like that?"

"I can be *ord-nry* if that's what you're looking for." Lark kissed her full on the lips before leading the way upstairs to her flat.

"This is a nice surprise. I hardly expected you to say yes."

"I bet you say that to all the girls." Inside the flat, Lark's first move was to draw the curtains in the sitting area. "There was no point in trying to work after I saw your text. I must have read the same page nine times before I finally gave up."

Channing tugged her into an embrace and sensed at once how the slimming skirt firmed Lark's hips and bottom. "Imagine how I felt. I've been sending out texts all day asking women for sex. Three of them said yes and now I'm bloody knackered."

"Oh, thank God. For a minute there I thought I was going to have to go through with it." Lark blinked coquettishly. "Tea?"

Staying ahead of Lark in the snappy comeback department was proving a delightful challenge, one she relished. "You're getting to be quite the Brit, with this dry wit of yours and offering tea to everyone who comes through your door. Next you'll be apologizing to someone who runs you down with their car."

"Sorry. So…tea?"

"I think not. I'd have to let go of you and I don't want to do that." As their eyes froze in a mutual gaze, the playfulness subsided and Lark's body went languid in her arms. "I like the way you smell. Leathery…is it men's?"

"No, it's called White Suede. Florals make me sneeze."

"And why have I never noticed it on you before?"

"Because I only wear it to cover hospital smells. Another reason not to do a residency. But I'll wear it more often if you like it."

If Channing had her way, it was all she'd be wearing soon. Her fingertips separated soft strands of hair as she closed in for a kiss, marveling at the perfect fit of her mouth on Lark's. With deliberate command over every touch and sound, every swipe of her tongue, she alternately inflamed and quelled their excitement.

Lark seemed to grasp her willful pace, answering every incursion and retreat until it was clear she was struggling to stand. "Come with me?"

"Anywhere."

They fell across the bed, where Lark's tight skirt bound her movements. "This definitely needs to go," Channing said, working the hook and zipper.

Lark slithered out and cast it carelessly on the floor. Plum-colored hi-cut briefs bared the sinewy muscles of her upper thigh, where the skin was silky smooth.

Channing's desire to savor the moment was no match for the urge to feel her swollen center against Lark's hip. She let herself be pulled down into another kiss, this one hungry and breathless. All the while her hand worked underneath the sweater—kneading, tickling, raking gently with her nails—until she cupped a satin-covered breast.

Somehow her trousers were open and Lark had slid beneath the elastic band of her bikini pants to grip her bottom. It made her want to tear away their clothes and touch every inch one to the other. Their first time had mattered...so would their second. The voice that had urged her to slow down and savor the moment now taunted her withering self-control.

"Do you have any idea how much I want you?"

"I think I do." Lark took her hand and placed it between her legs, where the cloth of her briefs was damp with arousal. She hurriedly loosened the buttons on Channing's shirt and pushed it off her shoulders.

Channing tossed it behind her along with her trousers, and helped Lark out of her sweater. Sweet torture that it was, she lay atop Lark, relishing the sleekness in all the places their skin slid together. Women were so divine. Kissing, caressing. After circling Lark's breast a tantalizing fourth time, she slipped beneath the satin and touched a hardening nipple.

Lark gasped and arched upward, allowing Channing the space to slither one hand beneath her and release the clasp. "Get naked with me. I want to feel you everywhere."

As the last flimsy barriers between them were tossed aside, she briefly cast her gaze upon Lark's nude form. Her upper chest was garnished with a faint cluster of freckles Channing had noticed yesterday. They required investigation, but later. What compelled her now was the feminine form, the soft swell of her breasts and tapered waist. And the beguiling triangle of hair the color of caramel.

"You are so bloody gorgeous."

There was no hope now of pacing herself, no reining in her passions to prolong their pleasure. She followed the musky scent of excitement and parted the luscious folds with her tongue. Salty, tangy. She drank the essence, reading every sound and twitch as a command, the language of sensuality.

With one hand tightly in Lark's grasp, Channing used the other to tease the opening. A finger barely inside, pulsing downward while her lips worked the taut bundle of nerves.

Lark's brow furrowed with concentration, lifted in surprise and furrowed again, though her lids never opened. Murmuring, whimpering. Her breath came in rapid, shallow puffs as her hips rose. Then a deep gasp that she held for several seconds before bursting with release.

Channing slid all the way inside to feel the walls clench her fingers. How she adored making love with this woman!

CHAPTER FIFTEEN

Lark hadn't slept with a lot of women, but she knew the difference between having sex and making love. One was performance, the other expression. Making love meant dropping the walls that let emotions through.

She and Channing had made love. Not the promise of eternal soulmates—they'd known each other less than three weeks. Yet they both seemed to recognize that what they had was special.

Special was enough for now.

Channing's stomach howled with hunger. "About that tea…"

A shake of laughter spoiled Lark's pretense of being asleep. "Does this mean I have to get up?" Her head rested in the valley between Channing's lovely breasts, which called to mind the nasty trio of men in the airport lounge. She felt delightfully, unapologetically smug.

"I could get it myself, but I'm not sure my legs will hold me."

"How many times did you come?"

"Hmm…five, I think," Channing replied. "A personal best, if you must know."

"Ta-da!"

"It helps to get an early start."

"And it's not even seven o'clock. We're going to shatter that record before the night's over." Lark whirled her legs over the side of the bed and sat up, searching briefly for something to cover herself before remembering she'd drawn the curtains in the other room. "We shall have naked tea."

"Four and a half minutes."

"I know, and milk first." As the water boiled in her electric kettle, Lark examined the contents of her refrigerator and shouted, "Will you eat tomatoes and leftover quiche Lorraine?"

"Off the floor if I have to." Channing, wearing only her bikini panties, darted into the living room to retrieve her bag. First she wriggled into a thigh-length cotton nightshirt, light blue with white piping. Then she produced a bottle of wine. "I raided this from Poppa's collection. L'Orval, 2001."

"I have no idea what that means but it sounds impressive." She put the quiche in the oven with focaccia and set up two plates with sliced tomatoes that she drizzled with olive oil and balsamic vinegar. Then she filled their mugs with boiling water and pushed them toward Channing. "I'm putting you in charge of these for the next four and a half minutes. Now if you'll excuse me…I'm feeling a tad underdressed."

"Don't overdo it."

Lark laughed to herself at the state of the bedroom before picking up and folding the pieces of clothing they'd strewn haphazardly about. Next she straightened the sheets and stole a peek at her phone. No voicemails, no emails. Now that it was after hours in the Cambridge office, she wasn't obligated to check again until morning.

Returning to the kitchen in paisley boxers and a tank top, she found Channing at the bar scrolling through her phone. "Anything interesting?"

"I keep thinking I'll hear from Mitch, the CEO at Albright. He promised to ring me after speaking with HR about the new position. I got the impression it would be only a few days but now it's ten and counting. Seeing as how Payton clearly doesn't want me to return, I suspect she's been trying to botch it. She could gut my chances like *that*." She snapped her fingers. "I can just hear her. 'Channing's not a team player. Channing's prone to overvalue depreciated assets.' Her word carries weight with Mitch."

"Surely the rest of them know you better than that. And I assume your work speaks for itself." It would be especially cruel for Payton to blackball her at work on top of breaking up with her. "There are other jobs in Boston, you know. Maybe something even better."

"I've a noncompete agreement, remember? Even if I could get Mitch to waive it, Payton still could tank my whole bloody career if she wanted to. Mark that as Exhibit A for why one should never have an affair with the boss, married or not. It does irreparable harm to the business relationship."

"What she's doing isn't just an ethical violation, you know. It's illegal. Think about it, she's actually punishing you for having an affair with her. Stand up to her and she'll be the one looking for a job, not you."

"Except that's not who I am, Lark. And Payton knows that. I could destroy her whole life if I wanted to but I don't. I couldn't live with myself even if she deserves it."

"Meanwhile she's exploiting that by dictating terms that mean you get screwed."

"Unfortunately that's true. But feelings for someone don't just go away. I still care enough not to wish her harm, though I'm not sure the feeling is mutual. Granted, it wasn't the smartest thing I've ever done, but I went into it with my eyes wide open. It was pure fantasy on my part to think she'd ever leave her husband. Like she was going to give up the big family holidays or the cottage on the Cape? Please."

Lark sat on the stool beside her, not touching but close enough to feel her warmth. She couldn't deny Channing's impetuous streak. Nor could she criticize it, since it was partly the reason she was here. Channing lived by impulse. Her feelings came easily and they set like concrete.

"I'm not still in love with her though, if that's what you're thinking."

"I wasn't…not exactly." Her face must have given her away. While she'd admit to a vein of jealousy, she wondered if Channing might be a collector of women, a serial monogamist who never quite let go of her ex-lovers. "I think you might be too decent for your own good. To be honest, I have trouble seeing how you could feel any warmth at all for somebody who'd dump on you and then run you out of your job. Payton's a real piece of work."

"It's my fault you have that impression. Kenny's the one who made me see that. Everyone I've told, which is basically just Kenny, Oliver and you, detests her because of the things I've said about her. But you've probably noticed that when any of you criticize her, I turn right around and stick up for her." She chided herself with an incredulous laugh. "If that doesn't already have a name in the psychology manuals, I suggest we call it Hughes Syndrome."

"Loyalty's not a syndrome, Channing." Though it was a weakness in this case, since it meant letting Payton push her around.

"It's not just loyalty. It's self-preservation as well. If I were to make a fuss at Albright, Payton and I both would end up in the shitter. She'd probably be fired, but they'd have to take me back on so it wouldn't look like they were condoning sexual harassment. But I'd likely never advance because they'd all be whispering behind my back that I'd bloody slept my way to the top."

"I get that, but it still isn't fair that you're the one who got screwed—figuratively, I mean. Payton's the one who crossed the major lines. Cheating on her husband was nothing compared to having an affair with somebody she supervised. In this day and age, that's just not done. She had to know she was putting your career at risk—and hers too. I know better than anyone that you're irresistible, but why on earth would a woman in her position do something so reckless?"

The oven timer dinged.

"Saved by the bell," Channing quipped. She poured the wine while Lark divided the quiche and focaccia. "You're quite right about one thing though. I *am* irresistible."

"Tell me something I don't know." Lark served her plate with one hand while the other casually groped Channing's backside. "So you seduced her and she fell for your charms. Been there, done that."

"Actually no. There was no flirting, no seduction by either of us. It simply happened of its own accord. It was a moment, an impulse. We could have stopped it right there, written it off as a misadventure, emotions getting out of hand, all that. Instead we took a couple of weeks to think it over and ended up deciding it was what we both wanted."

Lark thought back to the time during medical school when she and Bess had taken a break from each other, even going so far as to grant permission to see other people. Drowning in her studies, she'd barely had time to look in the mirror, let alone at someone else. Bess however became involved with another woman, a semi-serious relationship that had lasted several months. What brought that to mind now was Bess's insistence on telling her why she'd been drawn to someone else, revealing intimate details Lark had no desire to hear.

Oddly, she found herself voyeuristically intrigued by the particulars of Channing and Payton's affair. "It must have mattered a lot to both of you if you were willing to risk so much."

"Who thinks about consequences when all those brain chemicals are exploding? Payton once said we were like a pair of cats climbing a tree. They ascend quite easily but most have no idea how they're going to get down. I always had this sort of vague fantasy that eventually she'd leave Ben and come to live with me in my apartment. I failed to grasp all the obstacles in her path, since there weren't any in mine. She wasn't married only to Ben. She also had a whole extended family and way of life, and I don't think she ever saw me as being an accepted part of that. And I didn't exactly pine for it either, all the brothers and sisters, the grown children. If I'm honest, I only wanted her."

"So you were stuck in limbo waiting for her to decide. I can't imagine anything more frustrating."

"It was far worse than frustrating. When she wasn't there it was bleak, always bleak." Channing pushed her empty plate aside, and with her elbows on the bar, cradled her wine. "I probably shouldn't admit this...a part of me was actually relieved when she broke it off because I could never have done it. I'd said so many stupid things, like how I'd wait for her no matter how long it took, that I'd rather have stolen moments than not have her at all. Being pigheaded, I was determined to keep those promises, all the while growing more miserable every day. She absolved me from all that."

Lark found that oddly reassuring for a couple of reasons. First, it was the most convincing statement to date that Channing's romantic feelings for Payton were indeed a thing of the past. And second, Channing obviously possessed a strong sense of commitment. Lark needed both of those to be true for this relationship to feel like a possibility.

"Channing Hughes, I find you kind of fascinating." She dropped her hand to Channing's thigh and slowly walked her fingers underneath the nightshirt. "Maybe you noticed that earlier."

"You mustn't do that while I'm drinking, remember? I could choke and you wouldn't be allowed to help me because you're not a doctor."

"Bloody awkward," she said in her best English accent. "So tell me...what would I have to do to get you to feel all pigheaded about me?"

"I suppose that depends. You don't have a spouse tucked away somewhere, do you? That would certainly take the biscuit, now wouldn't it?"

"I have nothing tucked away anywhere." Lark pretended to pat her pockets. She didn't want their conversation to take a heavy turn. What if Channing—consciously or not—was drawn to women she knew would leave her eventually? She'd likely known Payton's family would ultimately claim her, whereas Lark came with a built-in expiration date. "I hope you're serious about coming back to Boston. Even if Albright doesn't work out, someone with your résumé could get a job practically anywhere. A whole different industry so you aren't in competition."

"Funny, Payton said the same thing, as long as I stayed in England. Though I'm not keen on starting at the bottom again. It's bloody hard climbing over all the whiz kids with their algorithms and game theories. What I'm best at is sitting down with clients, presenting the economic side, and making them feel confident."

Given Channing's handling of their tiff on the ship, it was easy to imagine that she set clients at ease. "How's this for an idea? If you want your job back at Albright—and it sounds like you might—make peace with Payton. Convince her that you aren't a threat, that you can put on your game face in the office and let the past be the past."

After a long silence, Channing abruptly picked up her glass and retreated to the couch. Her expression was hard to read, but the twist of her mouth hinted at an edge. "I'm not dismissing that, but I have to ask…what sort of sacrifice are *you* prepared to make?"

"What do you mean?"

"You asked what it would take for me to feel pigheaded about you. But you then proceeded to suggest that I swallow a rather bitter pill and crawl back to Albright, where I'd not only have to deal with Payton but also that Boyd Womack prat. I'm asking if there's another plan that doesn't involve me making all the sacrifices. What are *you* prepared to do?"

Before Lark would even attempt to answer, she needed to understand where Channing was coming from. Was this an actual negotiation or merely the voicing of a grievance? By her placid tone, she wasn't irritated or upset. Nor was she particularly inviting.

"You've got such a panicked look about you, Lark. I'm not asking specifically." She snickered and patted the space beside her on the couch.

"It's not panic. I'm trying to figure out where you're coming from so I'll know how to answer."

"I'm only raising the question because Payton asked quite a lot of me during the course of our relationship. We had only our secret trysts when we traveled together. Scraps, really. Never just a simple museum outing in Boston, and no holidays at all—ever. She would ring me occasionally when Ben was out but I wasn't to ring her. Meanwhile she had an entire other life that probably included having sex with her husband."

"In other words, all the hallmarks of a secret affair."

"Precisely, and it was even worse because she was my boss. I sucked it up while she screwed me financially, all so we could keep traveling together."

"And you got jack shit for it. See, this is why people who care about you despise that woman." It was difficult to reconcile the spirited, confident person sitting beside her with the passive mistress she'd just described. Even more curious was Channing's conciliatory acceptance of how Payton had ended their affair. "If you ask me, it's a miracle you didn't burn the whole house down, Channing. I'd have gone all Charlize Theron on her ass. How can you be so calm talking about all the crap she put you through?"

"That's my point. Not that I'm saying you're anything like Payton, but I can't go into another relationship in which I'd be expected to make all the sacrifices in order to keep it going. If I can't bring myself to go back to Albright...if there's nothing in Boston for me..."

"You're asking if I'd give up my job and move to England?"

"Or perhaps—and I'm totally making this up—setting out for someplace new in Europe or...or...California, somewhere we both could find jobs we enjoy. I'm not saying, 'All right, here's what I demand.' But if our relationship were to become serious, what's not on the table?"

It was thrilling just to hear Channing acknowledge their potential. "Obviously this needs to be said—our relationship is already serious as far as I'm concerned. My goal right now is to be with you as much as I can so we can figure this out. The answer to your question is nothing. If we decide we want this"— she clutched Channing's hand and squeezed—"everything's on the table. I'll do whatever it takes to make it work."

"All right then, lots of possibilities." Channing slid her hand inside Lark's shorts, going straight for the prize. "Perhaps now we can get back to shattering that record you were boasting about."

CHAPTER SIXTEEN

Channing swiped a band of steam from the bathroom mirror to inspect her neck for signs of excessive enthusiasm. *All clear*. Fresh from their communal shower, she called out, "I can't recall ever feeling quite so clean. I applaud your thoroughness, you little scrubber."

"I was looking for an earring." Lark appeared behind her in briefs and a crisp blue shirt, and carrying two cups of tea.

"My, this really is a full-service establishment."

"Don't forget to post a review. I love this, by the way," Lark said, bending to plant a kiss on the strawberry-shaped birthmark on Channing's hip. "If you believe the old wives' tale, your mother craved strawberries when she was pregnant with you."

"I'd totally believe that had it been a dollar sign." She relinquished the mirror and got dressed, noting that Lark had built a tower of sheets and towels for the housekeepers who would come through her apartment and refresh its appointments. "Does my invitation to return this evening still stand?"

"Of course. Why wouldn't it?"

"No reason. I just find it's always good to check the veracity of propositions uttered during sex."

Joking aside, she had every reason to trust where they stood. They'd circled seamlessly through heated sex, self-appraisal, silliness and now everyday routine like a couple who'd been together for months, perhaps years. Channing's only concern, oddly, was her lack of concern. The morning after her first night with Payton had brought a storm of anxiousness. She'd talked herself into believing Payton would regret what they'd done, that she'd renounce her feelings and leave her to sort herself. Why wasn't she equally panicked about Lark's imminent return to Boston? Either she'd bought into the future of their relationship or her subconscious had already accepted its demise.

"Such a serious face," Lark said as she pulled on a pair of trousers.

"I'm pondering my feelings for you."

"Okay, you have my attention."

"I'm feeling quite at ease."

Lark gave her a puzzled look and returned to the bathroom to finish her face and hair. "Is there any reason you shouldn't be?"

"No, it's very nice actually." With most of her life in limbo, Lark was a stabilizing force. "Kenny will be happy to hear that, since it gets him off the hook for spoiling our weekend. Should I tell him I had eight orgasms? He'd be positively green with envy."

"I always say there's no such thing as bad publicity. Have you decided what you're going to tell the Brownings?"

"Not about the orgasms...unless you think I should."

Lark gave her an incredulous look on her way to the kitchen. "Something for breakfast?"

If she'd had it to do over she'd have come out to Poppa as a teenager, and the Brownings too. Those were the years of Thatcher's Section 28, when most Britons considered gay life a "pretended family relationship." As her lies and deflections piled up, the topic grew more difficult to broach.

Following Lark to a perch on the kitchen stool, she sighed dismally. "I avoided them all day yesterday. Considering the fact that they avoided me too, I almost think they'd prefer I didn't say anything at all. Frankly I don't see the point in confronting them over it."

"It doesn't have to be a confrontation. You are who you are. They've loved you for thirty years...surely this won't change that."

"That remains to be seen, but I appreciate your optimism." More than anything, she was hurt. How could Cecil have looked at her with such contempt? "It's likely to hasten their retirement...which means I'd probably have to hire someone else to oversee the manor while it sits on the market waiting for a buyer."

"That's just sad if you ask me."

"I wish I knew what Maisie was thinking. Divide and conquer, you know? At least I don't have to feel bad about firing them, since they were leaving anyway. That would have been even more devastating."

When Lark presented her with toast with jam and sliced banana, Channing noticed a wry smile.

"All right, what have I said that's funny?"

"I was thinking of when we were walking through Heathrow and you made a wisecrack about my chattiness in the morning. You said it must be hard on my *cohabitant*. So is it?"

Channing grudgingly acknowledged yet again her appreciation of Lark's wit, dry and cutting without being cruel. "Smarty breeches. Aren't you late for work?"

* * *

The email from Mike Dobbins had landed in Lark's inbox just before midnight. *Let's discuss what this means*, with a calendar event for an afternoon conference call, and a file attachment containing lab results for eight of the Flexxene trial subjects, including the three who'd reported cardiac symptoms.

Upon being notified of each medical emergency, Lark had phoned the hospital staff in Cambridge to request additional blood samples, upon which Gipson labs would run exhaustive tests to determine Flexxene's effects. For comparison, she'd asked also for samples from three other subjects who were getting the drug and two who were not.

Dobbins had already screened the lab report and highlighted its most significant findings. Two of the emergency patients had only trace amounts of leflunomide, the metabolite produced by the body as it processed the chemical components of Flexxene. Such low levels suggested they hadn't received their scheduled dose. The third patient tested negative as expected, since he was in the placebo group that received an adhesive patch without the drug.

It was the second set of highlighted figures she found most astonishing—all three emergency patients had high levels of cotinine, the metabolite for nicotine. All reported being nonsmokers, and these levels were far too high to result from second-hand smoke.

"No way," she muttered.

A check of their files confirmed they'd been swab-tested prior to the study to rule out tobacco use. In particular, all three reported having never smoked. If PharmaStat had rigged its sample by submitting fake swabs, it appeared they'd also coached subjects not to mention their tobacco habits if they were audited. That would constitute fraud.

The last time she'd stumbled upon fraudulent practices, a small clinic in Dallas had brazenly faked its entire placebo group, submitting blood work from staff instead of actual subjects. Gipson referred that case for criminal prosecution and the supervising physician lost his license to practice medicine.

PharmaStat, with hundreds of millions in research contracts, had too much at stake to risk such unscrupulous behavior. But one fact was inescapable—any research process, no matter how exacting or rigorous, was only as strong as its weakest link. If a low-level employee like Wendi or Shane had felt under the gun to meet recruitment quotas by a certain deadline, might they fudge the data?

"Knock knock." Niya stuck her head in. "Lunch today at Curry King?"

"Afraid not. I just got some weird data from the lab. Looks like I have a bunch of calls to make before I conference with Gipson."

"The lab? Something to do with the trial? Can you tell me what it is?"

Lark shook her head grimly. "Not yet. I need to check a few things first. There's probably a simple explanation."

"Maybe I can help." Niya leaned across the desk to peek at the file, but Lark clicked quickly to close it. "I see. We're under suspicion again. Who is it this time?"

"I'm sorry, Niya. You know I can't share this. It's for your protection as much as mine."

"Oh, forget it. I might as well get started on my resignation letter. You know, Lark…I find myself going back and forth with you. Some days I actually think you're my friend." If not for the hydraulic closer, she surely would have slammed the door on her way out. From friend to enemy in a span of seconds.

Lark was left shaking and on the verge of tears. Hers was a maddening position, requiring her to investigate possible mistakes or misdeeds that might have been committed by someone she trusted. To exonerate Niya, she had to find evidence that would pin the trial failure on someone else.

She'd been through the list of everyone on the Flexxene team, from the hospital staff to PharmaStat's coordinators, and so far had found nothing out of the ordinary. Perhaps one of them warranted a closer look, an employee whose perfectionist work habits made her appear beyond reproach—Wendi Doolan.

* * *

The sound of crashing glass jolted Channing from Poppa's desk. "Maisie?"

She rushed downstairs to find Maisie whimpering at the mess, an entire stack of fine Wedgwood saucers broken to bits. "I'm so sorry, Miss Channing. I was taking them down so I could wipe the cupboard."

"It's all right. They're just dishes." Far more important was the bleeding gash on Maisie's hand. Channing grabbed a clean tea towel from the drawer and wrapped the wound tightly. "We need to get you to the medical center."

"I don't think it's that serious. Just a cut really...a plaster or two will do." She raised her apron to wipe the tears.

"You sit here. Don't touch any of this." She rushed back upstairs to fetch her phone, then took a photo of the gash. "I'm texting this to my friend Lark for advice."

"The woman who was here on Sunday?"

Channing bristled. This was no time for a confrontation. "She's a doctor. She'll know what to do."

"I'm sure you're right. She certainly set my mind at ease."

Odd...theirs had been only a brief introduction. "At ease about what?"

"Oh, that new arthritis medicine they were testing. I took it for a little while and it helped, but then came that article in one of the red tops about how they were using us like guinea pigs, saying the drug might cause a heart attack. Dr. Latimer said there was nothing to worry about."

"Wait a minute, are you saying—" Her phone rang, a call from Lark. "Did you get my photo?"

"That's Mrs. Browning, right? What happened?"

"She dropped some dishes and one of them bounced up and cut her. I want to take her to the medical center but she says not to worry. What should I do?"

"Start with basic first aid. Have you stopped the bleeding?"

She lifted the cloth. "It's still seeping a bit."

"Keep pressure on it and have her hold it above her head. It should stop."

Channing got Maisie situated at the table with her hand elevated and stepped into the great hall, letting the kitchen door swing shut behind her. "Maisie says she knows you, that she was taking one of your drugs that causes heart attacks. Did it not occur to you that I might like to know about that? She's practically my family."

"You know I can't discuss that with you, Channing. Everyone's entitled to privacy, but I'll say this—you don't have to worry about our drug. It's perfectly safe and I would *not* tell you that if I weren't a hundred percent certain it was true. Besides, she stopped taking it."

"Why the charade? Both of you pretended you didn't know each other."

"Come on, she was a patient in a confidential drug trial. It wasn't my place to say anything. When she pretended not to recognize me, I followed her lead. I'm sorry."

"Why would she…it doesn't make sense."

"That's a question for her, not me."

Channing groaned. "Must you always be so…so ethical?" With the phone tucked beneath her chin, she returned to the kitchen and inspected the wound. "All right, it's stopped bleeding. Can you look at the picture again? I don't care if you're a witch doctor. You have to tell me what to do."

"Let Maisie make the call. I'm sure she's seen her fair share of cuts and scrapes. I don't see anything that would alarm me if I were in fact medically qualified to say so, which I'm not." She finished with instructions for how to clean and dress the wound if they decided not to seek medical care.

"Please tell her thank you from me," Maisie said cheerfully.

"Maisie says thanks. So do I, Lark. Sorry I turned into my beastly self. I was frightened."

"It's okay. I'll be happy to come by later and give it a look if you want. I can even give you a ride to wherever you might be going this evening…if you're still planning on going out, that is. And back home tomorrow."

Clever. "Yes, that would be convenient. See you later then."

"She seems like a nice young woman," Maisie said as Channing dabbed her hand with a soapy cloth. "And pretty too. From Boston, is she?"

Channing's heart leapt at hearing she might have an ally in Maisie. "That's right. She's wrapping up her work here soon and going back. What's with this secret, the two of you pretending you didn't know each other when she came for dinner?"

"Oh, that…I felt so silly. I'd only met her the day before, for the interview in her office. I was afraid she might mention the plans we'd made for our pension before Cecil and I had the chance to tell you." She scolded Channing with a shaking finger. "All the while you were bottling up a secret of your own about Lord Hughes's estate. It was such a relief when we sat down and talked it out."

"Secrets are silly, aren't they? Both of us trying not to hurt each other's feelings. If we'd been honest from the start it would have saved us a lot of worry."

Maisie put the kettle on for tea as Channing swept up the glass. "Speaking of secrets...you've become close with Dr. Latimer."

Had Cecil not seen them together, such a question would have triggered what Channing called her "deflect mode." Keep calm, make the suspicious seem ordinary, and change the subject. There was no point to avoiding it now, as it was inevitable. "She's quite nice. Wonderful sense of humor too, very British. I like her very much."

"Your jaunt over to Amsterdam...it was one of those gay pride parades, wasn't it? I saw it on the BBC. Quite colorful, all the boats."

A deep shudder sent a rush of fresh heat to Channing's face. This was the conversation she'd dodged for fifteen years. "It was quite the party atmosphere. Great fun."

Maisie's trusting blue eyes flashed just the slightest hint of hurt. She'd held the door wide and Channing had been too cowardly to walk through it. It was the first time she'd considered that her pretense might be hurtful for someone who was waiting for her to open up.

"Yes, it was a gay pride festival. It's true, Maisie...I'm gay. I've pretty much known since I was about twelve, believe it or not. It was confusing for a while but I understand it better now. And I'm quite all right with it. Happy in fact. Not that it matters, since there's nothing I nor anyone else can do to change it." She tried to read Maisie's face, which somehow managed not a flicker of emotion. "I never told Poppa...it's possible he suspected but we never talked about it. That whole Thatcher thing and all. But anyone who knows me knows I've had a suspicious lack of boyfriends. There was always Kenny, who's…well, he's gay also. He's been with Oliver for several years now."

Maisie nodded slowly, her face still giving nothing away. "Cecil guessed as much about Lord Teasely. Saw him once when he was just a lad at the Plough and Fleece with some of his mates. Cecil said a new boy came in and they all kissed. It upset him a bit, what he saw. He doesn't understand how two men can fancy one another."

She thought again of Cecil's angry glare. "I'm sure it's difficult at first, especially if it spoils all the expectations, all those silly plans that Kenny and I would grow up and get married. Lord Alanford knew…and he made life miserable for Kenny at home, which is why he spent so much time here. I always assumed Poppa knew as well since Lord Alanford was his best mate, but he never said. He was always kind to Kenny. It's better now, the relationship with his family. Probably helps that they like Oliver so much."

The more she tried to normalize the discussion, the more it sounded to her ear like chattering. She needed Maisie on her side.

"The poor fellow, having to go through that," Maisie said. "He's such a dear young man."

"And full of mischief too, speaking as someone who knows him quite well."

Channing checked the wound one last time and confirmed the bleeding had stopped. As she fetched the first aid supplies, Maisie poured their tea.

"Cecil and I, we're old fashioned, luv. That sort of thing is more accepted now, I know. Still, it's a bit of a shock when you find out it's someone you know. You're used to thinking of them one way and now they're another way."

"A bit unsettling, I suppose. I always had a strong feeling it would be, which is why I kept it from you…and from Poppa as well. I didn't want it to cause problems between us. There were times I felt horrible about it, that I was being dishonest with you. But it never seemed worth the worry to upset everyone when I had no one special in my life."

Lark was special, but the rift with Cecil had left her feeling vulnerable about saying too much. If he was intent on judging her, she didn't want to bring that on Lark.

As if on cue, the back door opened to Cecil, who was carrying a box of groceries. It was instantly obvious he was perturbed, as he wouldn't meet her eye.

Channing stiffened at first but then chastised herself for her cowardice. "Maisie's cut her hand, Cecil. It's all right I think, but you mustn't let her do too much."

He promptly inspected the bandage and expressed concern.

"We were just talking about my friend Lark," Channing went on. "You're upset with me."

A scowl overtook his grizzled face, and still he wouldn't look at her. "It's not right, Miss Channing."

"Maisie and I were just saying it's a bit of a shock to suddenly discover—"

"It's not what God intended."

Channing sighed, realizing she'd have to try a new tack. "I do respect your right to your religious beliefs, and I know you feel them quite sincerely, but honestly…I don't share them at all. I've never been one for the church. How could I be when they seek to negate my very existence?"

"You are the one who's doing that," he said, his anger causing him to spit his words. "If your Poppa were here…he'd be ashamed of you."

Her face suddenly burned but not with the guilt he'd intended. What she felt was rage. "I'm truly sorry to have caused you such an upset, but I refuse to be ashamed of who I am. This is the real Channing Hughes, Cecil. It's who I've always been. If it was your intention to hurt my feelings, then you have. But if you're trying to bully me into denying my own existence, I'm afraid you've fallen miserably short. The only thing you've managed to accomplish is to lower my opinion of you. It's not how you treat people you profess to love."

He took a step toward her and shook his finger. "You are not the child I helped raise."

"I'm *exactly* that child—all grown up."

"Please, both of you. Stop this." Maisie's cheeks were streaked with tears. She'd spoken too late to stop the angry invective.

"I'm going," he said.

When the door closed behind him, Maisie fell into Channing's arms. "Darling, I'm so sorry. He doesn't mean those awful things. I hope you don't either."

Cecil had known Poppa better than anyone. It crushed her to think he might be right, that he'd have been ashamed of her. That wasn't the grandfather whose memory she cherished.

"It would take a lot more than that to change what I feel for you and Cecil. I love you both so much." Swallowing hard against the lump in her throat, she held Maisie's shoulders at arm's length and steadied her voice. "Are you disappointed, Maisie?"

"Not in you, luv. Never in you." Her voice was achingly sweet. "I'm a little sad…I'd have liked for you to have a little one of your own someday. I'd have loved that baby like my own grandchild."

"Don't count me out, Maisie. I may surprise us both someday."

CHAPTER SEVENTEEN

Wendi took the chair opposite Lark's desk and crossed her legs, causing a stylish platform boot to dangle like dead weight. "What can I help you with, boss?"

It was critical for Lark to get this interview right. If her renewed focus on Wendi turned out to be a wild goose chase, the stain of suspicion could end the young woman's career.

Certain facts were straightforward. Someone had switched out the transdermal patches for three study subjects, replacing them with high-dose nicotine patches that triggered an array of frightening symptoms. Automation and strict quality control measures at the Munich packaging and distribution center made it unlikely the switch had taken place there. Also a fact—in a marked deviation from normal procedures, those individual drug packets had not been subjected to the usual inspection upon delivery to the participating clinics. Without doubt the switch was deliberate. While the transdermal patches were similar in appearance, it strained credulity to think a single nicotine patch could have accidentally found its way into a packet with six trial patches, let alone into three separate packets.

Along with the facts were several conjectures. The switch likely took place at PharmaStat rather than at the clinic, since the affected subjects were at two different hospitals. Trial supplies were stored in a locked, climate-controlled dispensary at PharmaStat and delivered to the clinics once a week. Only a handful of people had access. And finally, whoever sent Shane with the deliveries probably had known he wouldn't examine the individual packets.

All that gave Wendi the opportunity and means. Did she have the motive?

"Wendi, I need to go over some questions I asked you earlier and make sure my record of events is correct. You handled most of the deliveries to the clinics, and you always inspected the contents of each package, right?"

"Correct, except for the two deliveries Shane made."

"And can you tell me the reason Shane was sent those two times? Since it wasn't his usual job, that is." According to Shane, Wendi had asked him to make the run because she was working against a deadline on a report for another client.

"Because I got slammed with reports." She scrolled through the calendar on her phone. "Here it is. Dr. Martin asked for an interim compliance report for Abbott Labs." Her hand shot to her mouth. "Oops, I probably wasn't supposed to say who it was for. Please don't tell Dr. Batra I did that."

"Don't worry about it. I'm not even writing it down. What about the second time?"

"That would have been the twenty-sixth. It was a…let's see, a subject recruiting update. For a different client. Not Gipson, not Abbott."

"So just routine reports."

"The reports themselves were routine. I've done dozens, probably hundreds of them. It's only a matter of pulling together the data on the page. I've a template for every project. And of course I check and recheck the numbers." She touched her chin pensively. "And I try to stay on top of the schedule. It's all on a white board in my cubby, the dates for what's due to whom. What caused the panic was that neither of those reports was scheduled, which is why I was slammed."

"What do you mean by not scheduled?"

"Apparently Dr. Batra was conferencing with the clients and needed to gen up on the status of their trial. At least that's what Dr. Martin said when he asked for the reports. I got Shane to sort the deliveries because I didn't have time."

"On both occasions?"

Wendi nodded.

Two last-minute special reports—both ordered by Jermaine Martin, ostensibly for Niya—upended usual procedures, exposing the trial to possible sabotage. Lark tried to shake off the implications.

"Wendi, something came to my attention in my discussions with the nursing staffs at Shire and Addenbrooke. They all remarked about your professionalism, how you're meticulous about the delivery process, opening every box to inspect the seals on each packet."

She grinned sheepishly. "I know, it's probably overkill. Some of them take the mickey, say I'm OCD. I've always done it that way though. It's how we were taught at Sheffield. Verify that treatment packets are intact, that they haven't gotten wet or spilled out in the bottom of the box. I found that once, believe it or not. A box cutter had sliced one of the packets open. It was contaminated and had to be replaced."

"It's a good habit, very conscientious. So it's not part of the training here at PharmaStat?"

"Only when it's stipulated by the client, which it hardly ever is. Dr. Batra seems pleased that I do it, but it isn't strictly required. As far as I know, I'm the only one who does."

There was nothing in Wendi's demeanor to suggest that she would do something that was not only malicious but dangerous. But whoever had done this was a master of deception.

"Wendi, I need to be blunt here. Something went really wrong with the Flexxene trial and we need to determine exactly where it all broke down. We're looking at possible tampering."

Her blue eyes opened wide in surprise and her freckled face began to turn red. "Oh my God, you don't think I—"

"I don't think anything. I'm still gathering information to determine how it could have happened."

"I can't believe it...I'm the one person who does things totally by procedure."

"Like I said, it's a good habit, Wendi. As far as I'm concerned, that makes you part of the quality control team."

Even so, Lark planned to check her story about the last-minute assignments. Drug tampering was only one aspect of her investigation. Whoever had done this had also laid a trail to implicate Shane and alerted the media with a bogus story about Gipson putting profits over safety. It would take a perfectionist to pull it off...and by all accounts, that described Wendi to a T.

* * *

Leon Downey had been a college mate of Kenny's at Queen Mary in London before dropping out for a career in real estate. Well-connected with the gay scene in London, Kenny said, especially in professional circles. Just the guy to help get Penderworth ready for sale.

Though foppishly dressed in a shiny black suit with patent leather shoes, he'd trudged through the seeping moss to view the exterior of the manor house from all angles. After a detailed inspection of every cupboard and closet within, including the Brownings' humble quarters in the old carriage house, he was to recommend simple repairs that might pay off with a higher asking price. He clearly was knowledgeable and market-savvy, but with all the charm of a plate of peas. Three times he'd called her Chandler.

"How soon do you think I'll be able to list the property?" she asked. Now that she'd made up her mind it had to be sold, she was anxious to see the process underway. Saying goodbye was a different matter, but they weren't there yet.

"It all depends on what you choose to do. People sell homes 'as is' all the time, but they don't usually fetch as good a price.

However it might be best to go that route in your case."

"So lots of repairs, huh?"

"More than a few, less than a lot. The foundation is quite good and the house has weathered nicely. If one merely wanted to live here, I'd start with a new roof to protect the structure and its contents, and add a few joists to level the second floor. Also, the entire parcel needs to be graded for drainage. Those are time-consuming, so a quick sale wouldn't be possible. But if one wanted to *enjoy* living here, there's also much to be done with the baths, the kitchen, the carriage house."

"So you're saying that 'as is' means the buyer takes care of the roof, the joists and the drainage...which means I could list it for sale right away."

"Yes, though I'd not recommend an actual listing, Chandler. Sorry...*Channing*. An historical property such as Penderworth attracts an undesirable element of, shall we say, sightseers. They run the agents ragged setting up tours purely to satisfy a leisurely interest in period homes. Very few of them can afford to seriously entertain a purchase of this magnitude, especially considering the cost of repairs and upkeep."

Little wonder Leon was Kenny's friend, given how much Channing wanted to smack him. "Very well, not listing but..."

He gave her a haughty cluck and said, "Any agent worth half his salt probably already has a list of buyers who are salivating for such a property as Penderworth. They'd sit down over a scotch whiskey and strike a deal within a week. Subject to your approval of course."

The thought of leaving the manor and all its memories in a week hit her stomach like a bad egg. There was an upside however—a quick sale would force her hand about returning to Boston.

As if conjured by thoughts of Boston, Lark drove through the gate and parked near the front door. She'd dropped by after work three days in a row, ostensibly to check on Maisie's wound, but also to pick up Channing so they could spend the night together at her flat.

"Hi, beautiful," Channing said, delivering an unabashed peck on the lips. Now that her secret was out, she couldn't be bothered with hiding her feelings.

"I'll go in and check on Maisie."

"She's in the kitchen. Be right there." Turning back to Leon, she said, "I'd like to explore my options, whether to do a few repairs or sell as is. You'll send me the list of recommended fixes?"

Time was a factor as well, since the cost of upkeep would have to be extended through the course of repairs. She could certainly afford to take a lower price if it meant selling right away. It would be nice to have at least a small nest egg after paying inheritance taxes. That could buy her time in London to scour the job market should she choose to stay. Or it could buy her time in Boston if she needed to make new connections.

Her overnight suitcase—the same one Cecil had carted upstairs on Sunday—sat by the door, packed and ready to go when Lark finished her examination of Maisie's wound. She'd toyed with the idea of having Lark stay over at Penderworth instead, in hopes of giving Cecil the chance to talk with her under less acrimonious circumstances. Surely he appreciated how she'd taken care of Maisie.

In the kitchen, Lark was drying the wound with cotton wool. "This is healing nicely, Mrs. Browning. Another day or two and it should close up. Just keep it clean and covered."

"I'm so grateful, a busy person like you coming all the way out here every day to check on a silly cut."

"You can thank Channing for that. She was pretty insistent."

The atmosphere at Penderworth had mellowed dramatically from two days ago, when Channing was frantic over both the injury and her confrontation with Cecil. The two of them had managed to stay out of each other's way, yet they remained at a stubborn impasse.

"What do you think, Maisie?" Channing asked. "Any sign of a crack in Cecil's armor?"

"Mmm…he didn't like the way that man talked to you just now, like you were a silly schoolgirl. I practically had to tie him to the table to keep him from going out there and telling him off."

Perhaps it was a good sign that Cecil was sticking up for her. "I didn't like it much either. But he's a friend of Kenny's, you know. And he offered good advice about repairs. Have you gotten an update from your brother concerning the guesthouse?"

"They're painting the interior this week so it should be ready soon. But we don't have to move right away, luv. It wouldn't be right to leave you here on your own."

Lark cleared her throat and tipped her head toward the back door, a not-so-subtle signal for Channing to go try to talk to Cecil again. It was gut wrenching to watch both of them suffer, she'd said, when a few caring words might be enough to soothe their row.

Stepping outside, Channing spotted Cecil in the gazebo, where he was scraping the rusty chairs with an iron brush in preparation for painting. Her slow walk toward him gave both of them time to decide what sort of mood they wanted to project.

"The property inspector, Kenny's friend…he was quite complimentary of the garden. Said it showed a master's touch."

Cecil grunted. "Stupid prat walked right through my tulip bed."

"If it's any consolation, I think he ruined his shoes." It flooded her with relief to see his wry smile, and she pressed her advantage. "Cecil, I can't stand this angry wall between us. This is hurting me so very much. I'm sorry for losing my temper. Of course I respect you. You're my family and I love you. And I have no doubts whatsoever that you love me too."

"I do, dear one." The fire in his eyes was gone but his face had fallen with sadness.

She took the brush and set it aside so she could hold his hands. "Then you have to accept me for who I am. I mean it, you *have* to. There's no other way for us to get past this anger. I can't simply will myself to change, even if I wanted to…which I don't actually. I swear to you that I'm still the same person you've always loved."

The pain in his face softened, a sign of how badly he wanted all of this not to matter. "I don't want to feel this way."

"Then don't. Wish for me to be happy as me, not as someone I can't be."

He slumped into the iron chair, his shoulders sagging. "It feels like I'm letting him down, Lord Hughes. I don't think he'd like this."

"It breaks my heart to hear you say that, Cecil. I'd have done anything in my power not to be a disappointment to Poppa, but this...it was never *in* my power. I truly believe he'd have understood, even if it was hard at first. But I know he'd have loved me just the same."

The moment stretched into an almost unbearable silence until he finally nodded. "All right then, Miss Channing. I'll do my best."

"Thank you. It means more than I could ever say." She stooped beside him and patted his forearm. "About Lark... Dr. Latimer. I care for her, obviously. It could be quite serious between us. She'll be returning to Boston soon and I'll have a decision to make. In the meantime, I would like it very much if she could see the very sweet, pleasant, warm person I know you to be."

"I'm not always pleasant."

His sardonic grin proved contagious and drew them together in a long hug. She had no illusions about how hard this would continue to be, but at least the searing pain had finally stopped.

* * *

Lark walked across the bed on her knees and collapsed next to Channing, who was tapping away on her tablet computer. Their collective mood was sullen given the issues that troubled them. Lark's trial review had taken her down an uncomfortable path, while Channing was coming to grips with selling Penderworth.

Channing paused and looked at her glumly. "Kenny had one of the partners look over my contract with Albright. He's relatively certain the noncompete is enforceable even here in the UK, which means there's probably zero chance of me going back to work at Lloyd's."

"Have you considered calling Mitch to say you haven't gotten anything yet from HR…maybe he could give them a nudge?"

"Oh, I didn't tell you. I got a note from him this afternoon. He apologized for taking so long. Apparently there's a lot of paperwork when they promote someone without advertising the position. He asked me to be patient—obviously he thinks that's in my skill set."

It was a tremendous relief to Lark to know the job at Albright was still moving forward. "At least you finally heard from him. Now you can stop worrying what Payton's doing behind the scenes."

"Something that occurred to me…Albright has an office in London as well. More of an outpost really, four or five people. Their primary focus is business development…financial networking to identify potential accounts. Perhaps they'd have need of someone with valuation cred."

Lark couldn't muster much enthusiasm for any job that would leave Channing in the UK, despite her promise to put all possible sacrifices on the table. Reality was knocking at the door in the form of her imminent return to Boston. Their relationship was at a fragile point. It didn't yet feel solid enough to weather the distance, especially if Channing were to shift her focus to a new job.

"You know, it's starting to look like I'm going to wrap up my project at PharmaStat early next week. I'm hoping Gipson will want me to stay a bit longer, maybe to get the trial back into the field, but it's possible they'll call me back to Boston. I'm talking like…five or six days from now."

Channing tossed the tablet aside and climbed atop her like a hungry predator. "What could you do to get arrested and then released on bail? Something where you'd have to surrender your passport."

"How about indecent exposure? I'll strip off all my clothes and run through the streets."

"That doesn't work here like it does in America. Seen one bum, you've seen them all." Her hands wandered inside Lark's paisley shorts. "Though your bum is quite exceptional."

Lark squirmed beneath her until she was sitting up. "I'm serious, Channing. Five days. How are we going to do this?"

Channing groaned and fell dramatically onto her back. "I don't know. But things will work out the way they're supposed to."

"Hunh…what does that even mean? It's not like we're on some giant game board where the Hand of God rolls the dice and marches us around. Anyone who thinks there's some master plan is full of shit." Her voice flagged with frustration she couldn't seem to help.

"So no magical fairy dust? I was so hoping there'd be magical fairy dust."

It was just like Channing not to take her seriously. "Not everything is a joke, you know. This is for real. If we want something to happen, we have to make it happen."

"Lark, we've already had this discussion, remember? We both agreed we'd make the necessary sacrifices if we want to be together."

"So do we?" She realized too late what a scary question that was, as it all but invited Channing to hedge. "Maybe the better question is what does 'be together' even mean? Can we be together if I go back to Boston and you stay here?"

Channing flipped onto her side and propped herself on her elbow. "Well, obviously not forever. Eventually people have to end up in the same place. Where that place will be though… that's a decision for another day. Right now my priority has to be to sort Penderworth."

It was true that she had a lot on her plate at the moment, but it stung not to be her priority. To say so would be selfish and immature. "I want to be your priority too."

"Very well then. I'll squeeze you in amongst sorting Poppa's papers, getting Cecil and Maisie moved, and selling the house." To her credit, she managed a tone that didn't sound the least bit sarcastic. "And there's sorting the contents as well, all the while searching for a job. But absolutely, you can be my priority as well."

"See? That wasn't so hard."

Channing laughed softly and reached to cuddle her again. "If you're feeling anxious, stop it. We agreed to make this work if we both want it to. *I* definitely want it to. Do you?"

That was the piece Lark needed to hear.

CHAPTER EIGHTEEN

To Channing's recollection, Sunday brunch at Breckham Hall had always been a formal affair. Bone china, cloth napkins embossed with the Alanford crest, servants in white gloves carrying covered dishes. She'd been a frequent guest throughout her teen years, her standing invitation from Lord and Lady Alanford meant to thwart Kenny having male friends visit for the weekend.

She was glad for Lark to have the extraordinary experience of such an opulent display, but it was obvious she was as stiff as everyone else. Even Kenny and Oliver appeared antsy to get back to London. They'd only suggested brunch because the earl and his wife were away for the weekend in Berkshire for the Ascot Racecourse, arguably *the* social event of the season.

The four of them sat clustered at one end of an elaborately dressed dining table that seated eight on each side. Their plates had been cleared, leaving only the task of replenishing coffee and tea.

"I can't imagine growing up in a house like this," Lark said.

"It was a bit like an institution, to be honest. This…" Kenny held up his hands gesturing to the elegant room. "It's not all that different from the dining hall at Aldenham, where Channing and I went to boarding school. All the buildings there were cavernous as well…and bloody freezing in the winter. Remember that?"

Channing shivered just to think of it. "It was worse than Penderworth if you can believe it. For some reason they diverted all the heat to the maths building. As if maths alone weren't enough to put everyone to sleep."

Kenny sneered. "I don't know why you complain so much about Penderworth. You have radiators, fireplaces. And unlike here, the rooms are small enough to hold the heat. I've always thought it cozy. At least my room was."

"Your room?" Lark asked.

"On the back corner by Lord Hughes's suite. I stayed over quite a lot, didn't I? Even kept some clothes in the wardrobe."

"Kenny used to row with his dad," Channing explained. His overnight stays had started the night he showed up on his bicycle with an eye swollen shut from a strike across the face.

"Dad didn't care for my choice of companions. Except Channing, of course. My staying at Penderworth now and then allowed him to gossip that his randy son was possibly shagging a beautiful girl, like any red-blooded English lad would do. Lord Hughes gave me my own key, said I was welcome anytime."

Oliver laid his hand in Kenny's lap, a sweet gesture of comfort. "Which is why I think Kenny has always been hopelessly sentimental about Penderworth. He's been out of sorts since Leon called and said you were considering selling the property right away as is."

"Oh, for God's sake." Channing pushed her chair back and stood. "Here we go again, let's all make Channing feel guilty about selling the manor, abandoning her heritage. Is nothing beneath you?"

Kenny came to his feet as well. "I wasn't actually trying to do that, but now that you mention it… I did offer to move into the place and take over the upkeep, you know. It's not as if I'm going to inherit Breckham Hall anytime soon. You know how the men in my family are—Dad could live to a hundred at least."

Oliver nodded pensively. "It would get us out of having to go deer stalking."

Noting Lark's perplexed look, she explained, "Any deer that has the misfortune of wandering onto the grounds of Breckham Hall usually ends up in a stew."

"Very well, Channing. If you're selling Penderworth, I'm buying."

"Kenny, you're not serious. It's bloody incestuous. Besides, your father's not going to let you buy someone else's manor."

"You may not have noticed, but I don't ask Dad's permission anymore. Granddad left me a trust."

"Oh right, and in return for your magnanimity, I'm to bear you a noble heir."

Oliver shook out a cigarette and flipped it to his lips, impressively catching it on the first try. "If anyone needs me, I'll be in the garden."

"Wait for me," Lark said. "I've decided to take up smoking."

Channing followed Kenny into the adjacent drawing room, where he sat on a piano bench and played the opening bars of "Für Elise," ending abruptly with four harsh chords that were distinctly off-key. "Oliver was right. I do have a soft spot for Penderworth. It saved my life, you know...and probably Dad's too."

"Bollocks. You never hit your father."

"Channing, he threatened to off himself if I didn't stop seeing men. He was terrified of the public humiliation. Mum would start packing to leave us both and he'd pull out his shotgun. Half the time this was a war zone, the other half it was a mental hospital."

She took the seat beside him on the stool and wrapped an arm around his shoulder. "You never told me that part."

"It was psychological terrorism. Getting out of here was the only way to dial it down." He laid his head on her shoulder. "I always felt safe at Penderworth. It sickens me to think of someone else living there...erasing us."

Erasure was a good way to put it, she thought, as though the Hughes family had never existed. "Funny you say that. I was thinking the other night about all those massive portraits, the Hughes and Penderworth bloodlines. I can't imagine them hanging somewhere else."

"Which is why I should buy it."

"That's insane. Why would you do that when you have all this?"

"Because you're Channing Hughes, my dearest friend in the entire world. Penderworth is your home, and I won't have you lose it just to pay the bloody death tax." He peered over his shoulder and lowered his voice. "And I especially don't want you making a premature decision about Lark because you're under pressure to find a job and a place to live."

A premature decision. In other words, he didn't want her to follow Lark back to Boston simply because it was the easiest solution. "So you obviously think I might be rushing into something. Can't you just trust my judgment?"

"After Payton?"

"*Not* the same. Not the same at all." Lark and Payton didn't occupy the same universe as far as she was concerned. "What could you possibly have against Lark? She's kind, she's funny. And she adores you and Oliver."

"I've nothing against her at all. Quite the opposite, in fact. I see it in both of you. Your faces, the way you touch when you talk to each other. It's genuine affection."

She'd seen those things in him when he first introduced her to Oliver. "It's more than affection…much more. But obviously you think it's too soon."

"I don't know if it is or not, Channing. But I want *you* to know. You have to be sure before you rush into such a critical decision as selling your birthright."

"It drives me crazy when you act mature." His words jogged a memory of her conversation with Lark, how she'd copped to coming to Payton's defense whenever someone else disparaged her. Apparently it was instinctual since she felt the same way about Lark. "Look, I appreciate what you're doing, really I do. If

I thought you were about to make a huge mistake, I'd try to stop you. Or at least to warn you. And you're right, I've got massive complications in my life right now, but here's the thing—Lark isn't one of them. She's the least messy thing I've got going. What you call the 'easiest solution,' I consider a cornerstone. It's what I have to work out first before all the other pieces can fall into place."

"So you love her."

"Yes…I actually do." What else could she call it if she was willing to arrange her whole life around being with her? "And I feel quite shitty for telling you that, considering I haven't yet told her."

* * *

"Sorry, sorry." Oliver waved the smoke away and moved upwind as they strolled along a worn path leading to a shade tree.

Lark wasn't bothered by it. Oliver's presence always set her at ease, partly because his ever-present jeans and hoodie made her feel adequately dressed no matter what she wore. She especially liked his moderating influence on Kenny when he went off on one of his outrageous schemes. "It's all right. The smoke reminds me of being with my ma, except I don't have to negotiate the oxygen bottle to keep from blowing us all sky high."

"Channing said she died recently."

"Late April. I moved back home a year and a half ago to take care of her. This is my first road trip for work since last fall. Looks like I might be signing up for a lot more if it gets me back here to Cambridge."

"So you don't think she'll return to Boston?"

"Hard to say. As much as it pains me to admit this, I don't think she wants to. Her history with Payton is just too toxic." Oliver probably knew that better than she did, since he and Kenny had served as Channing's sounding board for the last two years. "She was all set to go back until Payton called and begged her not to. I have to admit, it bothers me that she lets Payton push her around like that."

"You're jealous?"

"Not that exactly. Call it a protective instinct. I want to wring that woman's neck."

"Ah, got it. So what does it mean if she stays here? For the two of you, that is."

"I honestly don't know, Oliver. My company has offices all over. Nothing in the UK though. We talked about both of us going somewhere new."

"Kenny said it was an ironclad noncompete, that she might need to look into another line of work. So it's good you're willing to look at other places."

Lark laughed, mostly to herself. "You'd be surprised what I'm willing to do."

"I hear you, mate. Just like I'd do anything for the Viscount Teasely."

"Like deer stalking?"

"You laugh. Imagine my terror the first time I went slogging out there with Lord Alanford. No one for miles and he's carrying a bloody rifle."

As much as she liked Oliver, he wasn't the kind of confidante Niya had been before their friendship imploded over the Flexxene investigation. She had no one to confide her fear that the practicalities of trying to keep this relationship alive across three thousand miles of ocean would prove too difficult. It could vanish as quickly as it had appeared.

They'd wandered well away from the house to an area of the lawn that gave them a panoramic view of the property. She'd never seen a home so grand, rising like a castle against the horizon. "Can you imagine what it was like to grow up in a place like this? Horses, servants. And just look at that house. It's like a museum."

"Magnificent. Kenny puts on that he couldn't give a toss but I think he's rather impressed by it all. Mark my word, he'll be very proud someday to be the Eighth Earl of Alanford."

"He's a walking contradiction," she said, noticing that Channing and Kenny were waving from the courtyard. "There they are."

"They haven't killed one another. That's a good sign. You don't suppose they've struck some sort of Faustian bargain, do you?"

As they drew closer, Channing's and Kenny's smiles became clear. Either they'd settled the matters of Penderworth and babies, or they'd reached an amiable impasse.

"Breckham Hall is lovely, isn't it?" Channing asked. "I thought of you the last time I was here, the day I discovered I was a pauper. You'd remarked on how important I'd have to be to live in a house with a name."

"Our London flat doesn't have a name," Oliver said drolly. "Buckingham Palace was already taken."

"I'll be your queen, darling," Kenny said as the two men embraced. "Channing and I have the most marvelous news."

It would be surprising—but not shocking—if Channing had suddenly agreed to donate her eggs for their biology experiment. Their heartfelt pleas over dinner aboard the ferry had touched her deeply.

"Kenny's offered to buy a half interest in Penderworth."

"Forty-nine percent, actually, more than enough to cover her tax bill. Channing retains control and we split the cost of upkeep. It gives Breckham Hall access to the River Cam."

Lark couldn't join their celebration until she understood what it meant. Why else would Channing hold on to the manor unless she planned to stay in England? "So you'd own the house together…"

"Precisely," Kenny said. "She gets to live there for as long as she likes. Or perhaps Ollie and I will make it our weekend home. But if she ever decides to sell—whether it's a year from now or twenty—I can buy the remainder for a single quid."

"It's brilliant," Oliver declared. "This way you both get to keep it."

Channing was clearly pleased with the unconventional resolution. And why not? The stress of selling was nothing compared to the emotional toll of losing her family home forever. No matter what she eventually decided to do, Penderworth would be in loving hands.

Whereas Lark...she found it hard to be happy about Channing choosing her past instead of their future.

* * *

"And you're positive the Brownings won't come back early?" Lark asked.

Channing collected both of their bags from the boot of Lark's car. They had Penderworth to themselves for the next three nights. "Trust me, after what happened last time, they'd park outside the gate and sleep in the car before they'd set foot in this house. They won't be home till Wednesday."

"Hmm...then I may not see them again before I go."

"You really think you'll leave that soon?"

"The shit hits the fan tomorrow. I've done my part. Now it's somebody else's mess."

Channing left their bags by the foot of the steps and pulled Lark into the kitchen, where she put the kettle on for tea. "This PharmaStat business is going to be quite the scandal."

"Huge...we're talking shock waves through the whole industry."

"Yet it's not what's on your mind, is it?" She took Lark into her arms and kissed her forehead. "It was hard not to notice that your usual jovial mood fell rather sharply after Kenny and I announced our deal. Were you not happy to hear it?"

Lark smiled weakly. "I'm happy for *you*, Channing. It has to be a relief. But it hit me all of a sudden that I'll be going back to Boston in three days and you're putting all the pieces into place to stay here. "

"I'm doing nothing of the sort."

It was only natural that Lark would be worried, Channing conceded. She'd given her nothing but riddles and ambiguities, insisting the whole mess would work itself out. Lark was right— it was up to them to make their own future.

"Kenny bought me some time is all."

"So you won't be living here?"

"Honestly it's not even possible. There's no fairy dust, remember? It costs a small fortune to run a place like this and I don't even have a job."

She was charmed to see Lark fetch their teacups and pour the milk, as if she'd done it all her life. The way she'd taken care of Maisie, forgiven Kenny…these were all bits that added up to what her heart was feeling. Lark clearly needed reassurance, none of which would be convincing if Channing kept hedging about where she'd work and live.

"Look, Kenny's offer made me realize the extent of my attachment to this place. It once was my home, and Poppa's, and it's where my father was raised. So I'm inextricably tied to it whether I want to be or not. These last few days, ever since I talked to Leon, I've had this enormous sense of guilt over selling out my heritage to some total stranger in London who needs a country house to validate his status. But Kenny loves Penderworth too, possibly as much as I do. I could see him and Oliver raising a family here, a child who might slide down that banister the way we did." Out of the side of her mouth, she added, "Or climb up into one of the chimneys to smoke weed."

"You actually did that?"

"More than once. It was summer, of course. The ashes were cold."

"I love how crazy you are." Lark slid her arms around Channing's waist and up the inside of her shirt. It wasn't the sort of caress meant to arouse, though it was both warm and intimate. "Okay, here's what bothers me about going home. I'm afraid of how easy it would be for us to fall apart. What if we aren't solid enough? Right now we both want this…but how are we going to feel if I'm not here, if we're not together?"

"I can only tell you how *I'm* going to feel, Lark. I'm going to miss you, I'm going to text you every five minutes like I do now, I'm going to wait for your call. And all the rest of the time, I'm going to get things done. I've got the Brownings, Penderworth, there's the whole rest of the estate to settle, the books and papers. And then…" She kissed her brow again, smoothing her feather-soft hair. "And then I'll come to you. In Boston. And we'll figure it out from there."

Lark raised her head, revealing a surprised smile. "You'll come?"

"I will, in a few weeks. Perhaps this business with Albright will be settled by then. In the meantime, I might give Payton a call, try to calm her worries. No one could possibly suspect something between us if I'm dancing around in love with someone else."

"In love." Unmistakably a statement, not a question.

"Yes, in love…and you?"

The arms around her waist tightened forcefully. Suddenly she was lifted off the floor and briefly twirled around. "Yes!"

Channing laughed as she staggered to regain her balance. "I say we forget the tea. Let's go upstairs and make the most of our time in my fancy bed."

CHAPTER NINETEEN

The text came through at eight thirty a.m., just as Lark saw the limo pull into the parking circle by the fountain. *Just arrived at PharmaStat. Meet in lobby?*

From her vantage point on the fourth floor, she observed that Mike Dobbins had a bald spot. His hurried step to keep up with the tall, athletic Dr. Cooke was almost comical. Lark didn't recognize the third person but knew from their recent flurry of emails that he was Barry Sutton from Gipson's legal department. Things were about to get real.

Jermaine Martin stepped off the elevator as she was getting on. "You look very sharp today, Dr. Latimer," he said, nodding his approval at her blue suit, its sleeves pushed to her elbows. "I believe the American expression is 'loaded for bear.'"

By now the whole building knew something serious was afoot, as the rumors had proven impossible to contain in such an insular environment. PharmaStat's CEO had flown in from Geneva with a handful of corporate attorneys, and security had cordoned off several primo parking spaces for board members who were scheduled to arrive at eleven.

In the lobby, Dr. Cooke was first to greet her, transferring a briefcase to her left hand and extending the other. "Dr. Latimer, nice to see you. You've done excellent work here."

"Thank you. And please call me Lark."

"Kirsten." Blond and blue-eyed, she was the picture of authority in a loose-fitting tan pantsuit, its organic fabric still flawless after the overnight flight from Boston. "The others?"

"Already in the conference room having tea." She greeted Dobbins and Sutton in the elevator, noticing their suits hadn't traveled as neatly.

"Very well. Gentlemen, please go and make introductions, see if you can get everyone loosened up. Remember our goal here—de-escalate the situation and find a solution. It'll work in our favor not to have them on the defensive more than necessary. Lark, I'd like a word in private if you don't mind."

When Lark closed her office door, Kirsten sank into a chair and rubbed her face briskly with both hands. "I've been up all night looking at contracts, trying to figure out the best way to leverage this to get what we want. Before I go in there, I need to ask one more time how certain you are."

"I'm certain of the evidence, Kirsten. What conclusions we draw…those are above my pay grade."

Armed with findings from the blood work, Lark had abandoned her step-by-step verification process in favor of working backward from what they knew. There was no more room for doubt or tiptoeing around the obvious. Someone had tampered with the trial packets, replacing the intended treatment with a high-dose nicotine patch, the sort usually prescribed for heavy smokers trying to quit cold turkey. For patients not accustomed to the effects of nicotine, the symptoms perfectly mimicked a cardiac emergency—arrhythmia, dizziness, and nausea. Practically speaking, the list of PharmaStat employees who could have pulled off such a switch included everyone with security access to the third-floor drug vault, which was at least two dozen people.

Lark had considered several possibilities. A malicious prank by a disgruntled employee. A scheme to help a group of trial subjects win a liability settlement. Or the one that worried her most—corporate espionage meant to derail Flexxene's development so another company could seize the advantage.

With every investigative step she drew closer to the truth, until finally it was—even in the literal sense—staring her in the face.

"Let's get in there and get this over with."

Lark followed with her laptop, taking a seat next to Kirsten at the head of the table. Shane and Wendi had been called to the meeting and sat together at the back of the room, observers to the proceedings. The other two members of the Flexxene team, Niya and Jermaine, had seats at the conference table alongside the CEO and attorneys.

Niya sought to make eye contact and displayed a conciliatory smile. Their easy friendship hadn't been the same since the day she'd stormed out of Lark's office. Lark lamented that it was hard to really know someone until seeing them at their worst.

"Ladies and gentlemen, you know why we're here. Gipson Pharmaceuticals contracted with PharmaStat to conduct a Phase II trial for Flexxene…" Dr. Cooke owned the room as she methodically summarized Gipson's concerns regarding the execution of the trial. Reading from talking points, she laid out the case for malfeasance. "On behalf of Gipson, Dr. Lark Latimer conducted a review of protocols, and subsequently, an investigation of drug tampering. I'll turn this over to her for her report."

Lark began with an overview of her routine process, which included an exhaustive review of paperwork followed by interviews with subjects and clinicians, all of which had confirmed the team's adherence to protocols. "In interviews with staff members Shane Forster and Wendi Doolan, I discovered what I considered an anomaly in procedures." She explained in meticulous detail the differences between their handling of deliveries, and how those differences led to further inspection.

Shane burned with embarrassment as she described seeing a kiss in the parking garage that raised her suspicions. As all eyes turned his way, she exonerated him with confirmation from the IT department that his first exchange of texts and emails with the Haas-Seidel employee had occurred more than a week after the patient emergencies.

"Though I felt confident that Mr. Forster had not deliberately participated in the disruption of the trial, the coincidence remained troubling. It presented a potential opportunity for the introduction of tampering, since Wendi Doolan's habit of inspecting individual packets was well-known throughout PharmaStat and the participating clinics."

Wendi whispered something to Shane and shook her head to indicate her innocence.

Interrupting Lark's presentation, Kirsten distributed results of the blood tests that confirmed evidence of tampering, along with side-by-side photos of the two patches. She said, "At this point, we were certain someone in the chain of study had substituted a fairly common nicotine patch for the treatment patch for three of our study subjects. This introduction of nicotine triggered the cardiac symptoms that resulted in breaking the blind and subsequent suspension of the trial."

Mike Dobbins spoke up, passing around a chart he'd prepared. "Dr. Latimer's review of medical progress reports led our team to conclude this wasn't merely tampering, but a deliberate scheme to subvert the results of an otherwise promising trial. All three subjects who experienced these emergency symptoms had reported significant improvement in pain reduction and stiffness, the exact results Gipson hoped for from this innovative drug. The third subject however…was discovered to be in the placebo group."

His dramatic pause allowed them to consider the implications. Such pronounced gains during a trial were rare for placebo patients, though not unheard of, especially if the patient was susceptible to the power of suggestion.

It was Lark's turn again. "Our team concluded that whoever switched the patches had likely viewed the medical reports and assumed this placebo subject was receiving the actual drug. That led us to seek security records from IT showing who had accessed both the patient progress reports and the drug vault." Under PharmaStat's stringent security procedures, logins and swipes of employee badges tracked virtually every move.

There was a noticeable disturbance through the room as PharmaStat's decision-makers absorbed the damning testimony.

"On the Friday morning prior to the first two emergencies, a login belonging to Dr. Jermaine Martin accessed medical records."

He looked about nervously and nodded. "That's correct. The Flexxene team met every Friday in my office for a status update. Every Friday, not just those two. You can check my login."

"Throughout the course of the trial, treatment packets were picked up at the drug vault on Monday morning and delivered to the participating clinics. On the Monday preceding the first incidents, at seven fifteen a.m., Dr. Martin's security badge swiped the entry to the drug vault. Approximately two hours later Shane Forster picked up those drug packets and delivered them to the clinics. Dr. Martin's badge was used again the following Monday at seven twenty-five, after which Mr. Forster again made the delivery."

"No, that is wrong. It cannot be." Jermaine pounded the table and pleaded at his bosses with an anguished look. "My badge was lost. I reported it to security. They deactivated the other immediately."

Lark had recalled his lost ID, and included it in her investigation. "Yes, I checked your report, Dr. Martin. According to records, your security badge was in continuous use during the week between those two visits to the drug vault. It was reported lost on the day of the second visit."

"But I'm telling you, I did not go to the drug vault."

Lark continued by rote, willing herself not to look up, not to make this personal in any way. "Though the IT logs indicates Dr. Martin's badge was used at the drug vault, surveillance video indicates that someone else was using it. That video shows Dr. Niya Batra entering the drug vault, and in fact…tampering with treatment packets."

Niya sat stone-faced as hostility rose around the table. She glanced only briefly at Lark, her eyes flashing defiance. "I request an attorney."

* * *

Channing applied a touch of lip gloss and confirmed she was presentable to guests. Toby Singleton, the young man who'd helped pack Poppa's books, was on his way over with a couple of university representatives and one of their major donors.

"No," she said into the mirror, several times for practice. Poppa had left her nothing to donate but his work.

The group arrived in two cars, one a chauffeur-driven Bentley belonging to an elderly gentleman fastidiously dressed in a brown plaid three-piece suit. His thick white hair was bright against his tanned face. Channing recognized him at once as Sir Nigel Grimshaw, one of Britain's most celebrated billionaires. Fresh from a yacht off the Riviera, she guessed.

She recognized one of the women as Emma Cross, administrator of the economics library named for Poppa. "Miss Cross, Toby, nice to see you both again."

"Miss Hughes." Toby pumped her hand and gestured toward the second woman. "Allow me to introduce Miss Donaldson."

"Phoebe Donaldson. Like Miss Cross, I'm a library director too. Art and Humanities." She was slender and petite, with lifeless sandy hair that fell to the top of her shoulders. "And this is Sir Nigel Grimshaw. Sir Nigel is an avid supporter of the literary arts and one of our most generous contributors."

"Lovely place, your Penderworth," he said. "How fortunate you are to have an historic home directly on the River Cam. You can catch your own dinner."

"Thank you. Our caretaker fishes on occasion, but I like it for the occasional passing of swans." She was sorry to have him see Penderworth in its state of disrepair. On the other hand, if this was about making a monetary donation to the university, they could see for themselves that she lacked the means. "Please come in."

In the great hall by the stone fireplace, she'd readied a service of tea with biscuits purloined from the Brownings' cupboard.

Miss Cross opened the conversation with a statement of gratitude for the gift of Poppa's books and papers. "Professor

Lord Hughes's economics collection will long be the focus of scholars and historians. I appreciate his generosity and the amount of time you've dedicated to the task."

Working diligently for a few hours each day, Channing had separated the personal from the professional papers. "I have the rest of his work boxed up and ready for you. Perhaps Toby can collect them today."

Sir Nigel edged forward on the sofa and cleared his throat. "Miss Hughes, allow me to get to the point of our visit. As Miss Donaldson explained, I'm a proponent of the literary arts, and I feel strongly that Cambridge, as one of England's flagship universities, ought to maintain a splendid collection of English literature. Would you agree?"

"Of course." This was about the Romantic poetry collection, she realized. Toby had scooped it up with the rest as they'd hastily emptied the shelves. She was glad they'd taken photos to document the contents.

"I'm something of a bibliophile, if you will, a collector of rare books. I understand that Mr. Singleton here discovered among your grandfather's collection a number of works by the Romantic poets. Keats, Byron, Coleridge and others. According to Miss Cross, these books were removed from Penderworth in error. She confirmed that Professor Lord Hughes had not included them in the lot he intended to will to the university upon his death."

"That's correct, Sir Nigel. He meant only to gift his economics books and papers. In fact, the Romantic works had belonged to my father." She rose and walked to the wall of portraits. "Here he is, Henry Hughes, a wing commander at RAF Honington." Turning back with a smile, she added, "I'm told I have his eyes."

"Professor Lord Hughes had them too," Toby offered.

"That's right, a family trait. My father was killed in Kuwait shortly after I was born, a refueling accident. It happens he was a bibliophile too. Obsessed with all the Romantics. He and Poppa—that's my grandfather—they journeyed together all over the country to find them. Bookstores, estate sales, collectors. Poppa gifted me the entire collection for my tenth birthday."

Sir Nigel broke into a roguish smile. "That's fortuitous, Miss Hughes."

"I'm sorry, I don't understand."

"A property transfer that took place more than seven years ago carries no tax liability," Miss Cross explained.

"Ah, excellent." She'd been so focused on the house that she hadn't begun to sort its contents. Had there been tax implications, Lord Alanford would have told her. And speaking of the Romantics, she'd promised the earl a poetry memento.

Miss Donaldson, who'd been quiet so far, spoke with an air of authority. "When Miss Cross informed me of the collection, I took the liberty of inspecting them. They're in remarkable condition. Several are first editions, quite valuable."

"One in particular," Sir Nigel said, his voice rising with zeal. "An exquisite hand-printed copy of William Blake's *The First Book of Urizen*. It must be authenticated of course, but I'm quite certain it's an original."

"Blake's work is rich with illustrations," Donaldson added. Her efforts at professional detachment were no match for her obvious excitement. "Extraordinary. He etched his works on a copper plate and washed them with acid to lend relief. He'd print a single page at a time, then go back and add watercolor to the illustrations."

"A truly sensational work of art," Sir Nigel said. "One of a kind."

Toby cleared his throat. "Eight of a kind actually. That's how many copies are believed to exist, all of them with small differences. The last one put up for auction was 1999, Sotheby's of New York. It went for two and a half million dollars."

Channing shuddered. It was a staggering find for a dusty shelf in a rundown manor home. Surely there was a catch.

"Which is why I'm here, Miss Hughes." Sir Nigel gestured to the others. "Why we're all here, actually. A prize like *Urizen* would bring an incredible price at auction. Far, far more than what the previous edition commanded, because the number of potential bidders has increased rather dramatically. But collectors these days—let's be honest—few of them appreciate the magnificence of a literary giant like William Blake. Many of today's auction players are notorious tax dodgers who collect such offerings as trinkets, only to lose them for pennies on the dollar in a bankruptcy sale or criminal forfeiture."

Channing knew plenty of such lavish spenders from her work. Most were newly prosperous, having figured out how to leverage other people's money so they could live in opulence well beyond their personal wealth.

"I'd like to purchase your entire collection, Miss Hughes. Miss Cross here tells me that you've made a career out of determining what things are worth, so I'm confident we'll be able to agree on a fair market price. But as I said earlier, I myself am a bibliophile, a true collector. I believe there's more to a book's value than what it fetches in a sale. I'd be happy to show you what I mean if you're interested. I've an extensive private collection that's illustrative of my esteem for such works."

All four of them were tittering with anticipation, apparently waiting for Channing to breathe her approval.

Two and a half million dollars, twenty years ago. Figure inflation and rising demand—such a unique offering would bring at least three times that today. This would solve all of her financial woes, including Penderworth.

"I realize I'll need to overcome your sentimental attachment to the works, Miss Hughes. Perhaps if you knew more of my support for Cambridge…"

"Sir Nigel has donated hundreds of books and documents to the Arts and Humanities collections, and he makes his private collection available for scholarly study as well. At any given time a dozen of our graduate students are—"

"Further explanation isn't necessary, Miss Donaldson. I'm certain Sir Nigel and I will agree to terms. I'd be quite glad to know the collection was in such good hands."

"Delightful." His smile was bright against his tanned face. He'd probably return to the Mediterranean aboard his yacht the moment their deal was struck.

She'd retain a couple of pieces, of course, given the sentimental attachment she'd only just realized. Something for her, something for Lord Alanford.

"Very well, Sir Nigel. Let's adjourn to my grandfather's study upstairs so we can discuss the terms."

* * *

With Channing leaning back against her chest in the tub, Lark swirled the shampoo into the shape of an enormous pompadour. "This is a good look for you, a Spartan helmet. Hey, we need to do a breastplate too."

"Have you spoken to a therapist about your soap fetish, Dr. Latimer? Not that I don't enjoy a good surgical scrub now and then."

"Mock me all you want. I'll have you know I was top of my class in hand washing. A real gift for it, they said."

The bath attached to Channing's bedroom had a tiled tub and shower and well-lit vanity with abundant storage. The modern design, though both stylish and practical, stood out in the period home. Channing had explained that the room was added to her suite the year after she'd returned to England, when her grandfather discovered the peculiarities of girls and their ablutions.

Lark dug her fingertips into the taut muscles of Channing's neck and shoulders, eliciting a moan of pleasure. "How come you're so tight here? I thought regular sex was supposed to be the ultimate stress relief."

"But you don't have sex with my neck." Channing rubbed her soapy head against Lark's chin and purred like a cat.

"You're awfully sassy tonight, Lady Hughes."

"I picked up eight million quid today, tax-free. That sort of money makes anyone sassy." She stretched for the shower hose and passed it to Lark. "Do me."

"With pleasure." She rinsed Channing from head to toe with warm water, paying special attention to the intimate spots they referred to as nooks and crannies. "Your plan worked to perfection, by the way. I'm definitely much happier than when I got here."

"For the record, I was only kidding." Her solution to Lark's dismal mood had been for Lark to shower her with attention—making love to her, washing her hair, massaging her neck—whatever it took to get her mind off the mess at PharmaStat. "I figured if it didn't work, at least *my* needs would be met."

"Okay, you're done. Let me wash my hair and I'll be right out."

"Are you feeling any better?"

"I'm fine as long as I don't think about it." Lark had no words for how she felt about Niya. It was bad enough that Niya had destroyed their friendship. Her betrayal could have done irreparable damage to Lark's standing at Gipson. "Can you imagine if I'd trusted her all this time and defended her… and then somebody else came along and figured out what she'd done? They'd have me cleaning out my desk."

"You're torturing yourself with the worst-case scenario, even though it didn't happen. It sounds flippant to say let it go, but that's all you can do. Especially since you don't even know yet why she did it."

"I wonder how Jermaine's feeling tonight. It's amazing how close she came to hanging him out to dry. She almost managed to pin the whole conspiracy on him. Stole his ID, stood over his shoulder while he logged on for the medical data, even had him ask Wendi for the reports so it would look like he was the one behind it. She probably would have pulled it off if she'd known about the cameras. They added them last year after the burglary. But you're right, I need to let it go. I could make myself crazy over what might have happened."

"It's crushing to have someone you love, someone you trust completely, blindside you that way."

"You mean like Payton did when she broke up with you after promising she'd leave her husband?" Getting no response as she rinsed her hair, Lark turned off the water and peeked around the curtain to see if Channing had heard.

She was leaning against the sink, already dried and wearing a nightshirt. Her pensive gaze was a contrast to their earlier playfulness. "Payton never blindsided me, not really. Even in our best moments, a part of me always knew she'd go back to Ben. But Poppa's accounts were a different matter. I never saw that coming. What kills me is that he bloody knew I'd find out eventually. Not telling me was cowardly."

It was fascinating how the sudden windfall from the poetry books had triggered Channing's disappointment in her grandfather...or given her permission to express it. "Maybe it was like you telling him you were gay. He was waiting for the right time to say it."

"Hmm...I'd not considered my own duplicity. Am I supposed to feel shitty now, Dr. Gloom?"

Lark was blessed with enough dry wit to recognize the mockery in Channing's inflection. "I should hope so. I've had it up to here with your unicorns and rainbows. And your millions. You're choosing joy instead of misery. What kind of person does that?"

"Up to where? Show me the exact mark."

"Up to *here*." Suppressing a giggle from tickling herself, she drew an imaginary line from one nipple to the other.

"Are you sure the line goes that high?" Channing knelt in front of her and traced a finger around the triangle of her pubic hair. "Those randy unicorns, I've caught them wandering below but never higher than here."

"You might be right." Lark covered her hand and held it against her. "They're sneaky."

"You're shivering." Channing wrapped her in a huge white towel, silky and worn from years of use, and began to pat her dry. Here and there she'd pause to drop a kiss on the bare flesh, then quell the rising goose bumps with her warm breath. "These towels are older than I am. So soft...it's like drying yourself with a rabbit."

"A live rabbit?"

"Of course. You wouldn't dry yourself with a dead one."

Lark laughed. More of a snort actually, a sardonic chuckle. From the night they met, she'd fallen for that deadpan delivery and acerbic wit. No one had ever entertained her the way Channing did. What surprised her was how important it was, how their droll connection had become something she cherished. "I love how you make me laugh. Now I've already forgotten whatever it is you're trying to distract me from."

"Excellent. Then I shall commence stealing your wallet."

"Why would you do that? You're a multimillionaire."

"Odd, isn't it? You'll have to tell everyone I'm eccentric."

CHAPTER TWENTY

The willowy curtains of the canopy bed were tied off, letting the gray light of the imminent sunrise bathe their tangled bodies. Making love had been Channing's first conscious thought on this, their last morning together. In a few hours, she and her driver Ruth would be dropping Lark at Heathrow.

Over the last eleven days, Lark had surrendered her body's secrets one after another. This tightening in her thighs signaled she was ready. Not for teasing, not for titillating. She needed pressure on her clit right now—the rhythmic stroke of lips sucking the swollen knot in and out, with the predictable swipe of a rigid tongue. These would make her come in a matter of seconds.

"Oh, God…" She clutched a handful of Channing's hair, twisting it as her hips bucked sideways and the climax shook her. A deep gulp of air whooshed out from between her teeth in short bursts.

They both lay breathless for a couple of minutes, Channing resting her head on a thigh. "You taste womanly."

"I'd like to think that's a good thing."

"It's a glorious thing. It means you don't douse yourself with those bloody chemicals, the ones they say will make us feel 'fresh,' whatever that is. They treat our coochies like fruit we forgot to put in the refrigerator. There's even one that smells like strawberries."

"I'm sorry, did you just say *coochie*?"

"What do you call it?"

"I'm a medical doctor, Channing. We don't use such silly euphemisms. We say *hoo-hoo*."

Channing held her laughter for all of five seconds. "I'm going to miss you. Who's going to make me laugh?"

"The Viscount Teasely."

"All right, who's going to wash my back?"

"You got me there. But don't think I won't be inspecting it when you get to Boston. It better not be clean."

Channing climbed up and delivered a kiss before enveloping Lark in a possessive embrace. "That, by the way, is what I mean by a womanly taste. Everything about you is the way it's supposed to be. I like that you have *this*." She gripped a handful of pubic curls. "The woman I dated before Payton waxed it all away. Her breasts were so small, I started to worry she might not be of age. Can you imagine?"

"I'd show you some ID but a shady lady stole my wallet while I was in the shower." Lark nibbled on Channing's neck. "Maybe you'll wake up tomorrow and miss this. You can fly to Boston to surprise me in bed."

"I'll definitely wake up and miss you, but I'm afraid flying to Boston isn't going to happen right away. I've a lot more to do repair-wise now that I can afford it. Kenny's meeting me here this weekend with his friend Leon so we can discuss priorities." She'd been gobsmacked by his insistence on keeping their house deal even when he learned she no longer needed his money. The Brownings had cheered the arrangement since it meant Penderworth wouldn't be handed over to strangers. "He's got a contractor in mind already, someone Oliver knows. I'm actually thrilled I won't have to manage it, but I can't leave until it's all underway. Maybe you can pop back over for a few days."

"I'll be stuck in Boston for a while. Gipson's called for a desk audit of our PharmaStat trials—all of them. And whatever else it takes to calm our jittery stockholders. Who knows how long that list will be? But the first thing on *my* list is to find a place to live. It would be nice if I could find something that didn't require a lease. Maybe if I—"

"Excuse me?" Channing climbed directly on top of Lark and pinned her shoulders to the bed. "Are you saying you don't currently have a flat?"

"I've been living at Ma's for the last two years so I could help take care of her. It was just two months ago that she died." She made a feeble effort to squirm free before going limp in surrender. "When I found out I was coming here, I put all my stuff in storage. Chloe said I could stay with her and Bobby till I find something."

"It goes without saying, obviously—you should stay at my place when you get back. It's the top floor of a three-family house in Somerville, assuming that's convenient to your work."

"Are you kidding? Gipson's headquarters is near Malden Center. That's only two stops away."

"On the Orange Line. It's brilliant." Except Lark didn't seem to think so. "There's that little sneer of yours, the one you always try to pretend I don't see. Is there something about staying at my flat that concerns you?"

Lark shook her head, though a mild grimace confirmed she was holding something back. "No...it just seems kind of fast."

"You mean as opposed to spending every single night together since our first? Stocking the fridge for breakfast, sharing a box of tampons?"

"I know it sounds stupid."

"Stew-pid."

"Stew-pid. But it reminds me of my first year in medical school when I met Bess. We hadn't been dating that long, and our schedules were insane. One of the reasons we moved in together was so we'd have more time to—"

She put a finger over Lark's lips. "Do you regret that your relationship with Bess has ended?"

"No, of course not."

"All of our choices lead to eventual outcomes. Something to keep in mind as you chronicle whether anything you did was a mistake or not. Carry on."

"A fair point." Lark snatched her finger and held it. "But it was a problem at the time that we had no way to slow things down. Once you move in with somebody, the only way out is to break up."

"Or have your mother get sick, but that's kind of extreme."

"Heh…and you only get to use it once."

"The truth always comes out, Dr. Latimer." In the few times Lark had talked about Bess, she'd always seemed glad to have that relationship behind her. "Can I ask…if it became a problem that you lived together, why didn't you break it off? Please tell me you aren't one of those who suffers in silence at home but tells all your mates."

"We did break up, two or three times. But then we'd drift back together because we didn't know any better. If you've never had a good relationship, all you have to compare it to is what you grew up with. My ma was dysfunctional as hell and Bess's father was a womanizer. We felt comfortable with each other, but that's not the same as being happy."

Channing was impressed by Lark's evolved understanding of herself, having cycled through mummy issues of her own. Freudian implications aside, it was little wonder she'd been drawn to Payton's wisdom and maturity.

"Bess is happy now. Really happy. She met somebody last summer…they're actually getting married in August. My invitation must have gotten lost in the mail." Her caustic regard of Bess always stopped short of cruelty and actual harm, and Channing suspected the feeling was mutual. Lark's deep chuckle suggested there was a lot more to the story.

"I hope to hear all about Bess someday. There was talk you've recently met a woman as well. Any truth to rumors you're in love?"

"Was that in one of the gossip rags?" Lark asked, bringing Channing's face down for a kiss. "I wonder if they took pictures through the window. She's the sexiest, sweetest woman ever, and she has a gorgeous, strawberry-shaped birthmark right about"—her hands groped beneath the sheets—"here."

Channing offered no resistance as Lark urged her onto her back and attached her lips to a nipple. "Don't think I've forgotten what we were talking about, Lark. When I get to Boston, this is what I want waiting in my bed. My lease is up at the end of November. If there's a problem in our relationship, it will bloody sort itself by then."

* * *

Upon boarding at Heathrow, Mike Dobbins had coaxed another passenger—a younger man whose jeans and scruffy face reminded Lark of Oliver—into switching seats so he could sit beside her on the way back to Boston. Now instead of catching up on the sleep she'd missed as she and Channing said their early morning goodbyes in bed, she was stuck going over Gipson's legal and business strategies for handling the PharmaStat debacle.

A predictable wave of yearning struck her when the flight attendant delivered a pot of tea accompanied by a pair of shortbread cookies. Biscuits, Channing would have said. "How lovely. Thank you so much."

Mike snapped his fingers and ordered coffee, black with two sugars. The savage. "What pisses me off is that we wasted so much time and money on doing an onsite review when we could have just asked the lab. Always look to the science first."

It was too bad she wasn't sitting next to Kirsten, whose status as a senior officer of the corporation afforded her first-class flights. She was up there at the front of the plane with a couple of her PharmaStat counterparts, higher-ups who had the authority to satisfy Gipson's demands. Unlike Mike, Kirsten had too much class to trash-talk somebody's job while they were sitting right beside her.

If anything, Lark's review had favorably documented PharmaStat's professionalism and compliance with protocols.

Going forward, their enhanced security procedures would provide insurance against bad actors like Niya.

"For what it's worth, Mike, the review wasn't wasted. We'd have done it anyway, even if we'd gotten the lab results first. At least now Dr. Cooke has all the information she needs to get this matter resolved."

"I guess you're right. The weakest link in drug trials has always been people with no sense of ethics. I'm talking about doctors who fabricate data, recruiters who fudge the criteria. Remember that guy in Buenos Aires who 'lost' the results on all the subjects who suffered serious side effects?"

"Congratulations, by the way. Looks like Flexxene will go to Phase III early next year as planned. You should be proud of that."

"Thanks, I am. With luck we'll have this in front of the FDA by December."

Their odds of getting the drug to market went up markedly once it cleared Phase II.

Starting immediately, Lark would conduct a detailed review of every Gipson trial currently underway at the Cambridge facility. Future trials were off the table until PharmaStat put a new management team in place.

There was also the public relations issue. Gipson's VP of marketing had hired a crisis management firm weeks ago when the frightening news reports first appeared. They'd have to navigate this crisis too, and design a communications campaign to restore Gipson's reputation.

Lark was thrilled by Kirsten and Mike's decision to offer the affected participants a guaranteed slot in the Phase III trial, since one of those participants was Maisie Browning. Phase III involved thousands of arthritis patients worldwide, all of whom would be monitored for several years while using the Flexxene patch. Plus they'd all get the actual drug, since there was no placebo group in Phase III.

"You and Batra were friends, right? Did you ever have a clue she was up to something like this?"

Yes, Mike. I knew she was plotting this scheme to bring down Gipson but I kept quiet about it because she was my friend.

That's how she'd have responded to Channing, who would have laughed at her dry humor and poker-faced delivery. Doubting Mike's ability to recognize her facetiousness, she dutifully replied, "No one was as shocked as I was. I probably wouldn't have believed it if I hadn't seen the video for myself. Oh, here comes your coffee. I bet if you apologize for snapping your fingers, she'll bring you some cookies too."

He peered over at her cookies and pouted that there weren't any on his tray. "Excuse me, miss. I'm sorry for snapping my fingers at you earlier. Thank you for not breaking them off."

The flight attendant gave him a playful sneer before winking at Lark and walking away.

"Every time I think I'm ready to graduate from sensitivity training, I step in it again and get sent back for another round. Of course you didn't know what Dr. Batra was up to. She had everyone fooled, including her husband apparently."

"It floored me when they said she might have been having an affair with that guy from Haas-Seidel, Mike. She's always talked about Dev like he was the sweetest man on earth, like they were going to retire in Portugal. I'm not totally convinced this was an affair."

"It has to be something. There's no evidence that money ever changed hands."

When the clock on her phone marked four and a half minutes, she poured the tea into the cup over the milk. "Not yet, at least. But Niya lived four years in Geneva while she was working for WHO. I wouldn't be surprised if she still has a Swiss bank account."

Threatened with arrest for causing bodily harm to the three subjects whose treatments were switched, Niya had confessed to her part in the scheme. She'd named Torsten Shulte, a product manager at Haas-Seidel with whom she admitted having a "close, personal relationship," as her co-conspirator. Haas-Seidel was developing a transdermal patch called Ostefaan, similar to Flexxene in its molecular composition and delivery, but with a nominal corticosteroid Gipson scientists insisted was merely window dressing to subvert their patent. Ostefaan was at least eighteen months behind Flexxene in trials and bogged down in legal challenges. Getting Flexxene suspended from trials not only would have allowed Haas-Seidel time to catch up in development, it also threatened Gipson's legal standing as patent holder. Collateral damage to Gipson's reputation was icing on the cake.

While Shulte's motive was clear, Niya's was less so. Lark couldn't imagine that Niya had done it for the money. More likely, she'd simply burned out after years of so much responsibility. It would explain why she'd been so eager to offer herself as the sacrificial lamb even before the investigation revealed tampering. What if Dev had pushed her past her breaking point, insisting they both work another ten years before retiring? Perhaps it really *was* her exit strategy.

"I've been thinking about this Shulte guy," Mike said. "He's a product manager just like I am. He's got a handful of drugs that he's responsible for, but ninety-five percent of them don't even make it to Phase II. Ostefaan has a chance, right? I bet he thinks about it all the time. Like me with Flexxene. I can't go to the hardware store without thinking about Flexxene. I can't watch my kid's soccer game, can't make love to my wife without—"

"Yeah, let's not go there."

"Sorry…like I said, back to sensitivity school. Anyway, Shulte wakes up one morning and realizes he's basically hosed. Not only is Flexxene going to get there first, he's got all these lawyers up his ass about the patent case. He's thinking his bosses could pull the plug any day. Meanwhile his next pipeline drug is at least three or four years away. Career-wise, he's going nowhere."

The flight attendant walked by and wordlessly placed a plate of cookies on Mike's tray before continuing on to the first-class cabin. He beamed with delight.

"So you think he might have done this to save Ostefaan's chances?"

"Yeah, I do. Come on, which is easier to believe? That one guy sells out his principles or the whole company does?"

"Uh…Volkswagen?" It took all of her self-control not to swipe at his chin, where two days' worth of beard held a mass of cookie crumbs. "I don't have to tell you the numbers on Flexxene, Mike. It's worth billions. Niya Batra's not going to give up her whole career so her boyfriend can maybe get a drug to market in five or six years. Either she's getting serious money from Haas-Seidel, or it had nothing to do with money."

They could speculate endlessly. In the end, only Niya knew why she'd thrown away such an accomplished career and pristine reputation.

Mike however was suddenly sold on the Volkswagen comparison. He rambled that Haas-Seidel was trying to knock the US out of the British market. If Brexit resulted in European companies getting a competitive advantage, he said, they'd go after Johnson & Johnson next, then Pfizer. All the more reason Gipson needed to push back.

Lark found it all too depressing. It sickened her that, not even a month ago, she'd sat in the Crown and Punchbowl gushing over pictures of Niya with her granddaughter, aching at how her friend was being forced to bear the brunt of criticism. She'd praised Niya's brave actions and begged her to fight the scurrilous charges that had her considering retirement. Niya Batra—her hero, her role model—wasn't merely corrupt. She was reprehensible.

CHAPTER TWENTY-ONE

Channing found it amusing that, among the handful of her acquaintances who'd met Lark, it was her straight, married driver Ruth who admitted finding her sexy. "I'm into blokes but she's dishy. Such a cute figure…and those gorgeous eyes."

A chime announced a text message. If it was from Lark, it meant her flight was delayed.

Miss Hughes, it's Vanessa Easton. I got your number from our mutual friend, Oliver Bristow. Would love to have chat. Next week perhaps? V

Vanessa Easton. A capital manager, she recalled from the memorial event at the Crown and Punchbowl. And a handsome woman whose husband taught at Cambridge, who said she'd founded her company on economic principles learned from Poppa. Why would she… Perhaps because she was head of a company that might very well have use for someone of Channing's talents.

It was an intriguing possibility, assuming that's what this was about. The sort of work Vanessa Easton did was on a smaller scale than Albright, but right up her alley.

"They're just like the robber at Butch Annie's."

"Excuse me, what?"

"Her eyes. They're like the guy who robbed Butch Annie's."

"You mean the burger joint?"

"It was brill, just last year. Some wanker came in and robbed all the customers while they were eating. Made like he had a gun in his pocket and collected all their wallets in a sack. So the police came around and took down his description, right? Everyone remembered his eyes, that they were gold with little brown flecks. It goes out on Twitter and bunches of people start tweeting to the police that their friend Roger has eyes like that. So they go to Roger's flat and he's got this pile of cash on his bed and a sack of empty wallets. All because of his beautiful eyes."

"I'll be sure to tell Lark that story so she knows not to rob Butch Annie's."

She could have rented a car twice over for what she'd paid to have Ruth at her beck and call, but a rental car wouldn't have come with such vivid narration. All of Ruth's stories were captivating, even the royal gossip. Surely it was useful to know the line of succession all the way down to the grandson of the queen's second cousin several times removed.

"Bloody sakes, you actually know these people?" Ruth exclaimed as they started down the long drive that led to Breckham Hall.

"The Earl of Alanford lives here. His son was my best mate at school."

"My Toyota isn't posh enough to be in the drive. You want I should go back and wait outside the gate?"

Two luxury vehicles sat gleaming by the garage. Surely Lord Alanford would offer to have one of his drivers deliver her to Penderworth. Or she could ring Cecil to fetch her, since they'd be home from the Burys by now.

"I'll catch a lift home, Ruth. Thanks for the airport run."

The door was answered by Helena, a longtime employee of the Alanford household who'd served as Kenny's nanny when he was a toddler. "So nice to see you, Miss Hughes. Lord Alanford is waiting in the courtyard with tea. May I bring you anything else?"

"No, it's fine. Thank you." On the drive back from Heathrow, she and Ruth had stopped for a pub lunch in Hatfield.

Though Channing knew her way around Breckham Hall, Helena escorted her to the garden, a practice that always felt more like surveillance than hospitality. She wondered if they followed Oliver as well.

Lord Alanford rose from his shaded chair as she walked across the flagstones. "How wonderful to see you, Channing. Thank you so much for making time to come. I know how busy you must be."

There was no sign of Lady Alanford, who sometimes stayed at their flat in the city. In fact, Channing recalled Kenny saying they were catching a performance this week in West End.

"I was delighted when you called. It's been so hectic, I almost forgot I'd promised you a memento from Poppa's collection of Romantic poetry." She handed him a book by Keats that included "Ode to a Nightingale," the poem she'd excerpted at Poppa's funeral. "It's not a first edition, nor even in good condition, I'm afraid. It was one from which he read quite often, as you can tell by the worn cover. He'd be so pleased to know it was on your nightstand now."

He held the book to his chest as his eyes misted. "I couldn't be more pleased with your choice. I always felt it was the poetry that gave your grandfather his gentle side, which I very much admired. Lord Hughes, as we all knew, was an unflinching champion of the work ethic, but he saw the imbalance in our social system." Ever the gentleman, he held her chair before seating himself at the one adjacent. "Over the years he came to believe that economists, himself included, should focus their theories more on the common good. I believe it was his love of poetry that brought him to an appreciation of humanity."

Channing was too polite to call bollocks on his revisionist reflections, recalling all too well Poppa's full-throated defense of Thatcher long after civilized Englanders came to see her policies as needlessly cruel.

"Let me congratulate you on your meeting with Sir Nigel. He's always been such a generous patron of the arts and letters. I'm sure he was delighted at the find."

"He could hardly contain himself. They all were anxious that I might take it to auction, but I was impressed by Sir Nigel's promise to share the collection with scholars, as he's done with other works."

"A magnificent windfall, that was. Though in retrospect, I find it rather perplexing that Lord Hughes didn't mention this collection in his will. You don't suppose he was unaware of its monetary value?"

"Funny, I was going to ask you the same thing. He spoke often of the poetry itself but never its worth. But then I realized that the works were already mine. From my father, that is. Poppa presented them as a gift when I was just a child, but in hindsight I think it was to encourage my interest."

"Whatever the reason, I'm delighted by your good fortune. Almost as if Lord Hughes was watching over you."

"Quite right."

He sipped his tea and shifted nervously. "In light of your unexpected fortune, I thought we might discuss your present thinking on Penderworth. Perhaps you're reconsidering the offer Kenneth extended last weekend. He indicated that you'd tentatively accepted, though it's probably occurred to you that your new financial situation gives you more options."

"It has occurred to me, yes." Though any conversation about that would be with Kenny, not Lord Alanford, since Kenny said he planned to make the purchase from his trust.

"You might recall a promise I made when I executed Lord Hughes's will—that Lady Alanford and I stand ready to support you in any way, regardless of what you decide. I know it's been difficult, given both the practical and emotional issues. I have to say, I was impressed by the ingenuity of Kenneth's proposal. Obviously he wanted to make it possible for you to keep the manor and bring it up to standard—to live there if that's what you desire, or to hold in trust in the event you decide to return someday. Our son, it goes without saying, treasures your friendship."

"Just as I treasure his." Lord Alanford was saying all the right things to demonstrate his support, yet there was a feeling of suspicion that she couldn't shake. Did he have an ulterior motive? "I think Kenny's goal was to trap me into keeping it forever, since he knew I'd be crazy to unload it later for a single pound."

"You're probably right," he said, sharing her laugh. "Though I want you to know that if you'd prefer an outright sale to a deal that brings you only half what the manor is worth, I will gladly pay you full price for Penderworth."

"Is there some reason you think I ought not accept Kenny's offer?"

"Goodness, no. On the contrary, it would be fabulous all around. I'm only saying that if you're considering declining it in favor of getting full price, I stand ready to make that offer. If your concern is Kenneth, rest assured that I'd happily pass it on to him should he and Oliver wish to reside there."

It was the far better financial deal for both Channing and Kenny, but it assumed Kenny actually cared about the money. Perhaps he cared more about being able to say he'd purchased his own home. Or he hoped to share the costs with Oliver, as it might someday be the place they raised their children.

"Out of loyalty to Kenny, I feel I should discuss these options with him. Are you all right with me sharing this conversation?"

"Of course. I can join you if you like. What you want is most important, followed by what Kenneth wants. At the risk of sounding like Sir Nigel, my objective here is only to make a preemptive offer that precludes someone else acquiring Penderworth."

"You needn't worry about that, Lord Alanford."

His shoulders collapsed with relief. "That's wonderful news. May I ask then, are you any closer to a decision on what you'll do? He seemed to think you might return to Boston in the short term. Something about a promotion at your company."

"That's one consideration." She'd never spoken of her romantic life with either of Kenny's parents. The way they'd treated Kenny growing up made her distrustful. "Did Kenny happen to mention that I was seeing someone?"

"The doctor? Marjorie and I would love to meet her. Shall we plan dinner with the boys this weekend?"

His cheerful reference to "the boys" was endearing in light of his torturous history with Kenny. "I'm afraid she's gone back to Boston. I've only just dropped her at Heathrow this morning."

"A shame. You must let us know when she returns."

The conversation was almost surreal...welcoming the woman in her life with open arms the way he'd finally welcomed Oliver. It was only days ago that she'd told Lark about the night Kenny had shown up at the door, bloodied by his father's rage.

"Channing, is something wrong?"

"Lord Alanford, I need to ask you something about my grandfather...something you might find painful to talk about."

By his sudden look of shame, he'd followed the logical links from the subject of her girlfriend, and knew exactly where the conversation was headed. "It's all right. I fully accept that I brought that pain on myself, and on others."

His refusal to accept having a gay son had nearly destroyed his family. Even their eight-year healing process had been agonizing, Kenny said, as Lord Alanford's suffering and guilt had spiraled into depression. It was only after falling in love with Oliver that Kenny realized their path to reconciliation was through forgiveness.

"Back when Kenny used to stay with us"—a euphemism for his running away from home—"Poppa never talked about him being gay. Not with Kenny, not with me. He knew, obviously, because Kenny said he told him everything. For some reason, it just wasn't something he wanted to discuss. Kenny thought it was out of respect for you, his best mate and colleague. Whereas I always worried that it was a subject he couldn't bear to bring inside his own house for fear of opening the floodgates."

His voice lowered and he began the mindless distraction of turning his cup so that its handle played like a sundial against the saucer. "He certainly opened the floodgates in our house, as you put it. I'd never seen Hughes so angry. Actually rolled up his sleeves to take me on...all very ridiculous for two grown men to be circling one another with their fists up, as Marjorie pointed out."

What an incredible spectacle that must have been. Poppa would have been sixty years old to Lord Alanford's mid-forties. "I can't imagine such a sight. I never saw my grandfather raise a fist to anyone."

"No punches were thrown. At the time I thought I'd won the fight with my defiance, but I couldn't have been more wrong. As he walked out he said Kenneth needn't be my problem, that he was welcome to live at Penderworth. I'd certainly made the poor lad's life miserable here at Breckham Hall. No phone, no laptop. Small wonder he started going to your house on his weekends home from Aldenham. To be perfectly honest, I always appreciated knowing he was somewhere safe and not in a bathhouse with strange men twice his age."

She recalled Kenny raging over his father's baseless assumptions, saying he might as well do the things he was being accused of, cruising the dance clubs in London and tricking in parks. Instead he hung out with her at Penderworth, eating, sleeping and watching TV. And occasionally smoking weed in the chimney.

Given the earl's attitude at the time, it was unlikely her grandfather had confided his thoughts on her sexuality. "I don't suppose... Did Poppa ever mention that I might be gay as well?"

"Yes, of course."

She became aware of a pounding in her chest.

Lord Alanford folded his arms and crossed his legs primly, and though he spoke to her as he might family, it was clear he still struggled with layers of guilt. "You have to understand, it was a very difficult time for our friendship. I was furious that Hughes refused to condemn Kenneth's behavior. At the same time, he lost respect for me as a friend."

She hadn't known this righteous side of Poppa, though his valiant actions to protect Kenny spoke clearly of his decency. It was his silence that had made her wary of coming out. Words of unconditional support would have been of tremendous comfort.

"Your grandfather and I hardly spoke to one another during those last two years you both were at Aldenham. When Kenny chose Queen Mary instead of Cambridge for law school, he stopped coming home at all. You'd gone to university in the

States by then. The constant pressure of our quarrels was over, but Marjorie was heartbroken...as was I. We missed him terribly."

"He visited me several times when I was at Wellesley. My mum was living in Boston at the time. She adored him, and of course assumed he was my boyfriend. I told her no, that both of us were gay, but she's utterly incapable of processing anything but her own thoughts. I wondered if Poppa might have believed it as well, that perhaps Kenny had gone through a phase but was over it by college."

"Oh, I hardly believe he thought that." Lord Alanford laughed, this time a painless chuckle. "He and I met up for a pint at the C & P after you'd gone off to uni. He had several photos on his phone, one of you and Kenneth on a boat wearing silly pirate costumes."

"I remember...Halloween at Provincetown. Practically the whole town is gay."

"Hughes laughed and said it was a shame, the pair of you would have made beautiful children. But that you had about as much interest in men as Kenneth had in women."

"You're sure of that."

"Oh, absolutely. He said it was my fault you hadn't come out to him, that parents like me were the reason gay children hid their lives. He was looking forward to the day you did, because it would mean you'd found someone who made you happy. That's what he wanted for you—complete and utter happiness. He never understood how I could want anything less for Kenneth."

Tears escaped down her cheeks before she realized they were there. She'd never make sense of why Poppa hadn't spoken of it when Kenny brought the elephant into the room. But it was enough to know that Cecil was wrong about how Poppa would have felt about Lark.

* * *

Channing's building was on a tree-lined street just a block and a half from an organic grocery store and a row of small ethnic cafes. Even better, it was only three blocks from the Orange Line, which connected Lark to Gipson, and Channing to Boston's financial district. It was an absolute dream location, especially after the miserable rush hour commute Lark had endured for a year and a half from Ma's house in Mattapan.

They stopped in front of a neat Victorian painted the color of a stormy sky, with a white porch and shutters. It had three levels, including one partially below ground. Channing's top-floor apartment had a large bay window on one side and a small gray satellite dish peeking around the corner on the other. Parking was in the back, she'd said, accessible by an alley.

"Sixty-three," her taxi driver said, his voice muffled by a gnarly beard.

Her first reaction was that his fare was exorbitant, even with the Logan surcharge. Then she realized he was talking about the address.

"Thirty-one-fifty." A more reasonable fare, which Gipson would reimburse.

Her car, which sat in the garage at Gipson, would have to wait until the next day. Right now her body was saying it was nearly ten p.m. back in Cambridge, and that she'd been awake since four. Waving forty-five bucks, she coaxed the driver into carrying her massive suitcase up eight stairs to the porch and another sixteen to Channing's apartment. That was after keying in the four-digit code for Payton's birthday and kicking aside several pieces of mail that had come through the slot. It didn't help that the light for the stairwell was burned out.

She'd decided already that the rest of her belongings would remain in storage for a while, at least until the seasons changed. There wasn't all that much, since Bess had bought her half of the furniture when they split up. As silly as it was to be contemplating the state of her worldly goods, practically speaking it meant she could move into Channing's apartment completely unencumbered.

"Thanks, have a great night," she told the cabbie.

The apartment's interior was warm and inviting. Very warm in fact, since it had been closed up through the early part of summer. She quickly located the control for the climate unit and lowered the temperature until it whirred to life.

It was a cozy living room with a pair of love seats arranged at right angles to watch both the TV and the gas log fireplace. Only steps away was a modern kitchen with glass-paned cabinets and a large black granite island that doubled as an eating space. The walls of both rooms were painted a light sage against the dark cherry trim of windows, doorframes and baseboards.

As she crossed the hardwood floors, she noticed how the rugs and appointments—even the artwork on the walls—all seemed specially chosen for the space they occupied. Clearly Channing had hired an interior designer to style her home the way she styled herself, with perfection.

The bathroom was salmon-colored with a glass step-in shower and tile mosaics. Unlike the towels at Penderworth, these weren't monogrammed. They were luxurious, so pristine in fact that Lark wondered if there were others somewhere, worn and ragged, that were used for drying.

French doors led to an office suite in the smaller bedroom. The desk held a mountain of unopened mail, presumably placed there by someone who had access. A housekeeper or landlord.

In the master bedroom, a queen-sized bed invited her with its fluffy comforter and shams, but the odd touch was the matching pair of accent chairs by the bay window. Upholstered in a textured olive fabric, they looked comfortable but elegant—and hardly used.

She collapsed into one and dialed Channing's number. "Why do you have two chairs in your bedroom?"

"I was wondering if you'd gotten there yet. What do you think?"

"This place is gorgeous. If you break up with me, at least let me take over your lease."

"Always an angle. My cleaning lady comes on Mondays… Lucia. In fact, you can pay her."

"She's dumped a shitload of mail on your desk. How soon are they going to cut my water off?"

"That depends on how many notices I've already ignored."

It was possible Channing wasn't kidding. "For what it's worth, the AC came on when I figured out which button to push. If one of those was a panic code, the police will be here any minute."

"I pay everything online, but I always leave Lucia some extra cash. By the way, it's a bloody good thing you said that on the plane about stopping the newspaper. Can you imagine how many there would be if I hadn't called them the day we got to London?"

Though Channing had described her decision to quit Albright and go home to England as abrupt and reactionary, the unopened mail proved even more what an impulsive decision it had been. No wonder her boss was so quick to believe she'd been suddenly overwhelmed by her grandfather's death. Nothing else was rational.

"Are you going to answer my question? I want to know who this other chair belongs to."

"You, obviously. But there's only one bed. I'm afraid we'll have to share."

"If we must. Your bed is possibly the most blissful sight I've ever seen." She pushed off her shoes and lowered the zipper on her pants.

"Tell me about it. I came up to my bedroom immediately after dinner under the auspices of watching something on the telly. Instead I fell straight into bed. Do you have to be at work tomorrow?"

"Not until noon. Our whole team has been called to a meeting with the CEO and some of the higher-ups. A catered lunch. It's going to be nerve-racking but at least we'll have salmon and grilled vegetables instead of the usual turkey wraps."

"This really is quite the big deal, isn't it?"

"Huge. PharmaStat's our biggest contractor by far. *They* should have caught this before I did. If we can't trust their quality control process, we'll have no choice but to cancel all of our contracts."

"What you need, my love, is a little downtime. I think you should pull back the covers on that bed. All the way down to the sheet. Go ahead, I'll wait."

Lark laughed, but that bed was definitely calling her. She folded the comforter to the bottom, finding white sheets in soft pima cotton. "Okay, she's turned down. Do I get to lie down now?"

"You might want to draw the shades first. Then I think you should throw all those dirty, germ-y travel clothes on the floor and let those soft, satiny sheets caress your tired body and welcome you home. Shall I wait for that too?"

Hearing Channing call this place her "home" made her heart skip a beat. Technically, a surge of norepinephrine had done that, while dopamine had triggered a sense of euphoria. The cliché sounded better.

"All right, Lady Hughes...I'm buck naked and getting between these heavenly sheets. Are you going to sing me to sleep?"

"Trust me, you don't want that."

It occurred to Lark that she needed to up the minutes on her international calling plan.

"In the bedside table, bottom drawer..."

"Yes?" Lark flicked on the lamp and started digging through the contents of the drawer.

"There's a sweet little red device in there that I call Ruby... because she's a real jewel. I'd like to listen while the two of you get acquainted."

CHAPTER TWENTY-TWO

Voices from the kitchen drifted up the stairs and through Channing's open door. Her back protested the nine hours she'd been lying in bed, but otherwise she felt fully rested from her long day.

She wrapped herself in a summer robe and located her favorite beige slippers, which she sometimes wore outside the house. With her tablet computer in hand, she slogged to the kitchen to find Maisie and Cecil with the kettle on.

"Good morning, luv. Shall I make you some breakfast?"

"Just tea for now." Channing greeted each with a kiss to the cheek. "Come into the breakfast room so we can talk. Bring our pot of tea."

The Brownings exchanged troubled looks that jogged a memory of Poppa. It probably wasn't the talk they were worried about, she realized, but the unseemliness of joining her at the table. She recalled as a teenager scolding Poppa about how demeaning it was to have Cecil open his car door when he was perfectly capable of doing it himself. Had it not occurred to her, he asked, that Cecil wanted to open the car door? He'd made the indelible impression upon her that the Brownings, as honest, hardworking people, were proud to perform the duties for which they were paid. Whereas becoming too chummy would put them in the awkward position of feeling they couldn't occasionally negotiate for more compensation or changes in working conditions.

"Please join me, I should say. We won't have many more opportunities to share the morning, and I want to milk every single moment." She took her usual spot and waited for them to sit. "I bet you're getting very excited. Moving day is this weekend, yes?"

"Saturday," Cecil said. "Sorry we've had the car out so much. I suppose it's time for us to visit the Honda shop."

"We might get one of those cute little crossovers," Maisie said. "They're so comfortable and have all that room."

"About that…I should have told you this sooner. I want you to have Poppa's car…if you want it, that is. I can do the transfer online today but it could take a week or two to process. If you prefer the Honda, perhaps they'll accept it in trade." It was the least she could do for their thirty-four years of service.

"That is so kind of you, Miss Channing," Cecil said. "But what will you do about a car?"

"I can always call Ruth, or perhaps I'll rent one for a couple of weeks. Looks like I'll be returning to Boston soon."

"So you've decided to sell Penderworth and move back?" Maisie pouted and held her hand to her chest.

"Actually I'm only selling half of it—to Kenny. We'll bring in a contractor to make some repairs. It's possible Kenny and Oliver will decide to live here, at least on the weekends. But it will always be mine, and who knows? I may end up back here one of these days. That's my plan anyway."

Cecil grinned and bobbed his head from her to Maisie and back. "This is such wonderful news, dear one. Your Poppa would be so pleased."

The "moving back to Boston" part wasn't set in stone, but it certainly appeared so. She'd returned Vanessa Easton's text with a suggestion for a day and time but hadn't received a reply. Perhaps she'd guessed wrong about the reason for Easton's interest.

"Speaking of Poppa…" She didn't want to dampen their joy, but it was important to her to close the circle on what they'd talked about earlier. "I was worried about something you said, Cecil, that Poppa would have been ashamed of me had he known I was gay. I didn't want to believe that, so I asked Lord Alanford. They were friends, as you know, and they had a history on the subject with regards to Kenny. It turns out that Poppa knew about me all along, at least from the time I was a teenager. His only disappointment was that I never met someone who made me want to tell him."

Cecil's face was a mask of tearful shame. "I'm so sorry I said that to you. I had no right."

"It's all right, I forgive you." She stretched across the table and gripped his hand. "Look at me, Cecil. I'm only telling you this because Poppa deserves to have us remember him for who he was…a truly exceptional man."

"You're right, Miss Channing. Maisie and I found our pot o' gold the day we came to work here. We're so grateful for the life we've had."

"And I'm grateful you both were here to share it with me. Once you move to Bury, I won't be your mistress anymore." With her other hand, she clutched Maisie's. "I hope that means we get to sit like this even more, like family. That's who you are to me."

The poignant outpouring was more than Maisie could take, and she burst into tears. "That's enough of this sentimental mush, both of you. I have work to do."

Amidst laughter and cheer, they shared monstrous hugs before setting about their day.

Channing's world was brimming with "sentimental mush," she realized. After feeling almost impervious to sentimentality for most of her life, it was suddenly everywhere—Lark, Kenny, the Brownings. What she wouldn't give to have had this emotional awakening when Poppa was still with her.

Alone in the breakfast room, she poured herself another cup of tea and checked her tablet to find a late-night email from Mitch marked *Contract* that had an attachment:

Channing, I apologize for how long it's taken us to get the paperwork together on this. Please find our compensation package attached for the position of Senior Client Manager, Eastern Region. Ideally, we'd like to have you start by July 20, sooner if possible. The Grandover deal blew up on us. They got cold feet about the stock swap and it hurt us not to have you or Payton there to hold their hand through the merger. Isn't it horrible, this news from Payton? I spoke with her daughter yesterday and apparently they've known for months. The family has been told to expect the worst. I know you have a lot going on in your life right now too, Channing. It's times like this that make us realize the folks at Albright aren't just colleagues—we're family too. I hope to hear from you soon. Best, Mitch

* * *

Mike leaned over and grumbled, "Un-fucking-believable. Corporate espionage isn't even illegal in the UK."

"Let's hope that doesn't mean she gets a pass."

Still, there was enough evidence against Niya to send her to prison for a dozen years if Gipson chose to prosecute. Product tampering was illegal no matter where it occurred in the distribution chain. Niya had to know that surreptitiously infusing nonsmokers with nicotine would bring unpleasant and frightening effects. Her scheme would have been disastrous if one of her victims had suffered more serious consequences.

The meeting had been moved to a waterfront business hotel near Logan Airport in order to accommodate expansive teams from Gipson, PharmaStat, and Haas-Seidel, the three companies embroiled in the dispute. Tables were set up in a U-formation, with each company claiming a row. The powerful decision-makers—most of them white men, Lark noticed—sat at the tables, with their respective support staffs lined up in chairs behind them.

In all, Lark counted forty-two people in attendance. The roster included a sampling of board members, corporate officers, attorneys, and accountants—an indicator of how much money was at stake. While there was no one present who represented one of the science departments, several of the officers and board members were medical doctors. Lark thought it ironic that after playing such integral roles in the investigation and outcome, she and Mike Dobbins had been relegated to the back row. She was proud though to have Kirsten—not Gipson's CEO or general counsel—spearheading their company's position. If Gipson didn't name her CEO soon, someone else would.

"Ladies and gentlemen, it's possible Gipson Pharmaceuticals has suffered irreparable damage no matter what action we take today. The news story about life-threatening side effects received wide media attention throughout the UK. Our survey, which was conducted shortly after the article appeared in *The Sun*, found that eighteen percent of adults in the UK were aware of the story. That's nearly ten million people."

Haas-Seidel's CEO interjected, "To be fair, awareness has probably fallen considerably since the story first broke, and awareness isn't the same as understanding. Media users often are confused when it comes to specific details, especially over time."

Spoken like a man who felt at least partially responsible for the damaging article, since it was his employee who conspired to disrupt the development of Flexxene and fed the story to the press.

Kirsten showed little emotion on her face, and even less in her voice. "That's quite true, Dr. Vogel. What some of those readers remember is merely the existence of a scandal involving a drug trial. We owe it to our colleagues at Bayer, Merck, Abbott Laboratories, and so on, not to let the damage caused by this incident spill over onto their reputations as well. Working together for a resolution seems in everyone's best interest."

A board member from PharmaStat expressed alarm over the suggestion that the details be shared with other industry giants. He feared that PharmaStat, with research facilities all over the world, could be put out of business if drug companies no longer had confidence in their work.

An acrimonious back-and-forth erupted with one of Gipson's board members, during which Lark stole an opportunity to check her phone for messages. Nothing. No response to the three texts she'd sent, nor the voice mail she'd left during a bathroom break.

Her first text had been silly, saying Channing's pulsating showerhead could give Ruby a run for her money. The second was even sillier, reiterating her wish to take over the lease if they broke up. Those two she sent early this morning. By the time her group wrapped up lunch at the hotel, it was six p.m. in Cambridge, and still no reply. Fearing that Channing had taken her lease comment too seriously, she sent a third saying she couldn't wait to see her again and was already looking at fares for a long weekend.

She hated texting, hated email. People couldn't hear the inflection in your voice to know if you were joking. But then half the time she couldn't tell when Channing was joking, even if they were sitting face-to-face.

A groan somehow escaped her mouth and Mike gave her a nudge. "Don't worry, Kirsten's got this."

"Trust is absolutely essential for everyone in this room. I daresay the people who read that story and believed it no longer trust us. We can't fix that by lying to them or obscuring the truth." Kirsten paused, giving her words dramatic effect. As an obvious show of respect, no one moved to fill the silence. "So what happened here? Was this failure the result of systemic corruption in the industry? No—it was two people conspiring. Our clinical reviewer, Dr. Lark Latimer...where are you, Lark?"

Lark sat up straight and offered a small wave, feeling the eyes of everyone in the room.

"There she is. Back row, gray suit."

Technically it was taupe. Gray clashed with her hair and eyes.

"I asked Dr. Latimer this morning if she saw a way out of this. She said, and I quote, 'Just tell people what happened.' And she's absolutely right. Make public the news that two nefarious individuals took advantage of their positions for personal gain. That both have been fired. That all parties involved are taking action to ensure that neither individual is ever certified to work in this industry again. That we've taken steps to make sure mistakes like this aren't repeated."

Around the room were subtle nods, signs of agreement. Even PharmaStat's CEO, Pierre Dancourt—who arguably had the most to lose—grudgingly concurred. "Dr. Cooke is right. It is far too late to contain this. Secrets do not keep. The only way forward is to acknowledge our errors and demonstrate our resolve to correct them."

It was nearly five o'clock when the meeting finally broke. About half the attendees pooled into taxis and shuttles for Logan to catch evening flights back to Europe.

A small crowd clustered around Kirsten, following her to the elevator and into the lobby of the parking garage. Lark squeezed through to offer her personal congratulations for owning the room. "Lark, have you met Dr. Dancourt? This is Lark Latimer, who headed up our review team in Cambridge."

Lark knew PharmaStat's CEO only by reputation and wasn't surprised when he spoke out in support of Kirsten's strategy for full disclosure. As he handed her his business card, he thanked her for uncovering weaknesses in his company's systems.

Kirsten caught her elbow as she started to walk away. "Wait for me a sec, will you?"

She would never again wonder how Channing could have gotten involved with Payton. Dr. Kirsten Cooke, blond and athletic, soccer mom, the senior officer to whom their CEO turned with so much on the line. Had there been no Channing, had Kirsten needed a friend for one of the toughest days of her life, had they shared an intimate moment filled with sexual energy…she too would have had an affair with her married boss.

But that would never happen now. She had everything she could ever want in Channing. Who still wasn't answering her texts or calls. It was maddening.

Kirsten joined her on the walk to visitor parking, her slumped shoulders the only indication her whirlwind trip to Cambridge and back in three days was catching up with her. This woman had run the Boston Marathon four months after having a baby.

"How does it feel to be a rock star?" Kirsten asked.

"Me? If anyone's a rock star after today, it's you."

"Don't underestimate yourself. A lot of people are impressed that you got to the bottom of this when it so easily could have been written off as an unfortunate coincidence." Lowering her voice to a conspiratorial whisper, she added, "This wouldn't be a bad time to ask for a raise."

Feeling herself blush, she recognized the opportunity Kirsten's observation presented. "What if I asked instead about a transfer to the San Diego office?"

"A California girl? I thought you grew up here."

"My girlfriend and I are thinking about relocating...but only if it's a good career move."

"It's not my call, Lark, but I think Gipson would do its best to accommodate you. There is one issue though, which is what I wanted to talk about."

She didn't like the sound of that, nor the fact that Kirsten had felt the need to couch this "issue" in what might have been gratuitous praise.

"With regard to PharmaStat, I spoke with Pierre. We have a mutual interest in maintaining a strong research partnership. It's symbiotic—millions in contracts for them, without which Gipson would have a backlog of dozens of trials. We have to look at all the projects in the field right now with PharmaStat, but there are misgivings about you being the one to do that given your personal experience with this situation."

"Misgivings? I just turned in one of my best friends. You'd think that would get me a few checks in the integrity column."

"It does, Lark. Truly it does, and Pierre appreciates that greatly. But we're at a tenuous juncture and it's imperative that we mend this relationship. There's concern at Gipson that your involvement in further Cambridge trials might cause unnecessary friction with the staff there. They might not be as cooperative or as forthcoming. Your findings could be challenged, your recommendations rebuffed. Gipson can't afford to have that happen."

So no more assignments in Cambridge. No more chances to work in what was now her new favorite place to be. As depressing as that was to imagine, it was the logical end to the shitstorm stirred up by her review. Whereas people like Wendi and Shane had once thought of her as "the boss" they needed to please, she'd now be a spy to suspect, an adversary to resist.

"Can I at least say that sucks?"

Kirsten laughed gently and rested a hand on her shoulder as they reached her car, a minivan that probably held half a soccer team. "You're allowed to say that, but only to me."

CHAPTER TWENTY-THREE

Stepping off the elevator at Massachusetts General, Channing thought of Lark's habit of splashing on cologne to suppress the distinctive smells of a hospital. The lingering odor was proof there had been a vicious battle for life on this floor today, as if cancer needed another way to broadcast its horror.

At twenty after nine in the evening, the information desk on the fifth floor was dark and abandoned, except for the custodian whose vacuum cleaner roared beneath rows of padded armchairs. Families who earlier that day had fretfully waited in this room had long since gone home or taken their solicitude to a loved one's bedside.

The custodian turned off his machine and looped the cord around his shoulder for transport. She took a seat and watched until he stepped aboard the elevator on his way to being someone else's disturbance.

A call to Mitch's admin Robin, ostensibly for information on how to send flowers, had gotten her the room number, which she'd located on the floor plan in the main lobby. Down the hall and around the corner. Now after traveling 3,400 miles, she couldn't muster the fortitude to walk the last fifty feet.

Perhaps she shouldn't. The long day of travel had her on a razor's edge—anxious, confused, seething, heartbroken. It was clear Payton hadn't meant for her to find out. In this new light, her behavior of the last few months made sad, twisted sense.

The main question wasn't why Payton had kept this from her. It was whether she should honor Payton's wishes now or selfishly assert her own by going in there to show what a compassionate person she could be. Had she really come all this way to turn back now?

Her phone dinged again, this time to announce an email.

Hi sweetheart, I've been trying to reach you today by text and voice mail. I suppose it's possible one of us is having phone issues. Or maybe I used up all my data getting to know Ruby. Anyway, I'm a little bit worried (not a lot). If I don't hear from you by tomorrow, I'll give Kenny a call to make sure you're all right. If you're reading this—I love you! XXXOOO Lark

It was the fifth time today Lark had reached out to her. After Mitch's note this morning, Channing had been in no mood for levity but couldn't find the words to explain to Lark why she was dropping everything to rush to Payton's side. Then she asked herself why she even needed to explain it. If Lark had a problem with her feelings for Payton at a time like this, then she wasn't the person Channing thought her to be. In fact, by the time she'd gotten off the plane at Logan, she'd worked herself into a lather over things Lark hadn't even said, hadn't even done—all of which was absurd.

Night had fallen, enabling her to see her reflection in the window. She'd worn the black jumpsuit and heels, the outfit Lark liked so much. Funny that she'd bought it only hours after resigning from Albright as a reward for showing some backbone. She fluffed her hair, which had fallen flat from the dry air on the plane, and touched up her lips with gloss. It was probably the best she could do under the circumstances.

Her pulse quickened as she walked down the hall, causing her to regret that she'd not had a drink on the plane. Or three.

The room was dark but for a panel of fluorescent light at the head of the bed. Ben Crane lay on his back, his head wrapped in gauze and an oxygen cannula taped to his nose. Even from the doorway, she noticed his ruddy "moon face," characteristic of the steroid therapy commonly given to patients with brain cancer.

In the shadows beside him, Payton looked up from the glow of her e-reader, her face conveying alarm. She rose and checked on Ben before gliding noiselessly to where Channing stood. With her voice low and stern, she said, "I never wanted you here."

"I know, Payton. I'm not here to…" She didn't know what she could say with Ben so close. "I only came to say how sorry I am."

Payton whirled around and quickly called a number on her phone. Channing thought for a second she might be reporting her to security.

"Kathleen…hi, it's Mom. Is Tim there with you? I just wanted to give you both an update. Your father's quiet, he seems comfortable. I honestly don't think you need to come to the hospital tonight." She paced at the foot of Ben's bed, glancing furtively at Channing. "Enjoy the night off. Maybe if you come around tomorrow morning, I'll slip home and grab a shower."

Channing felt stupid—and guilty—when she grasped that Payton was confirming the immediate locations of both of her children so they wouldn't burst in while she was there.

"That's the last time I'm lying to my children about something to do with you," she said through clenched teeth.

How about not lying to me? She couldn't bring herself to say something so sharp, not with Payton in such obvious despair.

She followed Payton across the hall into a small room with several chairs and a table draped to look like an altar. A makeshift chapel, apparently. "I didn't come to cause you pain, Payton. I only found out this morning from Mitch that Ben was sick. He assumed I knew, by the way, and now he thinks you kept it from me because I'm still struggling with my grandfather's death."

In full light, it was obvious Ben's illness had taken its toll. Payton had lost weight, and her face was worn from worry and lack of sleep. Usually a smart dresser, she wore knit pants that bagged around her hips and thighs, and a long-sleeved blue T-shirt with an obvious grease stain on the chest.

"When your grandfather died, I really wanted to be with you for the funeral. Please believe that. I couldn't go then because Ben had an appointment with the doctor. He was having trouble with dizziness…he needed me to drive him. The same day you were burying your grandfather, we were hearing that Ben was already Stage IV and there was nothing they could do."

Channing had to fight not to take Payton's hand as it shook. "Why didn't you just tell me that?"

"Because I felt guilty. And then Kathleen…she and Mark told us that weekend their baby was due in October. Channing, she pulled me into the study and confronted me about us."

"That's ridiculous. How could she possibly have known?"

"It was that woman in Atlanta last fall. Remember at the hotel when I kept saying the woman across the hall looked familiar? It was one of Kathleen's friends from Brandeis. She recognized me from the wedding. She told Kathleen that she saw us in the restaurant and on the elevator. We acted like more than friends, she said, and then she saw that you stayed in my room that night. Channing, she followed the housekeeper into our room and sent Kathleen a goddamn picture of our bed."

"Bloody hell, last fall? Why didn't she say anything then?"

"She said it made her want to throw up. Then when her father got sick she took it out on me. I was afraid she'd tell him. She swore if I didn't break up with you, she'd keep me from my grandchild forever."

"So you were blackmailed."

"Blackmail, extortion…whatever you want to call it. But it didn't matter because Ben needed me. I couldn't see you anymore."

"But you could have told me. It would have broken my heart, and I'd probably have felt sorry for myself. But you can't possibly think I'd have been anything but supportive. I've always shown you compassion. Just like I've always been your friend."

"I couldn't take that chance, Channing, not after the things you said. That you'd love me no matter what, you'd wait for me no matter what. As long as there was a chance you'd put up a fight, I couldn't risk letting that happen."

Channing saw it clearly now—Payton had behaved similarly when she'd gone for the abortion two years ago, not telling Ben because she was afraid he'd want her to have the baby. Bottom line, Payton didn't give other people choices.

"And you couldn't just come out and fire me because that would have been illegal and I might have made a stink about it. So you made my life a living hell to get me to quit."

"That's not what happened. I couldn't travel anymore, not with Ben sick. I confided in Mitch. I told him you were fully capable of leading the team without me. And you were. I had no idea you'd walk away from such a challenge. But I assumed that was the end of it, so I called Kathleen that day and told her you'd gone. I thought it would ease her mind. I couldn't have you come back after that. I *can't* have you come back, even when Ben…" Her chin quivered. "It would be the end of my family, and I know that after all we've shared, you wouldn't want that for me."

"Mitch offered me the Eastern Region."

"Because he offered me VP of mergers when this is over. But I'm not going to take it. I'll say it's too much responsibility—which is true if you're gone and there's no one competent in charge of the Eastern Region." Payton studied her reaction, as if expecting gratitude for the compliment. She'd always been the best in the room at reading faces, which was what made her so effective at the negotiating table.

Channing sighed deeply, dropping her head to her hands. What Payton had done to her was manipulative and cruel. Now she expected Channing to pay the ultimate price for their affair. This was a unique moment in their history in which Channing had the power to say no. Payton deserved comeuppance—but on top of her suffering with Ben? Channing didn't have it in her to add to that mountain of misery, no matter how much she needed a job.

"You realize this leaves me bloody well fucked career-wise."

"Mitch came to sit with me over the weekend and we talked. This job offer is his gambit to get you back, but I know for a fact he'll release you from the noncompete if you decide to stay in England. He cares for you like a daughter, and he believes you're devastated over your grandfather's death."

"He's not wrong." Except her life was so much more complicated than that. "The irony is that I've met someone. And as luck would have it, she has a very good pharmaceutical job right here in Boston."

In a surprisingly candid moment, Payton revealed a look of jealousy. Channing had never thought her capable of recognizing someone else's advantage. "What does that mean, met someone? You're dating?"

"She's the one, Payton. I could very well see myself married this time next year."

"Someone who really appreciates you, I hope."

Channing chuckled, noting it was the first time she'd felt an inkling of warmth toward Payton in a very long time. Her description of Lark rolled off her lips like a corporate bio, calling attention to how vital Lark was to her company after solving a critical problem that might have cost them billions. Plus she'd grown up in Boston and recently lost her mother. "And she makes me laugh…except I can't let her see me laughing because she prefers that whole stoic Brit thing."

"Don't you dare let another woman make all the demands the way I did, Channing. I don't care how important she is. If she loves you, she'll give in to what *you* want, like moving to England to be with you."

It was a very "Payton" remark. There was the non-apology apology, the insinuation that Payton knew what was best for her, and the preemptive deal breaker that might imply Lark didn't love her enough. The trifecta. Bonus points for insinuating the only way for Lark to prove her love was to move to England.

Channing had patently outgrown her need for Payton's mentoring, both personal and professional. And with astonishing clarity, she realized as well that Albright was the last place she wanted to work. Mitch could hold her to the noncompete, but he couldn't stop her from taking a job that didn't involve insurance. Her Harvard MBA would open up a world of opportunity. Time to polish that résumé.

"Payton, I'm so sorry you have to go through this. It's terrible what's happening to Ben. I'm glad you have your kids to help you through it, and that you have Albright. I'll let Mitch know I'm not interested in coming back."

"But...but it's going to raise flags if that's all you say, Channing. Especially if you start job hunting in Boston. The only clean way to handle this is for you to tell Mitch you're homesick and you want to stay in England."

Payton couldn't stand not pulling the strings.

Channing shouldered her bag and took a step toward the door. "Take care, Payton."

* * *

Lark didn't know what to make of her day. Having Kirsten Cooke call her a rock star was a sterling moment she'd remember for a long time. It felt good to know she had the respect of her professional colleagues because of her role in such a momentous event for their industry.

After having drinks in the hotel bar with Barry Sutton, Gipson's general counsel, Mike Dobbins had called to gossip. According to Barry, all three companies were bracing for lawsuits from the victims of Niya's treachery. Barry thought they'd be called to give testimony and advised them to retain private attorneys to represent their individual interests. Gipson would provide counsel as well, Mike said, but a private attorney would make sure they weren't somehow scapegoated. Lark found the whole affair nauseating.

Back on the plus side, a job in San Diego was a possibility, along with a bump in salary. Channing had specifically mentioned California as a possible destination if both of them needed to relocate for a fresh start together. Could Lark really give up winters in Boston for Southern California? Yes, she bloody well could. The practicality of relocating was tougher to swallow, since it might be several months before Channing landed a job. Lark wasn't sure she could stand another week apart.

And what if they moved all the way across the country and Channing didn't like her new job? It was so much easier to think about both of them staying in Boston, but only if Channing could stomach going back to work at Albright. Lark wasn't even sure it was a good idea, since Payton obviously had an evil streak. Channing didn't need that in her life every day.

The worst part of her day—now at seventeen hours and counting—was the roiling anxiety over not hearing from Channing. Wendi had called from PharmaStat trying to locate the second set of keys to the Skoda, so there was nothing wrong with her international phone service. If Channing's phone had been on the fritz, she'd have found another way.

An emergency? It worried her that Maisie and Cecil had been working so hard recently to prepare for their move. Overexertion was dangerous for anyone, but especially for people their age. Except Channing would have called her, as she had when Maisie cut herself.

She refused to imagine an accident. Which left only one explanation—Channing was deliberately ignoring her. Either she refused to be bullied into replying, or she was trivializing Lark's concern. The thought of getting blown off made her furious. As long as Channing wasn't facedown in a ditch.

Lark should have been asleep. It was after eleven o'clock and she was less than two days removed from being five time zones away. Instead she was flopping around on the bed like a fish on the beach. And she wasn't in the mood to play with Ruby again, especially without an audience.

Suddenly the security alarm beeped, a continuous high-pitched trill that sent a shudder of fear through her whole body. Someone was breaking in.

After several seconds there were four beeps, followed by silence. Whoever was at the door knew the code or had otherwise disabled the alarm.

She threw back the sheet and tiptoed barefoot across the room to peek out into the living room. Light flickered from the stairwell, either from a flashlight or smartphone. Not a cleaning lady, landlord or security monitor. They didn't come in the middle of the night...unless they planned on robbing the place. No one but Channing knew she was here.

At least that gave her the element of surprise, as did the advantage of position. She tiptoed across the living room to wait at the top of the stairs. A fire poker would have been nice. Stupid gas logs didn't need one.

On the table between the love seats was a figurine, a woman carrying water on her head. Molded in concrete, she weighed four or five pounds, more than enough if Lark's hands stopped shaking long enough to land a blow.

As the footsteps grew louder in the stairwell, the stream of light danced upward and into the living room. Lark held her breath, preparing to strike.

Then a hand reached over the rail and fumbled for the lamp that sat atop the bookcase. Light flooded the area to reveal—

"Channing?"

Eyeing the figurine in Lark's raised hand, she said flatly, "Blimey, that would have left a mark."

"Oh my God, oh my God, oh my God!" She set her weapon down and hugged Channing fiercely. "What are you doing here? Never mind, I don't care. I nearly smashed you in the head."

"Good thing I don't keep a gun." Channing kissed her repeatedly all over her face and head. "I guess it's too late to yell 'Surprise!' Though in retrospect it was bloody stupid not to call first."

"It was but you're forgiven. I'm so glad you're here." It wasn't just Channing's physical presence that thrilled her. It was that she'd made such a grand statement by following her after only a day apart. "I love you so much. You have no idea how happy this makes me, you showing up here out of the blue. I can't imagine a sweeter surprise."

She couldn't resist a kiss, a real one. Passion soon led her to start working the buttons on Channing's jumpsuit until hands gripped her shoulders and gently pushed her away.

"I love you too." She scanned the room before turning on another lamp next to the loveseat. "I'm utterly knackered. Can we sit?"

Sit, stand, jump up and down. Lark was too excited to be still.

"I came to Boston to see Payton."

Lark felt suddenly lightheaded, as if the blood had drained from her face. A fight or flight reaction to fear.

"I got a note from Mitch this morning saying Payton's husband has brain cancer and he's in a bad way. Mitch assumed I knew but I didn't. It's why everything happened."

"Why what happened? What's everything?"

As she related her staggering saga, Lark processed an ever-widening array of emotions—jealousy, understanding, irritation, sorrow. The greatest was sympathy, which mitigated her anger at Payton for her selfish scheming. Facing such a tragic loss, even a conniving adulteress deserved compassion. That same sympathy also held in check her annoyance at Channing for rushing to Heathrow to grab the first seat for Boston. "What made you decide to go?"

"I've thought about that most of the day, especially on the plane. Obviously I care about her and I wanted her to know that she had my support."

As any decent person would, Lark conceded.

"And though I'm not proud to admit this, I came so I could confront her. When I learned how long Ben had been sick, I realized it was all tied together. I wasn't looking for an explanation or an apology. I just needed her to know that I knew."

Lark wondered if a part of Channing had hoped laying it all bare would make Payton reconsider. "How did it make you feel to see her?"

"It was piteous, seeing her so withered, and being shamed by her daughter that way. She was desperate for control. Control of me, of Kathleen...of the whole situation at Albright. I could see her panic over knowing others would decide all those questions."

To Lark it sounded like the fall of hubris. The quiet in Channing's voice might have been solemnity, or perhaps fatigue, but there was no celebration of Payton's comeuppance.

"Lark, that time you asked if it bothered me that Payton was married…I said no. But it feels different now that I know we were caught. We have to answer for it. If Kathleen wants to be mad at her mom, that's on Payton. I have no idea if she feels guilty, but I do. It's sad to me that Kathleen will always feel her father was dishonored. I truly regret my part in it."

"Sweetheart, I didn't judge you for that, honest. I thought what you said made a lot of sense, that Payton deserved the chance to know if she was on the right path without blowing up her whole life. We aren't responsible for other people's bad choices." She brought Channing's hands to her lips. "I have a ton of respect for you for saying that because it shows what an honorable person you are. I couldn't love you more."

"I don't know about honor. I've a price to pay as well." She slumped against the cushions and sighed heavily. "Going back to Albright isn't an option for me anymore. Please understand, Lark. I can't possibly work with her again knowing all she's done."

"It's okay. I won't ask you to. It so happens I have a lot more flexibility about where I work because of this PharmaStat fiasco."

"Clusterfuck."

"Touché. My boss said it was a good time to ask for a raise. I asked about a transfer instead."

"Something in the UK, I hope? Please, please."

"Our European office is in Munich. I mentioned San Diego, since you said something once about both of us going to California."

Channing, clearly agitated, stood and began to pace. This time the click of her heels on the wooden floor wasn't sensuous—it was impatient. "It's more complicated than that. The only way Mitch waives the noncompete is for a job in England. That's because Payton begged me to tell him I left because I was homesick."

Lark was only beginning to grasp the damage Payton had done to Channing's life and career, while knowing Channing was too decent to take her down.

"There are other things I can do, Lark. Investment companies, venture capitalists. Just not insurance valuation…and maybe not anything to do with consulting for mergers or acquisitions. The problem is that I won't get a glowing reference from Albright if they think my saying I was homesick was bollocks. Working four years someplace and not getting a decent reference is a red flag for potential employers." She perched on the arm of the opposite loveseat and folded her arms, a gesture of resignation. "Ultimately I'll need Mitch's blessing, but I can't march into his office right now and ask for it. It could take some time to finesse. I'm sorry."

Wait till she hears… Lark laughed sardonically, shaking her head. Now didn't seem like a good time to add that Gipson was pulling her from all work in Cambridge. The universe was conspiring against them.

"I love you, Lark. If you can please be patient…"

"I can be whatever you need. As long as you love me, nothing else matters."

"That's absolutely all I need to know."

Lark stepped into her open arms and finally allowed her heart to rest in knowing they'd make this work. The where and when weren't important—only the who.

EPILOGUE

The walk to passport control at Heathrow was as long as Lark remembered, but there was a jubilant spring in her step that belied an overnight flight. It didn't hurt that British Airways had answered her prayers with a last-minute upgrade from business to first. She'd come full circle. How was it possible this was just her first trip back since the summer? It would have been unbearable had Channing not been to Boston six times.

After breakfast on the plane, she'd slipped into the lavatory to change into warm leggings and a cable-knit sweater that reached her thighs. Knee-high leather boots and a lively scarf completed the look. Channing would approve. In fact, she might even "approve" as soon as they got to the car.

She'd left behind eight inches of snow in Boston, not unusual for mid-November. There were murmurs last night among the flight attendants over whether they'd even be able to depart, but then they joined the long line for de-icing and finally rumbled down the runway just before midnight.

"Now for the fun part," said Brian Petty, an industrial kitchens salesman from Cincinnati who'd shared her center row cubby. If pressed to describe him, she'd say he was well groomed, with close-cropped hair and neat fingernails. He'd started off the flight overly chatty, which she forgave once he admitted his borderline panic about flying over the ocean. "Hope you have your docs in order. I hear these guys do everything but take blood."

"You'd be surprised how much you can learn from someone's blood."

He chortled. "I guess you'd know that, being in the medical business."

The medical business...she needed to break her ridiculous habit of telling people she wasn't an actual doctor. Or maybe stop using a luggage tag. She'd detached the one from Gipson and left it in her seat-back pocket.

They turned the corner at the end of the hall and found themselves behind several dozen travelers in line at immigration. Apparently another flight had arrived several minutes before theirs, but Lark didn't mind. The wait only added to her brimming sense of excitement.

As they neared the front of the line, Brian grew increasingly antsy. Clearing his throat, straightening his tie and smoothing his hair...she recognized with alarm the signs of a man stoking his nerve to ask a woman out. "Look, I'm going to be in London for—"

"Gosh, I hope my fiancée made it down from Cambridge. She's picking me up to save me the bother of getting the train. There shouldn't be much traffic on a Sunday. I can't wait to see her."

"Oh, cool. So it was nice to meet you."

Lark's anticipation was building. She'd expected to zip through passport control. Instead the agent acted as if he were the last line of defense against an impending invasion.

"Do you have a permanent address in the United Kingdom?"

It was plainly written on her landing card. "Yes, it's Number Two, Penderworth Lane, Horningsea." She'd have to ask Channing why it wasn't Number One, since it was the only structure on the lane. Then again, they'd be living in the Brownings' cottage for at least the next year while the renovations were completed on the manor house.

"Your employer?"

"PharmaStat Industries, Cambridge Science Park." With a coveted corporate sponsorship that allowed her to stay in the UK for five full years.

To the surprise of no one, Jermaine Martin had been named director of PharmaStat Cambridge upon Niya's departure. Struggling to repair the trust that was shattered by the Flexxene scandal, he approached Pierre Dancourt with the idea to hire Lark as deputy director, a move he thought would give them instant credibility with US pharmaceutical companies. Even Kirsten admitted Gipson would have more confidence in PharmaStat Cambridge knowing Lark now had operational oversight of their drug trials.

Meanwhile Channing had started a new job as a valuation analyst at Easton Capital in Cambridge the first week of September. The work was similar to what she'd done at Albright, but the firm was smaller and more casual.

Lark dutifully answered the agent's remaining questions and felt a surge of elation when he stamped and returned her passport. Almost there.

Even after they decided to move heaven and earth to somehow end up together in England, Channing went ahead with Kenny's offer to buy half of Penderworth. It wasn't just the money, she said, but the desire to solidify their partnership to preserve the manor. If something happened to her, she liked knowing it would end up as part of the sprawling Alanford estate—provided the earldom didn't fall to the Irish mafia wing of the family. To that end, she'd also hinted to Lark that it might also be in her interest to help Kenny and Oliver with their science project.

Lark couldn't wait to start her new life at Penderworth.

Her fellow passengers crowded around the baggage carousel, but she had only a small rolling suitcase, having shipped most of her belongings two weeks ago when the apartment lease expired. Chloe had promised to send the last box.

Rolling through the final station, she dropped her landing card in the box—nothing to declare—and proceeded through glass doors that opened automatically. Up ahead, the woman she loved held aloft a sign that read *Welcome Home Dr. Latimer!* It was all she could do not to run.

Bella Books, Inc.

Women. Books. Even Better Together.

P.O. Box 10543
Tallahassee, FL 32302

Phone: 800-729-4992
www.bellabooks.com